DRAWN TO YOU

SWANSON COURT SERIES #1

SERENA GREY

WWW.SERENAGREY.COM

This book is a work of fiction. All names, characters, locations, and incidents are products of the author's imagination and have been used fictitiously. Any resemblance to actual persons, living or dead, locales, or events is entirely coincidental.

To readers.

Find love.
Live joyfully.
Be happy.

DRAWN TO YOU

On the night she discovers her ex's engagement, Rachel meets Landon, the most attractive man she's ever seen, who, for some reason, mistakes her for a hooker. The thing is, he's so sexy, and it's just one night...what harm can there be in giving in to the desire to lose herself in his touch? She's never going to see him again, even though he has given her the most intensely pleasurable night of her life.

Landon prefers his women beautiful and sophisticated, with no desire for commitment, so when his brother ignores his protests and sends him a hooker on his birthday, he's surprised by how willing he is to continue paying for her services. It should be easy, except she's no hooker, and she has no intention of letting him into her life.

As the billionaire owner of Swanson Court Hotels, Landon is used to getting what he wants, and Rachel is not going to be an exception.

CHAPTER 1

"*Y*OU should totally hook up with Chadwick tonight."

"What!" I exclaim. "No way!" I look up, meeting my cousin's gray eyes in the mirror. She's standing behind me, fixing up my mass of blonde-streaked, deep copper hair in preparation for Chadwick Black's birthday party, which she's practically forcing me to attend. Right now she's looking at me with her own particular expression of exasperation.

"Seriously, Rachel," she says, inserting another pin into my hair to hold up the style she's creating. "You need to have some fun, and from what you've told me, Chadwick is cute, sexy, and eager to give you just what you need."

"Me and every other girl in New York," I scoff. "Come on Laurie, it's not that bad. I have fun. I have you, Brett, all those beautiful books on my ereader, and an amazing job." I pause. "Well, not so amazing, but whatever."

Laurie laughs and pushes her back-length curly black hair over her shoulder. She'd just returned from work when I told her about Chadwick's party and at the time, I wasn't sure I wanted to attend. Immediately, she'd dropped everything and started to help me get ready, insisting that I had to go. She must be tired after a long day at the law firm where she works, but she still looks stunning. I like to think we look alike, at least features-wise—our fathers are identical twins after all—but in coloring, we take after our mothers. My skin is pale and a little rosy on a good day, while Laurie's has an absurdly beautiful light caramel tone.

"I'm sure you know how pathetic it is when me, my boyfriend, books, and work are your only claim to a fun-filled life," Laurie says, still smiling. "PS, when I said fun, I didn't mean the PG version." She meets my eyes in the mirror and lowers her voice to a theatrical whisper. "I meant sex."

I chuckle. "I'm not going to have sex with Chadwick. It's more than enough that you're practically forcing me to go to his party."

"Well, Brett is spending the night, and I don't

want to worry about being loud." She smiles mischievously. "Anyway, we both know that if I don't force you, you'll just sit in your room pining for you-know-who."

I shake my head. "I don't pine, and you can say his name."

"I know I can, I just wish you would forget it." She sticks another pin in my hair. "Forever."

"His name is Jack Weyland," I say stubbornly.

She rolls her eyes. "And he's an asshole."

"He's not."

"Is too."

We both laugh, reminded of when we were children. We practically grew up together, and have been inseparable our whole lives.

Her laughter ends in a small chuckle. "I don't know about you, but when a guy asks you out, leads you on, spends two months making you fall in love with him, and then when you finally tell him how you feel, he tells you that he loves you too, but...what were the exact words again?"

I don't reply. I don't want to remember. Sometimes, it's still too painful to think about.

Laurie is right—I spend way too much time thinking about Jack Weyland, the most renowned features writer at Gilt Traveler, a world-famous adventure traveler, and the man I've been in love with, silently and unrequitedly, for the last two years.

Immediately after college, I got a job at Gilt Traveler, one of the many publications owned by Gilt Magazines. I fell for Jack on my first day in the building post-interview when he walked past me in the lobby. I was starting as an assistant to Mark Willis, the senior features editor, and was on my way to the elevators when a tall, dark-haired, confidently handsome guy sauntered toward me, making me stare. He winked at me, and I almost tripped in my three-inch heels.

I didn't know who he was at the time, but I found out soon enough. By some divine providence, he also worked at Gilt Traveler. He was a gifted writer, good-looking, charming, and nothing like the guys I'd known in college. He asked me to dinner, making me the envy of all the girls at Gilt, because he had never dated anyone from the office.

It was magical—or so I thought. By the end of the week, I was sleeping with him. Before long, I knew I was falling in love with him. Stupidly, I told him how I felt, and he responded by telling me I was sweet and he loved me too, but that he could never commit to any one woman and would only hurt me in the long run if he tried.

"I mean it when I say I love you," he said earnestly, with the passionate expression that had always made me feel as if I was the most special person in the world to him. "It would mean a lot to me if we could be friends after this."

Laurie is still waiting for me to respond. I close my eyes, trying to block out the sad memory. "He said he can't commit to just one woman."

"That," Laurie says. "When a guy does that, he's an asshole, and you don't stay friends with him for any reason. You wouldn't even be going to Chadwick's party tonight if Jack was in town to say 'Hey Rachel, why don't we go hang out at this-or-that café. I'll be so charming and funny while I take pleasure in the fact that in just two months with me, I made you incapable of falling for anyone else.'"

We've had this fight a couple times, the one where she tells me how unhealthy my friendship with Jack is for me and I try to defend Jack and the fact that two years after he broke my heart, I'm still in love with him.

When I don't reply, Laurie—uncharacteristically—lets the matter rest. She sticks one final pin in my hair and steps back, looking at her handiwork. Most of my hair is held up in an up-do that's intentionally messy but stylish, with a few strands framing my face. It's lovely.

I meet Laurie's eyes in the mirror and smile my appreciation. "Thanks."

She smiles back. "No biggie. Now go to that party and have fun." She winks. "In case you change your mind and decide to rock Chadwick's world, I left a present in your purse."

Eyeing her suspiciously, I go to my bed and pick up the black clutch, opening it and rolling my eyes at the 'present'.

"I definitely won't need these," I say with a laugh.

Laurie shrugs. "The night's not over yet. Allow me some hope."

LESS THAN AN HOUR LATER, I'M IN FRONT OF THE Oyster Room, an exclusive restaurant and bar on the second floor of the Swanson Court Hotel. From the exterior, it's impossible to guess that there's a party going on inside.

Pausing in the corridor outside the doors, I catch my reflection in the glass and thank my stars for Laurie. She also helped pick out my clothes: a dark green dress the same color as my eyes. It has a suggestive décolletage and a hemline that ends just above my knees, paired with black heels that add four inches to my modest five-foot-five frame.

Satisfied that nothing is out of place, I push open the doors and step into a quiet anteroom occupied by a smiling hostess, who directs me to another set of doors that open directly into the restaurant. Inside, the party is in full swing, seemingly containing all the stylish, artsy, and creative young people in New York City. That's not surprising—Chadwick Black, the celebrant, is an award-winning photographer who sometimes does work for Gilt Traveler.

From the entrance, I glimpse a few people from the office and then Chadwick across the room, whispering something to an impossibly slender blonde who's giggling at whatever he's saying. Typical Chadwick. He loves to flirt, and he's been trying very good-naturedly to get into my pants for ages. I take a glass of champagne from a passing waiter, my eyes still on Chadwick. He's good-looking—very good-looking—with long brown hair, caramel eyes, and a charming smile that gives him the appearance of being the harmless, friendly-yet-incredibly-hot guy next door. I know better. His love for women is generous, nondiscriminatory, and definitely not monogamous.

He looks up from the blonde's ear and notices me. Grinning, he excuses himself and comes over. "Rachel honey," he exclaims above the loud pop music then kisses me on both cheeks before leaning back to look at me. "You look stunning."

"So do you," I reply, dodging a second round of kisses. "Great party."

"I know, right?" He takes my hand, and there's a flash as someone takes a picture. I don't have as much social clout as some of the other girls at Gilt, so I'm not worried that my picture will appear in any of the fashion or gossip columns.

Chadwick is still talking. "I have great friends who realize there's nothing more important than celebrating the fact that twenty-eight years ago, I came into this world for the benefit of women everywhere," he proclaims.

I chuckle. "You're so full of it."

"Yeah," he replies with a charming grin, "but you love me."

"I do."

"Then why won't you let me show you just how crazy I am about you?"

I swat him on the arm. "Because I love myself too much."

He sighs exaggeratedly. "Come on then. Let's introduce you to some of my friends." Pulling me across the room, he leads me over to a group of people talking and laughing over drinks and finger foods.

"Guys, this is Rachel," Chadwick announces, "into whose panties I'm trying to get." He winks at me, unrepentant, as his friends hoot.

Someone pulls at his sleeve and whispers something in his ear. "I'll be right back," he tells me before leaving to take care of whatever he's needed for.

One of the friends, a guy with messy brown hair and an unshaven face, tells me his name in a crisp

British accent. He also introduces the rest of the group. There's a painter, a curvy brunette who works at a tabloid, a food critic, and the typical blend of writers, artists, and other creative types. "We mostly went to college with Chad," British guy says. "How do you know him?"

"He does some work for us...for the magazine where I work."

"Which magazine?" The question comes from the painter, a petite woman with a pixie cut.

"Gilt Traveler," I reply.

"That's a good one." The tabloid writer, I think her name is Annabel, seems impressed. "What do you do?"

"I'm a features associate," I tell them. It's the official title for my real job, which is to write the tiny little articles the real features writers can't be bothered with."

"Sounds like a nice gig," someone says.

"Yeah, it is," I agree with a shrug.

"I can't wait for the moment when a bikini-clad model pops out of a cake," British guy declares, finishing his drink and immediately picking up another from a passing tray.

"Is that going to happen?" I ask, interested. I've never seen anything like that outside of the movies.

"Not likely. It's not a frat party." He sounds wistful.

Chadwick returns. "So have you guys convinced Rachel I'm worth at least a night of her time?"

"Are you?" one of the women says, tossing her hair. "Not from what I remember."

The rest of the group bursts into laughter, and I join them. Chadwick tries to look annoyed but fails.

"Chadwick, darling!" The soft voice comes from across the room, and we all look in that direction. The speaker is a vaguely familiar woman, tall and slender with a wild mass of dark blonde hair and mile-long legs shown off in a tight jumpsuit.

"Here comes Claudia," I hear someone say.

But I'm not listening. My heart is hammering, my eyes locked on the man standing beside the new arrival.

Jack Weyland.

What is he doing here? I think, panicked and elated at the same time. He's supposed to be in England, skydiving with Reese Fletcher, the sixty-year-old electronics billionaire daredevil. We spoke on the phone only a few days ago, and he didn't mention anything about returning to New York.

Yet here he is, with the most beautiful woman at the party, no less.

He hasn't seen me yet, so I have time to look at him. He's standing back, watching his date as she throws herself into Chadwick's arms, his expression that irresistible combination of boredom and mystery that only some guys can pull off. His dark hair is short at the sides and back, longer in front, with an appealing forelock falling onto his forehead. His body —perfect in a stylish shirt and dark pants—is fit and athletic. My heart catches in my throat, filling with the familiar, bittersweet ache I feel whenever I see him.

"Who's her companion?" Annabel asks.

"That's Jack Weyland," British guy supplies. "Now there's a guy who suffers from wanderlust. He's been all over the world. There was a three-episode special of his experience at the Spanish bullfights early this year. Never gave a damn before, but now I want to go to Spain." He stops his narrative to look at me. "He writes for Gilt too, so you should know him."

"Yes," I say quietly, still looking at Jack. Sometimes, like now, I still question why I agreed to stay friends. At the time, I thought that was what it meant to be sophisticated, to be able to act as if I didn't care, even when my heart was shattered. I've paid a high price for that sophistication in the last two years, smiling on the outside but dying inside while he went from assignment to assignment, writing magnificent articles, appearing on TV, and having affairs with women from all over the world.

He still hasn't seen me. His eyes are on his date, and I don't blame him. By now, I've placed her face.

She's a famous British model, and she's beautiful. Exactly his type.

"Chadwick photographed Claudia for some rodeo campaign back when they were both beginners," British guy is saying. "Made her famous as the 'risk-taking' model to watch back then. I think she's the only woman he never tries to sleep with—no offense to you, of course."

"None taken," I reply distractedly. I've already forgotten about Chadwick. I look from Jack to Claudia. She's only the latest in a long line of women he's dated over the years. With each one, it becomes more and more unlikely that one day he'll realize that maybe, just maybe his feelings for me are more than those of just friendship.

"If Chadwick is trying to sleep with her, he's in for a huge disappointment," Annabel says. "I heard she got engaged to some writer, maybe this hunk she came in with."

I take a sharp breath, my ears burning at the word *engaged*. At that moment, Jack sees me. There's a brief flash of surprise in his eyes, then he smiles and my whole body fills with longing.

"Yup, he's the one." One of the women holds up her phone, which has a popular gossip site open on the browser. I force myself not to look at the headline or the pictures.

Claudia is busy introducing Jack and Chadwick,

and as I watch, Chadwick starts to lead them both toward us.

"I'm going to go to the bathroom," I say to no one in particular. Finding a nearby table to place my champagne flute, I turn my back on all of them and find an exit. Outside the restaurant, I lean on the railing, breathing in cool, filtered air as I try to regain my composure. I let my eyes travel from the crystal chandelier hanging from about a floor above, down to the magnificent entrance lobby on the ground floor. It's a beautiful hotel, with classic architecture and evidence of careful, unstinting maintenance—too bad my first visit has been spoiled by having to watch the man I love with yet another woman.

I take a deep breath and start for the elevator, knowing I don't want to go back inside and see Jack with his beautiful date again. I'll have to apologize to Chadwick later, but I doubt he'll mind too much. There're probably one or two women already waiting to go home with him.

"Rachel."

Jack's voice stops me in my tracks. I turn around, trying to control the intense longing that fills me as my eyes land on him. "Hi Jack." I force a smile. "Didn't know you were back."

He shrugs. "It was kind of sudden." His gray eyes, travel over my dress then come back to settle on my face. "You look incredible."

"Thanks."

There's an awkward silence. Usually, we have so much to talk about. By now, I'd be quizzing him about his trip, about skydiving with Reese Fletcher, and he would be giving me his typical funny answers —but not today. Does he have any idea how I'm feeling? Is he aware of how much being his friend has cost me these two years? How painful it is for me whenever I see him with other women?

I doubt it. After he rejected me, I became much better at hiding my feelings.

"It's nice to see you," he says, moving closer. His lips curve in a small, familiar smile. "I wasn't expecting you to be here, but I'm glad you are. Don't tell me you're leaving?"

"I... Yes I am, actually."

"That's a shame." He looks disappointed, and for a moment, I imagine that maybe he was looking forward to spending time with me. That hope goes out the window with his next words. "You didn't meet Claudia."

Claudia Sever, the model he came with. The void in my stomach widens. "Is it true?" I ask. "Are you engaged?"

He smiles. "It's crazy, isn't it? Who would have thought I'd ever settle down?"

"Yes," I agree, my heart breaking. "Who would have thought?"

The silence stretches again. I'm supposed to wish him happiness, like a good friend would do, but I can't bring myself to say the words, not when I was still holding on to the hope that when he finally took that step, it would be with me.

I force a small laugh, and even to me it sounds fake and sad. "So what happened? You told me you could never settle down with any one woman."

He frowns. "That was a long time ago."

My eyes cloud. It's hard to understand how your feelings for someone can be everything to you, yet nothing to them. "Sometimes it still hurts like it was yesterday," I say softly.

"Rachel..." He closes the distance between us and places comforting hands on my shoulders. "You know I do love you."

The words come out of his mouth so easily, words that in other circumstances would mean the world to me.

"Then why..." I stop before I make a total fool of myself. *Why can't we be together? Why do you keep breaking my heart?*

"Rachel," he says firmly, "we're friends. You should be happy for me."

I push away from him, letting his hands fall from my shoulders. "We were more than friends, and it was good. It was wonderful. It was the best thing that ever happened to me." I stop talking, seeing the situation for what it really is - me, yet again throwing myself at a man who has made it clear that he doesn't want me.

His silence adds to my shame. I close my eyes. "I wish you all the best," I murmur before turning away and hurrying toward the elevators. I can feel tears stinging at my eyes, and I blink furiously to keep them from falling.

God! I should have thrown his friendship in his face when I had the chance.

Laurie tried to tell me, so many times. "He knows you're in love with him, and he wants to keep you that way, so you'll always be there. It's an ego thing. As long as you let him, you're going to be stuck in the same place while he chases the women who present a real challenge."

I didn't listen. I was too eager, too willing to take the little Jack offered. I thought if we spent time together as friends, he would surely see that we were meant to be more than that.

How pathetic!

The elevator doors slide open, and luckily, the car is empty. I step inside and press the button for the ground floor, unable to control the tears gathering as the doors swish closed again.

The ride is short. After only a few seconds, the elevator stops on the ground floor. By then, my face is wet with tears, and a glance at my reflection in the mirrored walls tells me I'm not fit to walk into the lobby. I dab at the mascara smudges on my bottom lid and without looking, I press a button to send the elevator back up. Hopefully, the ride up and back down again will give me some time alone to repair the damage Jack has done, both to my face and my heart.

BY THE TIME THE ELEVATOR STOPS AT THE TOP floor and beeps, my face is under control again. Now I just want to go home and forget everything about tonight—not that it will be easy. I'll still have to face Jack at work, and I have no idea how I'm going to do that. I sigh. No matter what happens, I'm so done being his go-to companion.

I hear another beep and realize a small box on the elevator panel is prompting me for a code. I frown. At the top of the panel, the button marked 'PH' is glowing. I'm on the penthouse floor, and the elevator probably needs a code to open the doors. I don't have a code, obviously, so I pause, wondering what to do.

I didn't even realize I pressed the button for the penthouse. I just wanted time to fix my face. I press the button for the ground floor, hoping that will work. The prompt for the code beeps again.

Okay, so what am I supposed to do now? There

must be an emergency button somewhere. I'm searching along the panel when suddenly, the doors to the elevator slide open.

And my breath stops.

Something happens. Either the earth drops, or it suddenly stops spinning. I feel unbalanced, as if I'm going to lose my footing. My hand finds the smooth metal handrail inside the elevator, and I lean on it for support while I stare at the Greek god standing on the other side of the open doors.

There's no other way to describe him. He's tall, at least a head taller than me, with long legs, lean hips, and broad shoulders shown off in a perfectly tailored dark gray suit paired with a snowy white shirt. There's no tie, and the top button of his shirt is open, exposing his throat and a little hint of well-muscled chest.

Dark gold hair frames his face. It's wavy and just long enough to tease his collar, with a few bright strands highlighting the dark waves. And his face! It makes me unable to remember what exactly I'm doing in the elevator. Dark winged brows, eyes a deep cerulean blue, and a Greek nose, slim and pointed like an arrowhead. His lips are full and sensual, and for some reason, they make me start to think of whispers, kisses, and those same lips tracing a path on my heated skin.

I stare, lost in the glittering depths of his eyes,

and unable to tear mine away. Strangely, it seems as if everything that's happened before this moment has somehow lost all importance. As if he can feel it too, his brow knits, a puzzled expression entering the eyes that seem to be stripping me and looking into the very depths of my soul. At that moment, it feels as if I know him...as if I've known him all my life.

I step back, my fingers curving around the handrail and holding on. Finally regaining the use of my lungs, I take a long breath, unsuccessfully trying to dispel the effect his undeniable masculine sensuality is having on me. It doesn't help that he's still looking at me, his eyes traveling up and down my body as if he knows exactly what he's going to do with it.

I close my eyes, trying to arrange my thoughts and ignore all the carnal images that have taken over my brain. Okay, so he's probably the owner of the apartment, the man with the passcode. He looks as if he was on his way out. He must have opened the elevator from inside and is probably surprised to find me right outside his apartment, staring at him as if I've never seen a man before.

"Good evening," I start, trying to find the words to explain why I'm here.

There's only a small flicker of his eyes to show he heard me. He considers me for a few more moments, and I wonder if he's going to acknowledge my words at all. Then one of his perfect eyebrows arches up.

"Well," he says finally, in a voice that's almost whispery soft, yet deep, raspy, and so incredibly sensual, it sends shivers down my spine. "You're not what I'd have chosen, but you'll do."

CHAPTER 2

I don't understand a word he just said, but that might be due to the fact that my brain is still discombobulated by his blatant sexiness. I watch as he steps back and inclines his head in a gesture that tells me he wants me to come inside the apartment.

"Come in."

I'm already stepping into the foyer before I wake up from the effects of his voice. I stop and frown at him. What does he mean 'I'll do?'

"Um..." I start, looking for words. What will I say? *I don't know who you think I am, but I was just hiding in the elevator while trying to repair the damage to my makeup from crying over a guy who doesn't give a rat's ass about me, and I ended up in front of your apartment. Now if you don't mind, I'd like to...* I hesitate. What exactly do I want to do?

I don't want to leave, that's for sure. There's something dreamy about being ushered into a million-dollar luxury apartment by a man who looks as if he just stepped out of a 'sexiest man alive' photo-shoot. He thinks I'll do? For what exactly? I want to know, and somewhere in a shameless part of me, I desperately hope I don't disappoint him.

He sees my hesitation. "Come in," he repeats in that mesmerizing voice. "I won't bite." There's a short pause. "Unless you want me to."

There's suddenly a weird, achy feeling low in my stomach. I pull in a gulp of air, my legs propelling me into the dimly lit foyer. He clearly thinks I'm someone else, but whoever it is, I'm more than ready to play the part, at least for now.

He leads the way through the foyer into a large living room with floor-to-ceiling windows that look out onto the city. As he walks, he shrugs off his jacket, dropping it carelessly on a sofa to join a discarded tie. "Have a seat," he says, turning back to look at me. Without the jacket, his broad shoulders, narrow waist, slim hips, and the hard muscles beneath his shirt are obvious—too obvious.

"Would you like a drink?" he asks.

It takes a moment for me to tear my mind from thoughts of his body. "Um..."

"Brandy, water, wine…?'

"Brandy," I tell him.

He gives me a small nod then walks across the living room to a bar by the side, where he pours two glasses then adds ice cubes. I manage to tear my eyes from his body so I can look around my surroundings. The room is tastefully furnished, the classic architecture complemented by a décor that's luxurious without ostentation. It feels like a home, a place you expect a family to live.

I wonder if he's married.

Well, it's not as if I'm planning to sleep with him, I tell myself, continuing my admiration of the room. Some of the furniture are classic antique pieces, and the walls are covered in some sort of textured finish. Paintings and pictures hang here and there. There's a family portrait featuring a couple that's obviously his parents, based on his resemblance to the man in the picture, and two children, boys.

He's clearly the older one of the boys. It's the same perfect face, only younger. Next to the portrait, there's a large black and white original of a beautiful ballerina, her posture graceful as she leaps through the air. It's the same woman in the family portrait, his mother apparently. At the bottom of the frame, I recognize the Andrew Marvell quote "A hundred years should go to praise thine eyes, and on thy forehead gaze."

"Here." I turn away from the image as that soft raspy voice pours over me again, making me shiver. He sounds like temptation, and I cannot imagine any woman who wouldn't agree to any suggestion made in that voice.

He hands me the drink, his eyes on my face, and I do my best to hold my hand steady when I take the glass from him. I almost fail when his warm fingers brush mine. It's just a tiny touch, but I feel it everywhere, from my fingers to my thighs.

Still watching me, he drops gracefully beside me on the sofa. I can't tear my eyes away from him. I feel almost as if I can look at him forever.

"You like ballet?"

"Hmm." I'm so lost in staring at him that it takes a while for his words to register.

He gestures at the print of the ballerina. "You seemed interested in the picture."

"I like ballet as much as any little girl who ever wanted to wear a tutu." I laugh nervously. Both Laurie and I attended classes, but I stopped only after a few months. I preferred to read, even then. "But I was looking at the quote in the picture," I continue. "It's from one of my favorite poems."

An eyebrow goes up, only a little, but it draws my attention to his eyes again. They look like sapphires, I decide, dark and rich, with an irresistible glitter in their depths. "Had we but world enough and time," he quotes, "this coyness, lady, were no crime." The corners of his sculpted lips lift in a small smile. "But you're not coy, are you? That would be inconsistent with your profession."

I frown, not sure what he means. He's doing a slow perusal of my body again, almost as if he's undressing me with his eyes. I should be annoyed that this stranger is ogling me so openly, but I'm not. Instead, I can feel my body responding. Heat unfurls in my belly, spreading until I can feel the insistent need all over.

What am I doing? A few minutes ago I was devastated because I found out that I'd been waiting in vain for Jack to decide I was the girl for him. Now here I am, letting another man turn me on, which, to his credit, he is doing just by looking at me.

I should explain that I'm not whoever he thinks I am and leave, but not yet. I want...

I want him to keep looking at me with that sensual, smoldering gaze. I want to keep hearing that sinful voice. I want to feel his hands on me.

I take a quick sip of the drink he gave me, breaking the contact with his eyes. I can't be considering casual sex with a total stranger.

Even if it is an insanely hot, sexy stranger who has me aching for him without even touching me at all.

I drag my eyes back to the print on the wall and the line of poetry, even though I'd much rather be looking at him. "The woman in the poem," I say, "was she being coy, or careful? Many people have tossed caution to the wind and surrendered to passion then come to regret it later." I'm rambling, but I can't stop —it's the only way to escape the spellbinding effect of being so close to him.

He doesn't reply, so I turn back to look at him. His eyes are on my face, a curious, speculative gleam in their blue depths. *How can his lashes be so long?* I wonder, half in admiration and half in jealousy.

"You're absolutely right," he says finally, with a small chuckle. "Though only my brother would find a hooker who talks about poetry on the job."

A what! I swallow a mouthful of brandy, and the hot fiery liquid goes down all the wrong places. I sputter, almost dropping the glass as I try to get my throat under control.

He's at the bar and back in what seems like milliseconds. "Here." He takes my brandy and hands me a glass of water. "Drink this."

I take the water from him and take a huge gulp. *He thinks I'm a whore!*

No wonder! He'd been expecting a hooker. I give the water back to him, unable to meet his eyes. I should tell him now that he's wrong, but his fingers close over mine. They're firm and warm and hard,

26

and even from that slight touch I can feel the heated pulsing intensify between my thighs.

He thinks I'm a whore!

"Are you all right?" he asks softly.

His fingers are still on mine, distracting me, making me think of all the other places where I want him to touch me. *It's only sex*, I tell myself, and heaven knows that after two years of being stuck in the friend zone with Jack, I could do with some of that, if only to get my mind to move on to other things.

I lick my lips, nervous at the thought of what I'm about to do. *He thinks you're a prostitute*! An inner voice of reason screams, but I don't listen. I can only feel the growing excitement in the pit of my stomach, and the aching need in my body.

"I'm fine," I tell him, venturing a small smile. "I just drank it too fast, but I'm fine."

"Good." His fingers are still around mine, and I wonder if he can tell that my heart is beating like a freaking drum. *I'm going to sleep with this stranger*, I think almost incredulously. I'm going to let him fuck me any way he wants because he thinks he's paid for that right, and I'm going to enjoy every minute of it.

He takes the water from me and sets it on the coffee table, his eyes never leaving mine. Suddenly, it's hard to breathe. Why am I doing this? I could tell him he made a mistake and walk out of here. I could tell him the hooker his brother sent is probably still on her way. I could go home to my empty bed and spend the rest of the night crying over Jack...

...or I can just let him fulfill the promise of toe-curling sex I can see clearly in his eyes.

"What's your name?" he asks.

"Rachel." My voice is barely more than a whisper.

"I'm Landon."

I'm doing this, I decide resolutely, smiling at him. *What happens now?* How do we go from exchanging names to entwined bodies and clawing sheets?

"Did Aidan tell you it was my birthday?"

Who? "Yes," I lie, guessing that Aidan is probably the brother.

He nods. "What are your rates?"

For a moment, I have no idea what to say. "It's already been taken care of," I murmur.

"Of course, but tell me anyway."

I pick a number off the top of my head that I think is exorbitant enough for a high-class hooker.

He looks impressed. "My brother is being very generous," he says with a small chuckle. He studies me for a moment. "So...what do I get for that?"

I pause. "The whole night."

"Anything I want?"

I take a lungful of air, pushing the small sliver of panic out of my mind. "Anything you want," I whisper.

His lips quirk. "Follow me," he says.

He leads me out of the living room into a wide hallway then up a flight of stairs to the upper floor. He walks gracefully, his obvious strength held firmly under control. He moves quickly, so I don't have time to admire the apartment or do more than be awed by the sheer size.

Upstairs, he opens the door to a large bedroom with soft grayish walls, large windows half hidden by long, heavy-looking curtains, and a perfectly made bed. A light from the bedside lamp on one of the nightstands casts a soft glow around the room, giving it an intimate ambiance. There's a lounge chair close to the windows, a writing desk and chair, and closer to the bed, there's a soft-looking armchair. I step inside the room, and Landon closes the door behind us.

"You have condoms?" he asks.

It's really not a question—what self-respecting hooker wouldn't have condoms? I start to panic, then I remember Laurie's present. *Thank the stars for Laurie*, I think silently, opening my purse to retrieve the roll of condoms before handing them to him.

He tosses them on the edge of the bed before going to sit on the armchair. I'm still standing by the door, and he motions for me to come farther into the room.

I walk toward him, suddenly very nervous. There's something incredibly sexy about the way he's leaning back on the chair with his body relaxed and his long legs splayed out.

He raises a hand to stop me before I get to him. "Take off your clothes," he says.

My fingers are trembling. Why are my fingers trembling? It's been a while, but it's not as if I'm inexperienced. I fumble with my zipper, trying clumsily to get it to go down. Finally, the dress falls at my feet, and I'm standing in front of this sexy man dressed only in high heels and my black lace panties and bra.

His face is unreadable. What should I do now? Go to him? Remain standing and wait for him to come and take what, as far as he knows, has been paid for? While all the thoughts are running through my mind, he arches a brow at me.

"All your clothes."

God, that voice! I take a deep breath and reach behind me to unhook my bra, freeing my breasts as I pull it off my shoulders before dropping it on the ground. His eyes drop from my face to my exposed breasts, and as if he's actually touching them, my nipples respond to his gaze, the pink tips tightening and extending. I hook my fingers into the elastic band of my panties and pull them down far enough so they can fall on their own, and then I step out of them.

His expression doesn't change, but his eyes don't

leave me. I watch as they move from my breasts down the length of my body.

"Get on the bed," he orders, his voice a little rougher than before.

The bed is a king-sized beauty. I imagine us, bodies entwined, rolling around on it. Swallowing nervously, I walk over to the edge, turning around to face Landon before I lower myself onto the soft sheets.

Suddenly, he gets up from the armchair, towering over me as he starts to first undo his cuffs, and then the buttons of his shirt. "Take off your shoes, Rachel," he says. "Pull up your legs and spread them. I want to see you touch yourself."

My lips part almost involuntarily, and nervously, I wet them with my tongue. This should feel weird, but as I watch him undo his buttons to reveal the perfectly defined muscles of his chest, I can only feel the insistent pulsing increase between my legs, making me eager to do as he says. I kick off my shoes and lift my feet to the edge of the bed, lying back and spreading my legs slowly, relishing the fact that his eyes are focused on me. My fingers reach between my wet folds, slipping easily over the most sensitive parts of me, and I close my eyes, letting out a small moan.

"Open your eyes." The words are a command. "Don't close them. Don't do anything unless I tell you to."

I obey. His shirt is off now, and the sight of the hard muscles and the flat board that's his stomach totally takes my breath away. His body is perfectly sculpted, not bulky, just lean, strong, and flawless.

His trousers soon follow the path of the shirt. At the sight of the hard, straining ridge in his briefs, I lick my lips again, transfixed. I want to see him. I want to touch him. I want to run my tongue over his nipples and lick the taut skin over his muscles. I feel unlike myself, as if the girl I am has disappeared, leaving a hedonistic alter ego to take over. I want him in my mouth, inside me. I want him to grab hold of my legs and hold me still while he plunges deep into me. The thought itself is almost enough to make me come. I release a soft, helpless moan and rub myself harder. My insides are throbbing with desire. I want to beg him to hurry. I move a finger down to the wet pulsing entrance to my body then slip it inside. My body clenches sweetly. I want more.

My eyes follow his movements as he pulls down his briefs to reveal the full length of his throbbing erection, and I moan again, begging him with my eyes to hurry. He reaches for the condoms, and I watch as he rolls one onto his hard, swollen length.

My breathing is coming in pants now, and I can't take my eyes off him. He advances towards me, his erection fisted in his hand. I've never wanted anything more than I want him inside me at this moment.

Kneeling on the bed between my legs, he reaches for my hand, stilling the movement of my fingers. Then he takes over, palming me while he slips two fingers inside me.

My body clenches eagerly and I groan, spreading my legs wider as his fingers slide in and out, stroking the sensitive places inside me. His thumb finds my clit, and he plays leisurely with the swollen mass of nerves, driving me crazy. I grab hold of the sheets, my hips moving shamelessly to meet his fingers.

"Don't stop." I moan, feeling the beginning of an orgasm. I need this so much. "Oh, please don't stop."

In reply, he inserts another finger and my brain shuts down. I cry out as my body tightens then shatters in a massive explosion of pure pleasure.

I don't even have time to catch my breath before he grabs hold of my legs and pulls me toward him, plunging into me with one swift movement. I cry out helplessly, surrendering myself to the pleasure as he fills me, thrusting deep with every rock-hard stroke.

I wrap my legs around his waist, urging him deeper. My whole body feels warm and sweet. I can already feel another climax coming as heat spreads from my core. He picks up his pace, his chest tightening as he pumps harder and faster. He grunts softly with each sure thrust, his eyes closed, his lips slightly open as he grinds his hips into me. I come with a loud moan, my body spasming as the waves of pleasure wash over me. He plunges deeper, a loud groan escaping his lips as his climax seizes him and leaves him panting, his chest heaving as he releases my legs.

M Y legs fall back on the bed, shaking uncontrollably. Even though the air in the room is cool, there's a sheen of sweat on my skin and on Landon's too, making his chest and arms gleam in the soft light of the room.

He pulls out of me, still slightly hard, making my body pulse with post-orgasmic pleasure. I sigh and fall back on the pillows, watching him through heavy eyes while he gets up and takes care of the condom.

He returns to the bed to join me, handing me a tissue. After I've cleaned up, he takes it back from me and tosses it. We're both silent, and I start to wonder what he's thinking. I shouldn't care. It's just a one-night stand after all—although, if I'm honest, it has turned out to be the best sex I've ever had in my life.

"I can't feel my legs." I almost don't realize I've said the words out loud, and when I do, I chuckle softly, slightly embarrassed.

"If it makes you feel any better," Landon replies, "I can't feel mine either."

We both laugh. Even his laugh is sexy, deep, and soft. He's so good-looking, so perfect, I can't even fathom why he would ever need a hooker.

"Can I ask you a question?"

"Go on," he says.

"Why would someone who looks like you ever need a hooker?"

His eyebrow goes up. "Looks like me?" he repeats.

I roll my eyes. "You know what I mean. Someone as hot as you are."

"Not to mention devastating in bed," he adds with a grin.

I hold up my hand. "I didn't say that."

"No." He's still grinning. "But you said you couldn't feel your legs."

"Okay, devastating in bed," I concede with a small laugh. "Why would you ever need a hooker?"

He thinks for a moment. "Are all your clients unattractive?"

Ha! My clients. I pause, wondering what to say. "Yes," I reply finally, imagining a string of lonely older men. "Some are too busy for relationships, others are just adventurous."

"Maybe I'm busy and adventurous."

My gaze travels over the raw beauty of his face. A man who looks like him wouldn't even need to snap his fingers for women to come running. He is obviously rich, too, and yes, devastating in bed. So devastating, in fact, that right now, all I want is to run my hands down that hard chest and over his stomach...

The silence stretches, and I wonder if I should go, or wait for him to tell me he's done with me for the night.

"Do you want another drink?" he asks. "Some water?"

I shake my head. "I'm fine, thanks."

He sits up to look at me, affording me a better view of his still naked body. He's still hard, I notice, excitement making me wet my lips before I realize he's watching me stare at his cock.

I blush, embarrassed.

"You're not tired," he asks, "are you?"

Slowly I shake my head.

"Good." He runs his hand down the side of my body, burning a path from my shoulder to my hip. I'm suddenly trembling, my skin tingling as he touches me. His hand moves to my back, sliding over my skin until he's cupping my butt.

My breath quickens, and he smiles at me. Gently, he turns me over so I'm lying on my stomach with my back to him. He runs his hands over my buttocks, softly stroking the sensitive skin before kneading each cheek firmly.

I let out a soft sigh, and in response he places his hands under my belly on both sides, pulling me up on my hands and knees. Then with one hand still on my stomach, he slips the other one between my legs from behind, feeling how wet I am before sliding two fingers inside me.

I close my eyes, my body twisting as he moves his fingers, spreading them even while he moves them in and out again. "You're so wet," he murmurs, his voice raspy, "so wet and so hot."

My body tightens and I move my hips impatiently, desperate for him to be inside me. I wait as he reaches for the condoms again, then his hands are on my waist, positioning me so he can slide slowly inside me.

He takes his time, pushing in slowly to the very hilt. His fingers tighten against my waist. "You're so fucking tight," he whispers, flexing his hips slowly as he slides out, then in again. "You feel so good."

His voice combined with the slow, sure thrusting of his cock inside me soon pushes me over the edge. My body starts to shake uncontrollably as hot pleasure builds in my core. He bends over me, plunging faster as he reaches for my breasts, teasing my unbearably swollen nipples. I cry out, my whole body tightening with the intensity of my climax.

He doesn't stop. Instead, he leans back up, gripping my thighs and lifting my legs off the bed. I clutch at the sheets, moaning weakly with each hot, sweet stroke. His grunts blend with my weak cries as he thrusts into me with an intense sexual abandon. Heat gathers in my core, pulsing, spreading, and my body tightens again as another orgasm washes over me. In the next moment, I hear his loud groan as he slams deep into me and comes.

He releases my legs and collapses on top of me. Our bodies are slippery with sweat as we both try to catch our breaths. He pulls out of me and gets rid of the condom.

"Now I definitely can't feel my legs," I whisper, half panting.

"Me neither," he says, surprising me by pressing a kiss on my shoulder. I smile at him and he smiles back, the expression on his face almost boyish. Then he falls back on the pillows on his side of the bed.

In the silence that follows, our breathing slowly returns to normal. *What now?* I wonder again. It's probably time for me to go. I stare at his naked body with regret. This has undoubtedly been the best night of my life.

"The elevator doesn't require a code to leave," he says, as if he knows what I'm thinking. "Just press the call button."

I don't say anything. I feel unaccountably sad. He

turns to his side to look at me, a small frown on his face. Then he gets up and picks his trousers from the floor. He retrieves a black leather wallet and removes a couple of bills, coming around to place them on the nightstand on my side of the bed.

"I know you've been paid," he says, "but consider that a bonus."

I give him a small smile, but I can't think of anything to say. Thank you? Is this when I tell him I'm not the hooker he was expecting? He comes back to lie on the bed beside me. "You can leave when you're less tired," he says, already dismissing me. "Don't forget to leave your number."

He closes his eyes, and I don't know if he's sleeping. Briefly, I toy with the idea of leaving my number, but I soon dismiss the foolish thought. He thinks I'm a hooker, which means he's probably already forgotten about me. I've had a beautiful night filled with great sex, and I can go back to my life and try to work on the things that matter, like getting over Jack.

I wait a while, then I get up and pull on my clothes. Leaving the money on the nightstand, I make my way back to the foyer. Like he said, the elevator doesn't need a code to leave, and in a few minutes, I'm out on the sidewalk hailing a cab to take me back home.

CHAPTER 4

SOMETHING is tickling my ear, very persistent in trying to drag me away from the dream where a beautiful man with dark gold hair and beautiful blue eyes is kissing a sweet path from my navel down between my thighs.

The tickling intensifies, and the dream disappears. "Go away," I mutter sleepily, covering my ear with one hand. The tickling moves to the skin behind my ear. Sighing, I open one eye, and then the other. My room is bright with early morning sun, even though it seems like I stumbled into bed at one in the morning just a few minutes ago. I still feel a little tired, but my body also feels light and sweet, with a delicious ache between my legs. As the memory of last night fills my head, I can't prevent the small smile that comes to my lips.

"So?" I turn around. Laurie is sitting on the other side of my bed, still wearing her favorite sleep attire of a thigh-length t-shirt. Her instrument of torture—a frilly scarf—is dangling from her hand. At the moment, one perfect eyebrow is raised questioningly, waiting for a reply to...whatever she's asking me.

"What?" I scowl at her, but she just smiles, ignoring me. At times like these, I start to rethink our decision to get an apartment together after college. At the time, we were so excited, refusing our parents' offers to help as we looked forward to finally striking out on our own. After two weeks spent looking at rat-infested apartments we couldn't even afford, my dad recommended a new agent, who showed us a beautiful apartment on Murray Hill. It was perfect and we both fell in love with it, only discovering later that the lease had already been paid by our parents.

We sulked and complained, but we moved in, because it was close to both our offices and we'd already fallen in love with it.

"You can always pay us back," Laurie's mom—my Aunt Jacie—had said diplomatically, enabling us to call a truce.

Now Laurie rolls her eyes, bringing me back to the present. "Sweetie, don't you think there's stuff you need to tell me?"

I shake my head. "No. It's Saturday, I want to sleep."

"Come on," she cajoles, lying beside me so her head is just inches away from mine on the pillow. "I want to know what happened last night." She taps the pillow in front of my face. "You can't just go to a party, sneak back in the a.m., and have nothing for me."

"I'll tell you anything you want after I get some sleep," I plead, even though I know it's useless. Laurie is an old hand at bugging a person relentlessly until the victim has no choice but to give in to her.

"You've slept enough," she argues firmly. "Come on...did you have sex with him?"

I frown, then realize there's no way she can know about Landon. "Who?"

"Chadwick, of course. Who else?" She peers at me. "I kinda assumed you finally gave in, throwing caution to the wind and all that."

I shake my head. "No, I didn't. You know I don't find him attractive."

She gives me an exasperated look. "A man with Chadwick Black's looks is attractive to everyone."

"I wonder what your boyfriend would think about that statement," I chide. "Where's Brett, by the way? I thought he was spending the night."

"He's asleep in my bed. He had a very tiring

night." Laurie winks. "So what happened? Why'd you come in so late?"

Even though she's my cousin and best friend, I find myself hesitating to tell her. There's something about what happened last night that makes me want to keep it to myself, to treasure every moment in my memories and bring them out to ponder when I'm alone, selfishly, like a miser over her hoard of gold.

But I know Laurie, and she knows me. There's no way I'll get away with lying to her.

I raise my tired body to a sitting position, resting my back on the headboard. Sensing that there's a good story coming, Laurie grins and slides easily into the lotus position, a commonplace feat I've never been able to accomplish. Unlike me, Laurie continued with ballet until she was fifteen. So, in addition to being stunningly beautiful, she moves so gracefully, it's a pleasure just to look at her. She retrieves her bowl of cereal from the nightstand, watching me expectantly as she continues her breakfast.

I sigh. "So I went to the party."

"Yeah, ok...and?"

"And..." I pause. "Jack was there."

"No!" Laurie looks as if she's swallowed something gross. "Please tell me you didn't sleep with him. Please tell me you didn't." She frowns. "Is that why the jerk was here last night? Did something happen?"

"Jack was here?"

She presses her lips together and rolls her eyes. "Yes, around eleven. He buzzed, but I didn't let him in. I told him you were out with Chadwick. I may have insinuated just a little that you were getting it on with the sexy photographer."

"I doubt he would have cared," I say with a frown, wondering what Jack could have wanted. "He's engaged."

"Jack?"

"Yeah," I tell her, "to Claudia Sever."

"That asshole," Laurie mutters. "I'm sorry," she adds gently.

I shrug.

"I thought he didn't have it in him to commit to one woman," she says drily.

"No, just me." I trace a pattern on the covers on my bed, the sadness from last night returning in an unwelcome surge.

"Stop feeling sorry for yourself," Laurie says. "You deserve so much better than a guy who keeps toying with you. Either he wants you or he doesn't. Seriously Rach, he gives you enough attention to keep you in love with him while he fucks everyone else but you."

"You're right," I say. "Now, do you want to hear the rest of the story or not?"

"Ohhhh, there's more." She loses her serious expression. "I hope it doesn't involve Jack Weyland."

Shaking my head, I start to tell her the rest,

watching her eyes grow wider and wider when I get to the part about Landon.

"Holy hell!" She whistles. "You had a one-night stand!" She starts to giggle. "And he thought you were a hooker. Wow! You're not the girl who left this apartment last night. Where's Rachel?" she asks dramatically. "Where's my cousin—what have you done with her?"

I smile. "I think I gave her something she really needed."

"Ha!" she exclaims, and then she frowns. "Landon...the Swanson Court penthouse... Was it Landon Court?"

"Who? I don't know, I didn't ask for his last name —you know, one-night stand and all that."

"No, you were too busy trying to get a ride on his disco stick." She snickers.

"Actually, two rides," I correct.

"Whore!" she exclaims, giggling along with me. "But seriously, Swanson Court, penthouse apartment. ..." She hands me her bowl of cereal and bounds up from the bed. My computer is on my desk by the window, and she lifts the lid and starts it up.

"What are you doing?" I ask, stealing a spoonful of her cereal.

"Hold on," she replies. "And don't eat my breakfast. You haven't even brushed your teeth."

I shrug and take another spoon, watching as the

laptop starts. Laurie opens a browser window and types a few words before hitting enter. The search results appear almost immediately, with a few images down the page. I wait while she clicks on something and then the screen is filled with pictures.

Some of them are of a building, which I recognize as the Swanson Court Hotel. The others are mostly of a man. I move toward the edge of the bed so I can see the screen better. There are pictures of him in suits, in tuxedos, a shot with his dark gold hair tousled, blue eyes vibrant. There's a picture on a large boat, one at an airport as he walks across the tarmac with a beautiful blonde woman who looks like a model, and lots more.

I get off the bed and move forward to check the search term Laurie used—It's *Swanson Court Owner*.

"Is that him?" Laurie asks.

I nod slowly.

"He's the fucking owner!" she whispers, uncharacteristically awed. "I've seen his name on the gossip blogs. He's always on those lists, the 'most eligible bachelors in the country' lists. He's a gazillionaire, and he's fucking hot!"

He is. I'm transfixed by the sight of him on my screen. Lauren goes back to the search results and I read some of the information on the screen. *Landon Court, hotelier, real estate magnate, billionaire owner of*

Swanson Court Hotels and residential apartments with branches all over the country.

He's beautiful, rich, and sexy.

And I slept with him.

"Wow!" I release a breath. "I had no idea."

Laurie clicks on the Wikipedia link and starts to read his biography out loud, but I'm looking at the picture at the top right of the page. This one shows him in a tuxedo outside a building that looks like the Met. He looks like a movie star, only more handsome than any of the ones I can name. In all the pictures, he looks detached, remote even, like a solitary man in a room full of strangers. I remember his smile from last night, and suddenly I feel privileged to have been on the receiving end of a familiarity he obviously denies the public.

Even if he thought I was a hooker.

"I can't imagine why he would want to sleep with a hooker," Laurie muses beside me. "No offense to you, obviously. You're not a hooker." She sticks her tongue out at me. "But he's been linked to lots of attractive women. I'm sure he can have anyone he wants without having to pay for it."

I remember asking him the same question. "Maybe he was being adventurous," I tell Laurie. "After all, I was supposed to be a birthday present."

Laurie sighs sadly. "Now I feel bad for your sake

that you didn't leave him your number. I mean look at that body! I'd pose as a hooker to hit that."

"Jeez Laurie. Remember Brett, your boyfriend who loves you? He's in the next room."

She giggles. "If he hears me, he'll probably challenge Mr. Rich and Handsome Hotel owner to a duel or something." Going back to the Wikipedia article, she starts to read again. "He's only twenty-nine," she says. "Fancy being so rich so young." She pauses. "OMG! His mother was Alicia Creighton." She turns to me, eyes wide. Then, realizing I have no idea who she's talking about, she shakes her head. "The prima ballerina. She died in a car crash before I started dancing, but my ballet teacher practically worshiped her."

"He must have been very young at the time," I say with a small frown. I can't imagine life without my mom, or even Aunt Jacie, even if they both drive me crazy at times.

Laurie reads on. "He supports various charities, and likes opera, ballet, libraries, and the theater." She looks at me. "Rachel, I believe this man is exactly your type."

"Don't be ridiculous," I say. "It was only a one-night stand. I'm never going to see him again."

"Said Cinderella, but then she got drunk and 'forgot' her glass slipper." Laurie does her thing where she winks continuously for a few seconds. "Seriously, if you had a chance to date him for real, you'd say no?"

I gaze at the Wikipedia picture. "I don't... After Jack, I don't need another guy to fixate on."

"Jack again," Laurie says wryly. "Forget about him Rach." She looks back at the screen. "A man like this would reboot you with his hard drive."

"Jesus!" I exclaim, shaking my head. I have no idea where Laurie picks up her references. The law firm where she works while attending her final year of law school is as old fashioned and staid as it is possible to be in twenty-first century New York, so it's definitely not at work.

I turn back to the screen. She's right though— Landon could help to wipe Jack off my mind, but then I'd likely fall for him. Who wouldn't? I'd be right back where I started, hung up on a man.

"It doesn't matter," I tell Laurie, pulling my eyes away from Landon's face on the screen. "I don't have his number, and he doesn't have mine. We hooked up for a night, and as hot as it was, we're never going to see each other again."

CHAPTER 5

*L*ANDON COURT.

No matter how hard I try not to think about him, I can't help myself. The memories, his name, everything just hovers at the borders of my mind, waiting for the slightest opportunity to come in and torment me with images from the night we spent together.

It's been almost a week, but I'm still no closer to forgetting him than I was when he was right in front of me.

Landon Court. Even the name is sexy, and his voice...it makes me shiver to remember.

"Top ten travel apps," Mark Willis, senior features editor, says musingly, looking at a sheet of paper on the table. It's Thursday, and we're in one of the small meeting rooms going over last minute articles for next week's publication on the website version of Gilt Traveler. "That one's yours Chelsea."

Chelsea, my fellow features associate, beams and makes a note on her writing pad. She's startlingly beautiful, with cornflower blue eyes and waves upon waves of platinum blonde hair. She always gets the simplest and most unchallenging articles, because of the combination of her wide-eyed sweetness, the fact that her father is a Kentucky billionaire oilman and rancher, and the southern accent she displays no desire to get rid of. She doesn't mind. She uses all the resulting free time to work on her historical epic novel about the power-hungry noblemen of renaissance Italy and the women who loved them.

The articles I write aren't much better. My last assignment was to write about a cruise on the Colombia River. I interviewed Evelyn Hart, a former Broadway star who'd taken the cruise. It was a promotional article, sponsored by the cruise company. Evelyn Hart even admitted to me that she'd spent most of the trip holed up in her cabin, recuperating from her most recent plastic surgery. Luckily, her assistant, who'd experienced the cruise while her boss was hiding out in her cabin, had been able to provide some details.

I don't really mind what I do. I was over the moon when I got a job at Gilt Publications, even though I didn't get my dream position in Gilt Review, the literary magazine where I'd hoped to work as an editor. There's just something about the organization and the atmosphere at Gilt that makes it more than just magazines. Gilt is a lifestyle, embodied by so many of the tastemakers who work here. From the enigmatic editor-in-chief of Gilt Style, who can make or break a fashion designer's career with just a word, to Grace Conlin, the no-nonsense boss at American Homes.

Mark looks up at me. He's a slightly built man with an earnest, serious face that sometimes makes me imagine he'd rather be teaching journalism at some Midwestern college than working at Gilt. "You have another promotional article. It's a place called Insomnia, the newest lounge in Manhattan, apparently. You'll write one of those 'Top Ten Reasons to Visit Insomnia while in New York' kind of articles. They requested you specifically."

I frown. "Really?"

He shrugs. "Your prowess at putting out promotional articles isn't going unnoticed, it would seem."

The words could be interpreted as anything between a compliment and an insult. I purse my lips and make a note of the assignment, resigned to my fate. At least I'll get to visit the 'newest lounge in Manhattan'.

As soon as I leave the meeting, I call the manager of the Insomnia Lounge and make an appointment for later in the evening. She informs me that a VIP access pass will be delivered to me so I won't have to wait in line.

By the time our conversation is over, I'm back in my office. My inbox is full of mail, and one of them is from Laurie.

Look what I found. His brother is even more delicious.

There's a link, and I click on it to see an article on one of the online gossip sites. There's a picture of Landon with a younger man as they walk out of a popular Manhattan restaurant.

Hotel Magnate Landon Court Celebrates Birthday With Baby Brother Aidan.

He's wearing the suit he had on when I met him, complete with the discarded tie I saw in his living room. He does look delicious. My eyes don't even go toward the brother. Instead, my mind travels back to that night in his apartment, to the memories my body isn't ready to give up yet.

I sigh. I'm not going to obsess over my one-night stand. I should be more concerned with planning how to act with Jack when I inevitably run into him again. Already the office is buzzing with news of his engagement. Chelsea, as nice as she is beautiful, and one of the few people who saw past my friendship with Jack to the fact that I was in love with him, already asked how I'm doing and assured me that she was always available if I wanted to bitch about Jack.

It's tempting, but the less I say or think about him, the better for me. He hasn't called me, and I haven't seen him since Chadwick's party, so whatever the reason he came to my apartment that night, it probably wasn't important.

The email from Laurie is still open on my screen. I type my reply.

Yeah whatever. I see how productive you are at work. Anyway, get ready, we have a VIP pass to Insomnia tonight.

She replies via text with a long *Yay!*

I spend the next few minutes answering the rest of my work emails. I'm almost done when my phone rings.

It's my mom.

"Darling." Her voice is low and smooth. "How are you?"

I imagine her washing paint off her arms as she speaks, phone tucked between her shoulder and her ear, her red hair pinned up. That's the image I always have of my mom. She's a successful painter, artsy and sometimes silly, the direct opposite of my dad, who is serious and a little nerdy. He was the business side of Trent & Taylor, the ready-to-wear clothing line he founded with his twin brother, my uncle Taylor, until they sold a large percentage of the company to a multinational chain. He totally adores my mom. Together, they're a walking true love cliché.

I grew up dreaming about having a love like theirs. I waited for it, and when I found Jack and fell so hard, I thought I'd finally found it. How wrong I was.

"I'm all right Mom. You?"

She laughs. "Oh! I'm fine. How's work?"

I shrug. "Perfect."

"It doesn't sound all that perfect from the tone of that voice—not that I blame you. You must be the only travel writer in New York who has never been outside the city for work."

"I'm not a travel writer, Mom. I just—"

"Write for a travel magazine. I know." She sighs. "I hope you can make it this Sunday. I'm making lunch. Laurie already confirmed that she's coming with Brett. She also said you're free this weekend so don't bother to give me an excuse. Your brother won't be there, but your uncle and aunt will."

I roll my eyes. Mom likes to plan these family reunions at least once a month, and she connives with Aunt Jacie to waylay us into coming. She probably told Laurie I'd already agreed to come.

"Fine. I'll be there."

I hear a pause in her voice. "Laurie told me about Jack's engagement."

I close my eyes, unsure whether to channel my annoyance toward Laurie for telling my mom, toward

Jack for breaking my heart in the first place, or at myself for letting him.

"Aren't you glad I finally got the wake-up call I've needed for almost two years?" I ask. My mom's opinion on my fixation on Jack has always been the same as Laurie's.

"Oh sweetie." She sighs. "I just hate that you're hurting. I remember how excited you were when you first started seeing him. Of course, you romanticized him, and you were more in love with your idea of him than with who he really was."

"You don't know that."

"I know more than you think I know. I'm your mother. Anyway, now you'll get over him."

"How's Dylan?" I ask, eager to change the subject. My baby brother is the apple of my mom's eye.

Her voice perks up. "He's fine. Sometimes I worry that he's studying too hard..." She launches into a long monologue about my brother, and thankfully doesn't bring up Jack again before she has to go.

Afterward, I wonder what she would have said if I'd told her about Landon. She'd probably have been excited and, like Laurie, disappointed that I hadn't left him my number. Again, I can't keep my mind from drifting back to that night, and a wave of heat courses through my body. It was only sex—great sex, yes—but thinking about it, it felt like so much more.

Maybe if I had come clean and told him I wasn't

actually a hooker, we could have come to some sort of mutually beneficial and sexually rewarding arrangement. Maybe I could have kept on pretending to be a prostitute, hooking up with him whenever he called. I'd be Rachel Foster, Gilt employee by day, Landon Court's whore by night.

The prospect is disturbingly appealing.

Shaking the thought out of my head, I turn back to my screen. Landon Court has probably forgotten that I exist, which means the only reasonable thing to do is to forget about him too.

CHAPTER 6

*T*HE VIP pass allows us to bypass the long queue outside the lounge. Once inside, a hostess clad in a revealing but classy mini-dress leads us through the club to a raised area overlooking the dance floor, where she shows us to our table.

"The manager will be with you soon," she tells me before her eyes shift to Brett as she surreptitiously checks him out. "Drinks are on the house."

"Thank you," Brett drawls in reply.

The hostess smiles, her eyes still alternating between his wiry muscles and his face. "I'll send a waiter," she says, and then finally leaves.

As soon as she's gone, Brett lets out a whistle. "This is some swanky joint," he says, grinning at me and already nodding his head to the music. He's tall and fit, with curly black hair and intense dark eyes.

Like Laurie, he's a great dancer. He used to be an associate at the same firm where Laurie works, but he left to pursue a career in fitness. He co-owns a trendy gym close to our apartment, but hasn't been able to get either Laurie or me interested in squats, lunges, or whatever other exercise move people are doing these days.

"The staff shouldn't make eyes at the customers though," Laurie says drily. "That hostess was totally checking you out."

Brett leans over and kisses her nose, making her laugh. "I didn't notice. Only got eyes for my baby."

"Seriously, you should get these kinds of assignments more often, Rach," Laurie declares, flirting hostess already forgotten as a waitress approaches our table.

We order drinks. "So where's the manager?" Brett asks. He has one hand on Laurie's lap, and she's leaning into him. Even in public, they're unable to keep their hands off each other. They're the third nauseatingly happy couple in my family, my parents and Laurie's parents being the other two. Soon Dylan will fall in love and join them, and then I'll probably have to buy a box full of cats and resign myself to my fate.

"She's probably on her way," I reply to Brett's question, looking around at the suits in the VIP area as I search for a woman who might be the one I spoke to on the phone. The song playing segues neatly into another one, a new track with what Laurie would call a 'sick' beat. She's practically dancing on her seat. If I weren't here, she would be on the dance floor with Brett.

Our drinks arrive. "Why don't you two hit the dance floor?" I suggest.

"And leave you here all alone?" Laurie shakes her head. "We'll finish our drinks first."

They down their drinks in record time while I nurse mine, knowing I have to keep my head straight for my interview. Luckily, I don't have to urge them to leave me again as the manager arrives just as Brett sets his glass down.

The slightly built woman who joins us is dressed in dark pants and a white formal blouse, a sharp contrast from the hostesses. "Rachel Foster?" She gives me a questioning look before extending her hand. "I'm trying to match you to the picture on your magazine's website. I'm Marjorie Lake."

I shake her hand. "Nice to meet you. This is my cousin Laurie, and Brett, her boyfriend."

"Great!" She smiles at them. "You guys having fun?"

"Mmmhmm." Laurie nods. "Your DJ is something else."

"We're going to dance," Brett says, getting up and holding out a hand for Laurie. "See you later."

Marjorie settles down beside me on the soft leather seats, which are arranged in a cozy semi-circle around a small table. "We already prepared some material," she says, "pictures, notes, highlights... I have a printout, but I've also emailed them all to you."

I go through the material she gives me, asking her questions and typing my notes into the document app on my phone. "You seem to be doing so well already," I remark when we're done. Judging by the line of people outside and the number of famous faces I've spotted in the VIP area since we arrived, I'd guess Insomnia was already one of the top ten lounges in the city.

"Yes," Marjorie agrees. "We do already have a lot of buzz, but I suppose senior management wants to expose the club to a larger client base."

"Well, you can never have too much exposure."

I check my phone to make sure I've received her email with the attachments, then I hand the stack of material back to her. "Thanks for taking the time to talk to me."

"No problem." She gets up. "Enjoy yourself," she adds with a smile before leaving.

Taking a sip of my drink, I look toward the dance floor, trying to find Laurie and Brett among the people dancing. After a few moments, I spot Laurie giving Brett some mini twerking action while he grins from ear to ear.

"Mind if I join you?"

I look up at the good-looking guy in front of me. He's tall and fit, dark-haired, and confident in the manner of a guy who knows how good-looking he is. Something about him reminds me of Jack, and that alone is enough to make me shake my head and smile apologetically.

He shrugs and walks away, leaving the raised VIP area for the bar, where a couple of women are sitting alone. I down the rest of my drink and resume watching Laurie and Brett. I know I can't spend the whole night watching them, and I can't leave early and ruin the night for them either. Maybe I shouldn't have sent away the guy who approached me.

"You want another one of the same?"

I look up at the waiter standing by the table, leaning toward me. I should have another drink, get a little buzzed, and let it loose on the dance floor. If I party 'til I'm exhausted, maybe I'll fall asleep as soon as I get home and won't lie awake thinking of Landon Court.

Just the thought of his name and my body awakens, demanding more of the pleasure from that night.

I shake my head. It's a good thing I'm never going to see him again. Letting him get into my head is nothing but a recipe for disaster. What's the point of thinking about someone who's so hot, obviously rich, and probably not available?

"Why are you still sitting here?" I hear Laurie exclaim. I was too deep in my thoughts to see her approach the table. "Come on Rach, you have to dance."

She collapses on the seat beside me, breathless and, exhilarated from dancing. There's a light sheen of sweat glistening on her skin, just enough to make her look soft and dewy. "Where's Brett?" I ask.

"He's getting some water at the bar," she replies. "Come on. You know you love to dance."

"I'll be right back," I tell the waiter, getting up to follow Laurie to the floor. Down there, the music is loud and pumping, and the beat is almost impossible to resist. Laurie starts to dance and I join her, grinning as the DJ plays hit after hit. After a while, I completely lose myself in the music, forgetting about work, the fact that I'm only going to get a few hours of sleep before work tomorrow...I forget it all, except for Landon Court.

I pretend I'm dancing for him. That with every move of my body, I'm reeling him deeper and deeper into my spell, like a dancing siren, or Salome with her seven veils. I pretend that I'm seducing him with my dancing, teasing him, tempting him to take me somewhere and drive my body to madness again.

When a pair of male hands settle on my hips, I

want to close my eyes and pretend it's him, his hands, and I almost do, but I'm not uninhibited enough for that, so I tap the hands away. I hear Laurie shout, "Go girl!" as I dip it really low, then shimmy back up. The guy behind me lets out a whistle, and I look up with a smile. Then for some reason, my eyes go toward the VIP area, and I see a man seated alone at a table, drink in hand, watching me.

The man is Landon Court.

All the air escapes from my lungs, leaving me frozen. What is he doing here?

Even from that distance, I can feel his eyes on my body, like heat burning into my skin. The expression in them is sensual, carnal even, as if he's thinking of the things he wants to do to me, or remembering the things he has done to me.

He looks away, his eyes dropping to the glass he's holding. I manage to drag in a deep breath before he tosses back the contents and spears me with his gaze again.

He's too far away to say anything to me, but like someone compelled, I go toward him, leaving the dance floor as I'm drawn to him by some deep desire in me I can't control. I'm already standing in front of him before I realize how awkward it is. We're strangers—strangers who've had sex, but still, as far as he's concerned, I'm a hooker.

He's wearing dark pants and a deep blue sweater,

looking effortlessly handsome, sexy, and sophisticated. His hair is tousled, gleaming gold in the lights, and he's still looking at me with that sensual gaze that makes me wish that instead of this public place, we were back in his apartment, tangled up in his bed.

He smiles, almost as if he can see what I'm thinking in my eyes.

"You're a great dancer," he says lightly, looking up at me through lashes that are much too long for a guy. Why is everything about him so sexy? It's unfair to everyone else.

"Thanks." I shift on my feet, wondering what the hell I'm doing standing in front of him like I'm being inspected. I should say something and go back to my table, but even as I struggle to find something, anything to say, it feels as if my body is reaching toward him, wanting to relive the contact of that first night.

He reaches out a hand to me. "Come on," he requests. "Join me."

I take his hand, feeling my body pulse as soon as my skin comes in contact with his. He pulls me down to sit beside him on the soft leather seat, and my nose fills with the scent of him—body wash and a faint whiff of spicy cologne.

He doesn't let go of my hand, keeping it on his thigh as he beckons a waiter to bring us both drinks.

"What are you doing here?" I ask.

He inclines his head toward me. We're so close I can feel the heat from his skin, and when he speaks, his warm breath fans my neck. "I was in the area."

Trembling, I take a shallow breath and move back a little, turning to face him. It seems like too much of a coincidence that he's here, at the same lounge, on the same night. "Really?"

"Really," he replies. There's a gleam in his eyes that I don't quite understand. I want to flatter myself that somehow, he's here to find me, but how is that even possible? He leans closer to me and I lose the ability to think of anything but how much I'd like him to kiss me now. My lips part, almost involuntarily, and he lowers his eyes, his fingers tightening around mine.

He wants me. The thought is exultant. Whatever this thing is I'm feeling, this unreasonable desire I can't even justify, he feels it too.

The waiter arrives with the drinks, and I watch with regret as Landon pulls back, releasing my hand.

Suddenly my throat feels parched. I take a long sip of my cocktail. "So are you on the prowl or what?" I say it lightheartedly, even though the thought of him picking up another woman tonight causes an intense pang of jealousy inside me.

He considers me for a moment. "Are you working tonight?"

I almost reply that I am, but then I remember that he doesn't know what I actually do. "Working?"

"Are you working the joint?" he repeats, his penetrating gaze steady on my face as he waits for me to reply.

I swallow hard and look away. Of course, as far as he knows, I'm a hooker. Why else would a hooker be in a swanky club if not to pick up men?

"Not tonight," I reply. "I'm here with my cousin and her boyfriend."

He doesn't look as if I'm telling him something he doesn't already know, fueling my suspicion that his presence here has something to do with me.

"Does she know what you do for a living?"

I lean back, resenting the lies I can't stop telling. "No."

The tempo of the music changes, and Justin Timberlake starts to sing about mirrors. I move farther away from him on the seat as the silence stretches between us. The weight of the knowledge that my deception has gone further than I intended makes me shrink from him. It feels almost as if he knows, as if with his eyes, he's challenging me to come clean, but that's just ridiculous.

I decide to go back to my table. Laurie will be back soon anyway, and somehow, I think it's better if she doesn't find me at the same table as Landon Court. I'd have no words to explain that one.

I start to get up, but his hand snakes out, reaching for mine.

"Don't go," he says.

I fall back on the seat, momentum bringing me closer to him than I originally was. He's turned toward me, and my body is angled toward his, so close that all I can see, feel and breathe is him.

His eyes are on my lips, and I can feel the tenseness in his body, like an animal about to spring. There is an aching tightness spreading from my belly, making me breathless.

I lick my lips again, and a breath escapes him.

"Don't do that." He says it like a warning.

"Why not?" My voice sounds thick and husky.

His eyes roam my face. Hooker or whatever he thinks I am, he wants me, and his desire is calling out to mine. I can feel one of his hands on the side of my thigh, warm and firm, and I know I want more. No matter what he proposes, I won't resist.

As if he can sense my capitulation, his body relaxes. He strokes a finger across my cheek, his lips rising in a small smile. "I think your cousin is looking for you."

For a moment, I can't focus on what he's saying, too intent on wanting him to keep touching me. Then I hear Laurie's voice.

"Rach!" She sounds confused. "I was looking for

you." She's holding Brett's hand and frowning in Landon's direction. "Why'd you move tables?"

"I... This is Landon," I say, watching as her eyes widen, only for a second, and then her face is composed again.

Landon rises to his feet, managing to do so gracefully despite how tangled up our limbs are. "Please join us," he says, extending a hand to Laurie. "I'm Landon Court."

"Laurie." She gives me another questioning look as Landon and Brett shake hands and exchange names. I raise my shoulders in a gesture to show her I'm as confused as she is and then look away.

"We were just going," Laurie says, looking at me. "Do you want us to wait or..."

"No." I steal a glance at Landon then look back at her. "Just wait for me, I'll be right out."

"Nice to meet you Landon," Brett says politely. "We're right outside, Rach."

I watch them leave then turn to Landon. "I'm leaving," I say.

"I gathered," he replies, a small smile on his lips. He's holding my hand again, making no move to release it.

"It was nice to run into you," I say softly.

He chuckles. "It was nice to run into you, Rachel."

He's holding my gaze, making it hard for me to

breathe. After a few seconds, he releases my hand, and I wait for him to ask for my number, to ask if he can see me again, but there's nothing.

I get up, stung by how clear it is that he has no intention of pursuing the obvious attraction between us. "Goodnight."

I can feel his eyes on me as I walk away. Outside, there're still people trying to get into the club, and on the sidewalk close to the entrance, Brett and Laurie are kissing. I walk toward them, pissed off at Landon, and at myself for caring so much. So what if he doesn't want to see me again? I shouldn't care. He's just a one-night stand I should already have forgotten.

As I walk toward Laurie and Brett, a sleek black car pulls up on the sidewalk beside me. The driver, a bulky guy with a crew cut and sharp eyes, steps out of the car.

"Miss Foster?" he asks.

"Yes?"

"I'm here to take you home," he says. "Courtesy of the Insomnia Lounge."

"Hey," I call to Laurie and Brett, momentarily perked up by the fact that I won't be walking home in my four-inch heels. "Our ride is here."

CHAPTER 7

A few days later, my article about the Insomnia lounge is up on the site. I refresh the page for like the fifth time, reading the new comments. Most of the people commenting have been there, and have nothing but praise. The people who haven't been leave comments about making sure to visit next time they're in the city.

Not bad.

There're a few pictures of the lounge published with the article, shots of the VIP area among them. Just looking at the pictures, I can't help thinking about Landon, the way he held my hand, and how intoxicated I was by his presence.

God! I have to stop thinking about him. He's just a crutch. He's just something I'm subconsciously using to occupy my mind while I deal with getting over

Jack, the person who has occupied it for the past two years.

The person I haven't thought of for days.

Right now, it's Landon who's occupying the prime place in my thoughts. Landon who didn't even bother to ask to see me again, because in his mind, I was just a hooker on her day off.

The words on my screen start to look blurry, and I turn toward the window, a tiny slice of glass that provides me a limited view of other office buildings and a little sky. He wanted me—I'd felt it, in his touch, in his voice, in the heat from his body that found its way into mine, making my whole body thrum with need for him.

He wanted me, and yet he chose to do nothing about it. Now, I feel silly for allowing myself to toy with the idea that somehow, he'd found out who I was and was there to see me.

Even Laurie had been thinking along the same lines.

"I thought you said you didn't leave him your number," she asked me on our way home in the car the club had provided.

"I didn't."

"So...he just appeared at the same Lounge you had to go to for a work assignment? It was a coincidence?"

"What else could it be? He doesn't even know my last name."

"That seems very unlikely," she pronounced before transferring her attention back to Brett.

But it was a coincidence, and he hadn't even been interested enough to use the opportunity afforded by that coincidence. I was so desperate for him, I'd have followed him back to his apartment, his car, or any dark corner without a thought.

My door opens, jerking me out of my thoughts, and I look up to see Jack standing at the entrance to my office.

I haven't thought about him in a while, but now that he's standing right in front of me, it hits me that all the romantic hopes and dreams I've centered on him for the past two years have resulted in nothing, and there's a small ache that comes with that realization.

"Hi." There's an uncertain frown on his face as he looks at me. His shirt is tucked into jeans, and he has a deep blue jacket slung over one shoulder. As much as I would prefer not to admit it, he does look good.

"Hi Jack."

"You busy?"

That has always been his standard question. Usually, I say no, and then he comes in and sits on my desk. We talk, and he makes me laugh so hard my stomach hurts. Now I can't even imagine laughing at anything he says.

I give him a humorless smile. "I am, actually."

"Rachel." He draws out my name as he walks into my office. "Don't be mad."

Don't be mad. That's all he has to say. I snort. "I'm actually not mad, Jack, but I'm really kinda busy at the moment."

He stares at me then comes around the desk, leaning on it as he smiles down at me. "I've missed you, you know."

"Yeah, the way you always do. You missed me when you were dating that flamenco dancer in Spain, that Italian swimmer you spent a month sailing with, the Brazilian model... You always miss me, but never enough to—" I stop, annoyed with myself for even allowing the outburst. "How's your fiancée?"

"She's great."

"Good."

He suddenly reaches for my hand, taking it in his. The touch is intimate, but not strange. I realize how often he's touched me like this over the past two years, gestures of intimacy that keep me hoping, yet make no promises.

I stare at my hand in his, and I find myself thinking of Landon, about how different it feels to be touched by him. There's something potent about

Landon's touch, something that sets me on fire and makes me want to toss away all my inhibitions.

"Rachel," Jack is saying, "I know we have a history, but it was a long time ago. What I need now is for you to be happy for me. I need to know we can still be friends." His eyes are imploring as they hold mine. I know the look well; it's one he has used successfully to break down my resistance over the years. Usually, it would make me succumb to whatever he was suggesting. Right now, though, it just makes me think of Laurie's words. *He knows you're in love with him, and he wants to keep you that way, so you'll always be there.*

My desk phone rings, freeing me from having to respond to Jack. I pull my hand from his and pick up the phone, holding the receiver to my ear. "Hello."

"Jessica wants you." It's the brusque and efficient voice of Carol Mendez, secretary to Jessica Layner, editor-in-chief of Gilt Traveler.

In all my time at Gilt, Jessica has never requested me specifically. In fact, I don't think she's ever said more than two words to me. "What for?"

"You can ask her when you get here," Carol snaps, and I hear a click to signify that the conversation is over.

I get up from my chair. "I have to go," I tell Jack.

He looks disappointed. "All right, but we should talk later, Rachel. I can't stand this...distance."

I watch him leave, frowning as I pick up a tiny notepad and a pen. *He's going to have to get used to the distance*, I decide resolutely. There's no way I'm letting our relationship go back to the old dynamic, where I wait on the sidelines hoping for little crumbs of his attention.

~

AS THE EDITOR-IN-CHIEF, JESSICA HAS THE LARGEST corner office on the floor. It's actually a suite, with a large closet/dressing room, a private seating room for when she doesn't want to be disturbed, and the main office, from where she commands us foot soldiers. I arrive at Carol Mendez's office first. "Jessica's in," she tells me, barely looking up from her computer.

"Thank you," I reply, wondering what Jessica Layner could want with me. To be honest, she's rather intimidating. I spent my first year at Gilt terrified of her. She's very fashionable, tall, and slender, with sharp eyes that don't miss a thing, an attractive face, and a body any woman would be proud of at any age. She's in her late fifties, according to Wikipedia, but Mark Willis once confided that she's a few years older than her official age.

From Carol's office, I enter the short hallway that leads to Jessica's. The walls are lined with pictures of Jessica with various politicians, Hollywood stars, and world leaders. Further intimidated, I smooth my sleeveless cream silk blouse and black knee-length pencil skirt then run a hand over my hair before opening the door to Jessica's spacious office. I see her as soon as I enter the room. She's sitting at her desk, facing the door with her back to the windows, her signature mane of back-length, expertly colored blonde hair framing her face like a halo.

There's a man sitting opposite her on the other side of her desk, wearing what looks like a very expensive suit. Something about his profile, even from behind, makes my stomach tighten. Even so, I'm so concerned about what Jessica has to say to me, that I don't spare more than a quick glance at the thick waves of dark gold hair and the obviously good-looking body in the suit.

I take two more steps inside the room, my eyes on Jessica, but something makes me turn back toward the man. At the same time, he raises his gaze to meet mine, and for a moment—longer than a moment—my heart actually stops beating.

Landon.

I forget about Jessica as my eyes drink him in. I forget everything but him. I feel elated and confused at the same time. Blood surges under my skin, making me weak, and still he keeps on looking at me, his deep blue eyes holding me like a prisoner.

What is he doing here?

There is a small smile on his face. It looks harmless, friendly even, but beneath the surface, I can sense the danger.

He knows. There's no surprise in his face at seeing me, only that smile that tells me he knows exactly who I am and that I work here.

"Rachel." Jessica's voice sounds far away, and it takes a concerted effort to force my eyes to break away from Landon's gaze and go to her. "I'm glad you're here," she's saying, as if she has forgotten she sent for me. "This is Landon Court."

He gets up and faces me. I suck in a breath, feeling as if I've been kicked in the stomach. There's just something so raw and feral in his beauty. In the light of Jessica's office, all the burnished gold in his hair gleams brightly, contrasting with the darker parts. Captivated by the sexy smirk curling his lips, I stand frozen as he extends a hand toward me. "It's nice to meet you Rachel," he says in that deep raspy voice.

I let him take my hand, as if I'm not already confused enough without having to deal with the jolt I feel when his skin touches mine. "It's...It's nice to meet you too," I stammer, turning a confused glance toward Jessica.

"Landon was in the building for a meeting, and he stopped by to say hello to an old friend—"

"Definitely not old, Jessica," he says to her

without letting go of my hand.

She smiles indulgently in a way I've never seen before, and I look from one to the other, wondering what the hell is going on. "Thank you, Landon." She turns back to me. "He wanted to thank you for that lovely article on the Insomnia Lounge."

I turn from Jessica—who has never noticed anything I've ever written, much less described it as lovely—to Landon. I'm finding it difficult to comprehend what's going on.

"I don't understand..." I say, feeling stupid. "Why...?"

Jessica smiles. "Landon owns the place. We had a little discussion earlier in the week and decided an article about it would be the right fit for our website..."

I can hardly hear what she's saying; I'm staring at Landon.

He owns the place.

"...and Landon requested that you write it. Luckily he'd read a couple of similar articles you've written..."

He requested for me to write it. He arranged for me to be there, and then he appeared. That meant he'd known who I was, had known since early in the week, and he'd had the nerve to ask me if I was working the joint!

Jessica keeps talking, but it's almost as if she's not

in the room. I can only see Landon, the contrast between the polite smile curling his lips and the steeliness in his blue eyes. *You lied to me*, he seems to be saying. *What are you going to do now that I've found you?*

I jerk my hand back from his, annoyed. I may have lied to him—no, I may have *omitted* that he was mistaking me for someone else, but no way did that mean he had the right to use my work to get me to his club under false pretenses, to practically seduce me again, all the while pretending he didn't know who I was.

I don't need this. After Jack, I don't need to even be in the same room with a man who wants to play games with me. I take a deep breath, doing my best to calm the emotions raging inside me, and then I school my face into a polite smile. "I'm glad you liked the article, Mr. Court—"

"Landon," he interrupts smoothly, cocking his head slightly as he gives me another small smile. "Of course I liked it. You're obviously very good at what you do."

I pause, momentarily distracted by the pure suggestiveness of his statement. "Mr. Court," I say deliberately, "I had a great time at your club, and the article reflected that. If that is all, I have to get back to work." I smile politely at Jessica before turning around and heading for the door.

Outside Jessica's office, I pause for a moment,

breathing deeply and trying to compose myself before I cross the short hallway to the door leading to Carol's office.

I'm about to open the door when I hear Landon's voice behind me.

"Wait."

It's a terse command, and if I had any self-respect, I would ignore it, but I stop, my hand on the door knob. I don't want to turn around, but almost as if I have no control over my own actions, I find myself turning to look at him.

He takes a step toward me, and my breath quickens. "Why the rush, Rachel?"

I lick my lips. "I have work to do."

"You said." He gives me a look. "Although this is a strange workplace for a hooker."

I pull in a sharp breath. "Why didn't you tell me that you knew?"

"Why did you lie to me?"

"I didn't lie to you," I say evenly. "You made an assumption."

"And you didn't think that maybe you should have corrected my mistake?" he asks, his voice edged with annoyance. "I spent the weekend wondering why you didn't leave your number, but I thought it didn't matter, since I could always get it from my brother. Try to imagine how surprised I was when I called him and he had no idea what I was talking about."

When he assumed I was a hooker, he also assumed that I was a birthday present from his brother. I didn't even want to start thinking about how strange that was. "Look," I start, "I'm sorry for the inconvenience, but you had no right to get me to your lounge under false pretenses just so you could... How did you even find out who I was?"

He shrugs, not bothering to reply. Of course, with the depths of his pockets, he probably has access to resources I can't even imagine. "You had every chance to tell me you weren't who I thought you were," he continues. "Why didn't you?"

I stay quiet. There's no way I'm going to admit that I wanted him so much, I was willing to pretend to be a hooker. "Why are you here, Landon?"

He moves toward me, and in a few steps, he's right in front of me. I try to step back, shaken by the surge of desire I feel, but my back is against the door. He closes in on me, enveloping me with his body and his presence, making me feel as if I'm losing control of myself.

His voice is hard. "I'm here because you owe me an explanation. That night at the hotel, why did you stay? Did you know who I was?"

I shake my head, trying to dispel the effect of his body being so close to mine. "I didn't, and I don't owe you anything. I wanted a one-night stand, and you wanted a hooker. We both got what we wanted. Why can't you leave it at that?"

He leans downward, one hand resting on the door beside my head as he brings his face close to mine. I lose my train of thought, my eyes locking on his sensual lips. They are so close. I wet my lips, nervous and aroused, and as if he knows, he smiles. "I didn't get what I thought I was getting," he murmurs, "and in any case, my hooker didn't get paid, did she? That's unacceptable to me Rachel. I always pay my debts."

"Maybe your 'hooker' decided to make it a charity case," I snap.

He laughs. The sound is rich, sexy, and it warms me to my toes. "I'm sure I don't strike you as someone who needs charity."

No, he does not. I take a shaky breath. "Well then," I say with a calmness I don't feel. "Back to my original question. Why are you here?"

"Maybe..." he says slowly, moving his body closer still, so that between the door at my back and him so close to me in front, I can hardly breathe. "Maybe I want to fuck you again."

Raw heat floods between my thighs, making my knees go weak. My lips part as I drag in a ragged breath. He's not even touching me, and yet, I feel as turned on as if he was. Desperate, I turn my face to the side so I can't see his perfect face, his mesmerizing eyes, the perfect curve of his lower lip. His breath fans against my ear and I close my eyes, trying to find the words to tell him to leave me alone when all I want is for him to fulfill the wild desire coursing through me.

"If that's why you're here," I say slowly, "you're wasting your time." I swallow. My even tone belies the fact that my body is already his, from my straining nipples to my aching sex. "Jessica could walk into this hallway any moment, so if you don't want her to come in and find us like this, I think you'd better let me go."

He smiles, his eyes communicating exactly what he thinks of my dismissal. He knows I want him—how could he not, when my whole body is straining toward him as if drawn by a magnet. His eyes hold mine for a long moment, until I'm sure I'm going to lose the ability to breathe.

"I couldn't care less about Jessica finding us," he says, "and I never waste my time." He places a hand on my waist, and at the contact, I let out a gasp. But he only lifts me from the door, molding me to his hard body just for a second before he sets me back on my shaky legs. "I always get what I want, Rachel," he says softly. Then he reaches behind me and opens the door, walks past me, and leaves me standing there with my heart racing and blood pounding in my ears as I try to get my traitorous body under control again.

CHAPTER 8

"I still can't believe he actually said that," Laurie says without taking her eyes off Adam Levine being super sexy on *The Voice*.

"Me neither." I frown into my box of Chinese takeout. "I mean who even says stuff like that?"

"What exactly do you have a problem with?" Brett asks. He's sitting beside Laurie on the couch, feeding her from his own takeout. "Is it the wording, or the intention conveyed?"

I scowl at him. "I have a problem with everything —getting me to go his lounge under false pretenses then pretending he didn't know who I was. Just who does he think he is anyway?"

"Hush," Laurie complains as some teenage girl with knee-high suede boots starts to sing a country number.

"I think you should fuck him," Brett whispers. "You obviously want to, and you already did before, so..." He shrugs.

"I agree," Laurie adds, looking away from the screen long enough to give me an encouraging smile.

"Definitely not," I reply, getting up. "I'm going to bed. Apparently, you two have no idea what a one-night stand means."

"There's no law that says you can't have a repeat," Laurie calls after me. I ignore her and dump my takeout box in the trash then go to my room to get ready for bed. When I finally lie down and close my eyes, all I can think of is Landon, and those words repeating in my ear like an erotic refrain.

I want to fuck you again.

In a shameless part of me, I admit that I want the same thing. I've wanted it since I set my eyes on him at the Insomnia Lounge. Thankfully, there's another part of me that's sensible enough to be infuriated at him.

I always get what I want.

"Well, good luck with that," I mutter to myself, tossing on the bed. I'm most definitely not going to sleep with him again. I'm not interested in a guy who thinks he can own the world just by wanting it. It doesn't even matter how sexy he is. I won't be adding myself to the list of women he can get into bed just by saying something as raw as 'I want to fuck you again.'

Out of curiosity, I open the browser on my phone and run a search on him with 'girlfriends' as one of the keywords. The articles that come up in the results are mostly from the New York gossip sites, with pictures of him with various women, including a few famous ones. The articles allude to romantic connections between him and some of his dates, but most of the allusions seem to have been based only on rumors. I wonder if he approached all the other women as directly as he approached me.

I want to fuck you again.

Jesus!

I put the phone away and close my eyes. There's no point in reading about his past relationships when I should be banishing him from my mind, memories of great sex and all.

The first step is to stop thinking about him, and I will, starting tonight.

I try my best, but by the time I finally fall asleep sometime later, I've already failed miserably.

I DO BETTER THE NEXT DAY, BURYING MYSELF IN work and writing up a storm. At lunchtime, I walk down to a nearby deli with Chelsea and Sonali Nagra, a cute new Indian intern who speaks with a British accent despite growing up on Park Avenue and who insists that her home is in Mumbai even though she's been there only once in her life. Her dream is to work at Gilt Style, the most popular of the Gilt magazines, and after that, to launch her own couture line. Over lunch, we gossip about people from the office and laugh about the more ridiculous articles Chelsea has had to write lately.

"I finally saw Jack Weyland yesterday," Sonali exclaims at some point, running perfectly manicured fingers through her coal black hair. "He looks even better in person. I swear when I got scorned at Gilt Style, I accepted the position at Traveler just so I could work with him."

Chelsea looks from Sonali to me, and I shrug, making it clear that I don't care if we talk about Jack.

"You shouldn't have taken the position then," Chelsea says sympathetically. "He never dips his dick in the office ink."

"Plus he's engaged now," I add, chuckling silently at Sonali's obvious disappointment.

"I'm more worried about his attitude about office relationships than his engagement," she replies, her eyes serious. "Claudia Sever has broken three engagements in the past two years, and everyone knows the person she really wants is Reese Fletcher, the billionaire. They've been on and off for ages."

I wonder if she could be right. When it comes to gossip and fashion, Sonali always knows what she's talking about. However, instead of the sick relief I would have felt in the past at the knowledge that Jack might soon be available again, I just feel uninterested.

"Speaking of hot men, I saw Landon Court in the building yesterday," Chelsea grins. "Now that's a big girl's Jack Weyland. I wonder what he was doing there."

I feign ignorance by keeping silent as they both speculate about the person whose name I've already decided to banish from my thoughts.

"I wouldn't mind the brother," Sonali says with a sigh. "He's doing a play on Broadway right now, though it's still in the preview stage. Some of my friends went, hoping to catch a glimpse of him." She lowers her voice. "There's something about guys with tragic stories. My mom says both brothers were in the car with their mother when she had the accident. Landon pulled Aidan out and then had to watch as the car burned with his mother inside."

"That's so awful," I exclaim, unable to imagine how painful it must have been, how painful it must still be for him.

Sonali shakes her head. "Yes, but they were both uninjured. Poor things."

"Yes, poor things," Chelsea says. "But enough

with the sad stories. I still want to know what Landon Court was doing in our building."

"Maybe he's planning to take over Gilt," I quip. "Takeovers are the new conquests."

"Well, I wouldn't mind working for him." She grins. "Or under him, depending on what he prefers."

It's an innocent statement, but my reaction to it, a mixture of possessiveness and fierce jealousy, startles me. I shouldn't care if my beautiful colleague finds Landon attractive. He's nothing to me.

"I doubt he's available," I point out, unable to let it go.

"Yeah." Chelsea sighs. "But a girl can dream."

WE WALK BACK, WITH SONALI DOING A RUNNING commentary on every hot guy we pass on the street. By the time I get to my office, I'm still laughing a little, but my thoughts soon go back to Landon and the things Sonali said about his mother's death.

I do a quick search on my computer, looking for old archived news reports from twenty years ago. It's not hard to find a report on the accident.

Even before I start to read the article, my heart breaks at the picture of two boys—both wrapped in blankets, the little one looking confused while the older one, Landon, has the most heartbreakingly sad expression. Next to that is a picture of a beautiful couple, his parents.

I start to read the article. The car skidded off the road and somersaulted a couple of times. According to an eyewitness–a teenager who stopped his car a few minutes after the accident occurred and called an ambulance–Landon emerged from the car carrying his little brother, but the car started to burn immediately after, and by the time the ambulance reached them, it had been too late for Alicia Creighton Court.

Oh Landon. To witness all that! He must have been devastated.

My desk phone starts to ring. Reluctantly, I abandon my perusal of the article and answer the call.

"Hello."

"I'm just confirming that you're back from lunch." Carol Mendez's voice is, as usual, brusque and efficient.

"Why?"

"Jessica wants to see you."

I frown, a sense of déjà vu creeping into my spine. "Now?"

"Well, not tomorrow." I hear her say something, not to me. Then her voice comes back on the line. "Sit tight. She's on her way."

I hear a click as the line goes dead. Jessica Layner is coming to see me? If that isn't strange, I don't know what is. I close the browser and arrange a stack of sheets on my desk, wondering what she wants. I just know, somehow, that this has something to do with Landon.

Jessica pauses at the door to my office, her eyes taking in the space as if she can't quite believe how small it is. She looks stylish in a cream sheath dress and scarlet heels. There's a rumor that the powerful women in the Gilt organization are perpetually in competition, which is why they always look on point and demand perfection in every single aspect of their magazines.

She takes a step inside the room and closes the door behind her. I get up from my seat, and she waves a hand. "Oh sit," she says lightly. "I'm not the president."

I sit my ass back on the chair, confused. She walks to the window and stares out. "You haven't got much of a view have you?"

"It's adequate."

She shrugs, then turns around to looks at me. "There's a hotel in San Francisco, the Gold Dust Hotel. It's one of those old, classy places." She looks at me to see if I'm following. "Landon Court purchased it some time ago from the original owners, and it's been undergoing renovations ever since."

I wait for her to continue, not sure where I come in but already knowing deep down that Landon has initiated something I won't like.

"I've already heard that it's going to be a top destination in San Francisco, and he has the most renowned interior designers as part of the project team," she says. "About a month ago I approached him about doing an article in Gilt, a glimpse into the new hotel for our readers. He wasn't interested." She pauses. "Then last week, his assistant calls to arrange a promotional article for a lounge he owns. And yesterday, he was here, asking to see you and offering me the article about the Gold Dust."

I frown. "I'm not... I don't think it has anything to do with me."

She raises her perfect brows. "You don't?"

I shake my head. "Maybe he decided he needed the publicity for his hotel after all."

Her eyes assess me for a moment. "When you applied to Gilt, you wanted a position at Gilt Review—why?"

I studied English Literature, and I've always wanted to have a career that had something to do with books and literature. "I thought it would be the right fit for me."

She waves a hand in a dismissive gesture. "There's no such thing as a right fit. You have to take owner-ship of wherever you find yourself, make it fit you." She stops and gives me a look. "You've applied your-self very well here. You won't have a problem going to

San Francisco to write about the transformation of the Gold Dust, will you?"

I choke on air. "You want me to go to San Francisco to write about Landon Court's hotel?"

"Don't you want to?"

I swallow. "I'm not sure... I've never handled anything like that."

She gives me a questioning look. "I would have thought you'd be sick of all those promotional articles by now. You're not a hack. This is a real assignment. It's going to be a main feature." She walks over to my desk. "I'm not in the habit of visiting associates in their offices, but I want to know if there's a conflict, any reason you can't do it."

I hesitate. Do I really want to tell my boss I don't want to take an assignment because I think the owner of the property I'm going to be writing about, a billionaire with properties around the world, wants to get into my pants? And Landon, *God!* I wonder if writing the feature would mean seeing him again. I can't lie to myself—I want to see him, especially after the article I just read about him. "I would love to do the feature," I hear myself saying. "I'm glad you considered me."

Jessica nods. "The travel arrangements are being made on his end. You'll be meeting with Tony Gillies at the Swanson Court Tower to discuss logistics. Is that okay?"

"It's fine."

'That's all then." She taps a perfectly manicured nail on my desk. "All the best."

～

AN HOUR LATER, I'M CLIMBING OUT OF A TAXI IN front of the impressive mixed-use office and residential high-rise that is the SCT building. As I walk toward the revolving doors, I catch a glimpse of myself in the reflective glass walls. I'm wearing a gray pencil skirt, a light green silk blouse, and black pumps with my hair held back on one side with a rhinestone barrette. I pause for a moment to check that the little makeup I applied before leaving the office looks okay, and then I mutter an unladylike curse and keep walking, unwilling to accept that Landon is the real reason I'm so concerned about my appearance.

Screw him, I think resentfully as I give my name to the security at the front desk. They're apparently expecting me, and they hand me a visitor's pass to enable me to cross the turnstiles between the doors and the elevator bank.

"Sixty-second floor," one of the guards informs me.

"Thank you," I reply, still thinking of Landon. I have no doubt he has engineered this whole thing

97

because he thinks he can use it to get me into his bed, but I'm determined to disappoint him.

On the sixty-second floor, the elevator doors slide open, revealing a spacious reception room with a large marble desk and a TV screen overlooking a plush seating area. I step out of the elevator a second before an almost invisible glass partition between the elevator bank and the reception area slides open, allowing me to walk toward the reception desk. There, an immaculately dressed girl with cropped black hair and glasses is waiting for me with a friendly smile.

"Good afternoon, Miss Foster," she says cheerily.

"Good afternoon," I reply, waiting as she scans my visitor card. While I wait, another set of glass doors slide open and a sharp-looking guy steps into the reception area. He's about my height, and like the receptionist, he's perfectly dressed in a trendy suit, his short curly hair neatly framing his face.

"Hello," he starts, extending his hand. "You must be Miss Foster from Gilt. I'm Tony Gillies, Mr. Court's assistant. We'll be discussing the logistics for your trip in his office. Please follow me."

In his office? "Landon—Mr. Court is going to be there?" I ask, suddenly tense.

"Yes." Tony nods and then starts to walk, giving me no choice but to follow him through the sliding glass doors into a long wide corridor with glass partitioned offices on one side and conference rooms on the other. At the end of the corridor, there's another set of glass doors that lead into a large office with two desks and a sitting area. One of the desks is occupied by a woman speaking into a set of headphones in a language that sounds like Italian, though I can't say for sure because I'm totally hopeless at any language that's not English. She doesn't look up when we enter.

"Please take a seat," Tony says, the picture of formal efficiency. He glances at his watch. "Mr. Court is in a meeting at the moment, but it will be over in a few minutes. Would you like anything to drink?"

I shake my head. "No."

He nods then retreats behind the second desk in the room. As I wait, I use the time to look around. On one side of the room, there's a wall of some sort of frosted glass with a door in the middle. I'm guessing it's the door to Landon's office when it opens and three men pour out of the room beyond, talking quietly among themselves. Through the open doorway, I catch a glimpse of Landon seated at the head of a conference table. He's looking at some papers on the table, a frown of concentration on his perfect face. I can't tear my eyes away from him. I would keep on staring, but the doors close, blocking him from my view.

"We can go in now." Tony is already standing by

my side. I also stand, nervously smoothing my skirt. Why am I so anxious? I have nothing to be worried about—nothing apart from being in the same room as Landon again.

I follow Tony to the door, waiting as he holds it open for me to walk inside. Immediately, my eyes settle on Landon. He's now standing beside the conference table, tapping an impatient finger on the glass surface. He's removed his jacket, which is now hanging off the back of the chair he just vacated. In just his light blue shirt and slim black pants, the strength and fitness of his perfect body is obvious— much too obvious.

I step into the office, and he looks up. His hair is slicked back, making him look even more intense. As his blue eyes land on me, he breaks into a smile. My heart misses a beat at the transformation of his face, and my steps falter.

"Come in Rachel."

I steady myself and keep on walking. The office is easily larger by far than any I've ever been in. Aside from the conference area, there's a sitting area with plush leather chairs and a glass coffee table. A large desk sits on a slightly raised area, almost like a dais, with the skyline of Manhattan as a backdrop. There's a wall covered with screens, which, at the moment, are all tuned to different news channels and financial reports from around the globe.

He has already pulled out a chair, and he stands behind it as he waits for me to sit. I walk toward him on shaky legs, cursing myself for the uncontrollable effect he has on me. One look and I forget all my resolutions.

Tony busies himself with setting up the projector, oblivious to the tension between Landon and me. I take the offered seat, trembling slightly when Landon's fingers deliberately brush my shoulders before he returns to his own seat. After a few seconds, Tony joins us at the table and starts up the slideshow of pictures of the new hotel, showing the stage of refurbishment already accomplished. The décor is a little more light and modern than the New York hotel, with more glass and brighter colors, but whoever the interior designer is, they sure know what they are doing.

Landon doesn't say a word as Tony goes over the description of the amenities being provided, the design firms involved, and what Swanson Court International hopes to achieve with the new hotel. Then he goes into the history of the property. Formerly known as The San Francisco Gold Dust hotel, it was built in the twenties and has been in the Sinclair family for generations. Landon recently acquired the property from Evans Sinclair and will reopen it as The Gold Dust, a Swanson Court Hotel.

I take notes, asking questions and documenting

the clarifications as well as highlighting areas for further research. Tony has done a great job on the presentation, showcasing the extensive and indigenous art collection that's part of the property, the high-class spa, the famous chefs, and the celebrity fitness trainer who will be joining the hotel. I have no doubt that for the people who can afford it, it's going to be worth every penny.

Finally, we get to the end of the slideshow, and I look away from the screen to find Landon's eyes on my face.

"Is that all?" he asks. He's talking to Tony.

"Yes."

"Thank you. You can leave us now," he says. "Miss Foster will communicate any requests for additional information or clarification."

Tony nods and exits the office, leaving me alone with Landon. I avoid looking at him, feeling the tension in the air thicken with each passing second.

I start to get up. "I should be going."

His hand on my arm stops me. "No, don't." He moves his chair from the head of the table to directly beside mine, arranging it so he's facing me. "We should talk."

"I know what you're doing," I say heatedly. "You engineered this assignment so you can get me to spend time with you." I glare at him. "Well, guess what, this time you're not going to get what you want. You're wasting your time. I'm not going to let you get away with manipulating my job just so you can fuck me."

His eyes flare at my heated words, but instead of responding, he presses a button on the desk, turning the frosted glass of the office walls even more opaque. "Let's see," he starts, "I generously agreed to a request your boss made a long time ago. How is that manipulating your job?"

"And the article about the Insomnia Lounge?" I challenge.

"I brought you there to give you a chance to tell me the truth, which you didn't take, for whatever reason."

"Maybe because I didn't want to. Maybe because I was perfectly fine with you thinking I was a hooker. Maybe because I had no intention of ever seeing you again."

He leans forward, his hand still on my arm. Suddenly I feel helpless against the magnetic pull from his body. Who am I fooling? I want him. I want him so badly I can taste my desire.

"Quit lying to yourself," he says quietly.

I let out a soft breath through parted lips. "I don't know what you mean."

"Tell me the truth, Rachel," he challenges. "What do you want?"

I don't answer, so he continues. "You see, I know

what I want. I want you. I didn't ask Jessica Layner to give you the feature, but I hoped she would, especially after I told her I was a fan of your work. I'll be in San Francisco for a week, and I want you there with me. I want to fuck you every day we're there. I haven't stopped thinking about it since that night at my hotel. I want to make you come until you beg me to stop, and I know you want the same thing."

I swallow hard. His words are doing something to me. Already, my nipples are hard and aching, pressing insistently against my bra. I wonder if he can see them through my blouse, even as I hope desperately that he can't. He hasn't even touched me and yet, I already feel breathless with desire. My cheeks flush and I close my eyes, frustrated by my inability to control my body around him.

"But if you'd prefer not to," he continues, "then we won't see each other in San Francisco. You'll do your work, return to New York, and probably never see me again. Is that what you want?

I want him to kiss me, that's what I want. I want to lean forward and close the gap between our lips. I want to taste the warmth of his mouth. I feel bewitched, confused, a second away from forgetting my own name. I can hear my breath coming in soft little pants, like there's no longer enough air in the room.

"What do you want?" he repeats.

I open my mouth, not sure what I'm going to say, and immediately his lips close over mine, warm, demanding, and skillful. His tongue traces my lower lip then dips into my mouth, teasing, caressing, stroking the desire that's already burning inside me into a frenzy of hot, uncontrollable need.

He pulls away and I moan in complaint, leaning forward, aching for more. "This is what you want." His voice is warm and seductive. I stare at him through glazed eyes, wondering why he's stopped kissing me. "Your nipples are hard, Rachel." He lifts one hand to stroke one of the hardened nubs through my top, as if to prove his point, and a low moan of pleasure escapes me. "Between your legs, you're wet and aching for me, aren't you?" His eyes are blue fire burning into mine. "I know you want me to fuck you, right here, in this office, on the floor, on my desk, against the wall—anywhere. You wouldn't care. You just want me inside you, right now."

At his words, acute desire shoots through me like a lightning bolt. My body clenches needily, helpless against the mental assault of his words. Almost as if I'm under a spell, I reach for his face, pulling it down toward mine.

He claims my lips hungrily, getting up and pulling me to my feet in the same movement. He lifts me up, pulling my skirt up so I can wrap my legs around his waist as he carries me over to his desk.

As soon as my butt touches the surface of the desk, his tongue plunges into my mouth, tasting and plundering while his hands cup my breasts through my blouse. I reach for him, my hand moving from the hard slab of his stomach to the perfection of his chest. Loosening his silk tie, I toss it away and start to unbutton his shirt, but he stops me, holding both my hands to my sides while he bends his head to my breast, grazing my aching nipple with his teeth.

My skin is so sensitive it feels like it's on fire, and the throbbing between my legs is making it impossible for me to think. I groan, freeing my hands from his so I can thread my fingers in his silky hair. I want more than just this teasing. I want him inside me, as soon as possible.

I arch my back, lifting my breasts closer to his face. He groans, coming back up to cover my mouth with his, his tongue mating with mine as his hands move down to my hips to push my skirt up around my waist, exposing me from the waist down.

He strokes warm fingers over the damp lace of my panties, finding my pulsing clit and rubbing it through the lace. I tear my mouth from his, unable to hold back a small cry of pleasure.

"Do you like it when I touch you like this?" His voice is rough, his eyes blazing with desire.

"Yes," I whisper helplessly, rubbing my hips against his fingers.

He smiles and pushes my panties aside, giving his fingers access to stroke me. I'm already so wet, they slide easily through my folds, slipping inside to tease me with the promise of what will come later.

I brace my hands on the desk and spread my legs for him, inviting him deeper, but he pulls his fingers away and drops to his knees in front of me.

He's still holding my panties aside, giving him access to lick every inch of me. I cry out at the warm touch of his tongue, gripping the edge of the desk tightly. He pulls back then hooks his fingers into the lace of my panties. In the next moment, I hear a ripping sound, and then his lips touch me again, followed by his tongue, the sweet velvety warmth sending me straight to heaven.

"Landon." His name comes out of my lips in a long moan. His tongue flicks over my clit then travels down to the quivering entrance of my body, teasing me and making me want more. "Oh God, Landon."

He responds by sliding two fingers inside me, teasing my pulsing walls and making my body clench and shudder. His tongue continues to tease my clit, bringing me to the brink of orgasm time and time again until I'm crazy with the desire to have him inside me.

I rock my hips against his mouth, begging him with my movements to give me more. He pauses long enough to look up and grin at the desperation on my face before he starts to torture me again.

"Landon," I beg. "I can't..."

He ignores me, sucking on my clit as he crooks his fingers, finding the tiny mass of nerves along my walls and stroking it masterfully. My body tightens, spasming uncontrollably as I cry out, losing myself in a hot pulsing orgasm.

Almost immediately, he's on his feet, my face in his hands. "I love the way you taste, Rachel," he whispers before sucking on my bottom lip. "I want to lick every inch of you. Tell me you'll come with me."

My eyes are still dilated, almost unable to focus. Somewhere deep down, I remember that I shouldn't be doing this.

When I pause, he kisses me again, his tongue delving into my mouth. His fingers find my nipples, swollen and aching in the confines of my clothes. With an impatient sound, he rips the front of my blouse open and pulls down my bra, exposing my aching breasts. His mouth covers one nipple and I almost weep with pleasure. I hear him undoing his belt, then his zipper, and when he releases my lips again, I look down at the perfect length of him, aching to have him inside me.

He reaches for something inside his desk, and the next moment I hear the sound of foil tearing. *He knew this would happen,* I think through my aroused brain. He knew and he prepared for it, even when I was lying to myself, telling myself I wouldn't sleep with him.

I watch him put on the condom, the need and excitement stronger than my thoughts.

"I want to fuck you without one of these," he says softly. "Will you let me, once I prove that I'm clean?"

I nod, desperate with need. Right now, I just want him inside me. I'd say yes to just about anything if it meant he'd enter me again.

He positions himself at the quivering entrance to my body. "Tell me you'll come with me to San Francisco," he whispers again, his voice rough.

I roll my hips, hungry for him. "Yes," I whisper. "Yes."

His hands find my waist and he moves me toward him. At the same moment he pushes forward, sliding slowly inside me and filling me completely.

"Yes!" I cry out as the first immediate pulse of my orgasm rolls through me. My legs weaken, and I moan helplessly, coming apart at the seams. He grips my thighs, pulling me to the edge of the desk as he pulls out, almost to the tip, then plunges into me again. He lowers his head to my breasts again and I groan, my body clenching almost unbearably around the sweet, hard strokes of his cock.

I brace my hands on his shoulders, feeling the tense, bunched up muscles even through his shirt. He lifts his head to look at me, and his eyes are focused on me, the intensity almost blinding. His expression of clear and utter arousal feeds the unbearable heat between my legs. He starts to move faster, his pupils dilating as he drives mindlessly toward orgasm. Heat fills my body as another climax builds, the whole world turning to nothing but the sure strokes of plea-sure between my legs. My head rolls back and I cry out as my body stiffens, my orgasm seizing me as Landon plunges wildly into me, all control gone as he rides the waves of my climax to his own. He comes with a loud groan, his whole body shuddering with his release.

My heart is racing. I take deep gulps of air. The air in the office is cool, but we're both sweating. Landon expels a deep breath and slowly pulls out of me, making my body shudder as residual tremors shoot through me. My face is buried in his neck, and as I catch my breath, I inhale his spicy cologne, hot sex, and a scent that's just him. I have to restrain myself from placing kisses all over his face. I close my eyes, trying to weigh the languid satisfaction I feel against the mortification of the knowledge that I just slept with him, even though I told him I wasn't going to, even though I know I shouldn't have.

He starts to adjust my skirt, pulling it down and smoothing it. My panties are ripped and unsalvage-able, and he just takes them off me and puts them away in his pocket. He adjusts my bra and tries to do the same with my blouse, but with two buttons missing, there's nothing even he can do. There's no way I can go outside looking like this.

He leaves me on the desk and wraps up the condom in a tissue before tossing it in the trash. By the time he turns back to me, he's already fixing his clothes, and there's no sign that he just fucked me senseless on his desk. He looks as immaculate as he always does, and I look like a wreck.

He comes back to the desk and takes my arms, gently pulling me to my feet. "Come on," he says, "let's get you decent."

"Unless you have a blouse exactly like mine somewhere in this office, I don't see how you can manage that."

His fingers touch the silk of the blouse. Then he smiles and takes my hand. "I doubt a blouse like that would look as good on me as it did on you," he says before pressing a button on his desk.

"Mr. Court?" Tony's voice flows into the room through a set of speakers I can't see.

"I'm going out," Landon says curtly. "Reschedule the Clifton meeting."

He presses the button to end the conversation without waiting for a reply, and then he leads me toward a door I hadn't noticed before. It opens to a small but airy room with a set of seats and large windows that share the same view as his office. A stairway leads from the room to an upper floor.

"Don't tell me you have an apartment here as well," I say, following him up the stairs.

He frowns. "I do."

"How many apartments do you have?" I ask, curious.

"A few." He's smiling. "The apartment at the hotel belongs to my family, and I spent some of my childhood there. This is where I mostly live these days, especially when I'm busy with work."

The apartment is smaller than the one at the Swanson Court hotel, but it's still large. It's evidently a bachelor pad, simply but tastefully furnished with a few personal touches.

"This is convenient," I comment. "Every workaholic's dream. Why leave work when you can live at work?"

"One more dig at me, and I'm going to have to fuck you again, just to keep your mouth otherwise occupied." His expression is bland, as if he's only commenting on the weather, but stupidly, my body responds by remembering the pleasure of a few moments ago and wishing for more. "Make yourself comfortable," he offers, gesturing toward the living room. "There're drinks in the fridge, over there." He points in the direction of the kitchen. "I'll be right back."

He leaves me and disappears inside the apartment. I walk over to the kitchen, which looks modern, if underutilized. Retrieving a bottle of sparkling water from the fridge, I uncap it and take a long drink. I'm twisting back the cap when Landon returns with a deep green sweater.

"You can wear this," he offers, handing me the sweater.

I take it from him. The material is soft and smooth to the touch. I remove my blouse and shrug it on. It's a little big, but it smells like him and feels heavenly against my skin.

Landon folds up my blouse and hands it to me. "It looks better on you than it ever did on me."

I scoff. "Somehow I doubt that."

"I love it when you pay me compliments," he says with a heartbreakingly beautiful grin.

"I was only making an observation."

He shrugs. "I love your complimentary observations."

I chuckle despite myself. "So what now?"

He takes a strand of my hair and curls it around his finger. "Now that there's no question of how good we are together, I hope you'll finally agree to spend more time with me."

I look up at his face. "You mean sex."

"Lots of it."

I shake my head. "Actually, I meant, what happens right now."

He chuckles and releases the tendril of hair, letting it fall back to my face. "Now, I take you home."

There's a private elevator from the apartment to the garage on the ground floor. He left his jacket and tie behind in his office and in just his tailored shirt and pants, he looks more casual, but still sexy as hell.

He leads me to a sleek silver Jaguar convertible, low to the ground with leather bucket seats and a softly purring engine.

He keeps the top up, sliding on a pair of dark glasses as he navigates the car out of the garage. Even driving, he's powerful, controlled, his fingers light on the steering wheel as he moves through the late after-noon traffic.

In front of my apartment building, he turns to me. "About San Francisco," he says. "I want us to go together. I want you to stay with me, spend the whole time with me when you're not working. If that's not what you want, you don't have to do it because of what happened today."

I nod, knowing I want that trip with him. I want it so much it hurts. "What happens after it's over? When we come back?"

He taps a finger on the steering wheel, making me

wonder what he's thinking. "What do you want to happen?"

My mind goes to Jack and all the feelings, which are hard to recall at the moment, but still there, unresolved. "I don't want a relationship," I tell Landon. "This is just sex, and I don't want to pretend it's anything more."

He doesn't reply, so I continue.

"I also want exclusivity, for as long as it lasts."

"Not a problem," he says with a shrug.

How long will that be, exactly? I wonder. How long until he gets whatever desire he has for me out of his system and moves on? I don't want to be rejected again; I won't be able to take it. I swallow.

"And it lasts only as long as we're in San Francisco," I add quickly, before I change my mind.

"A week?" The words are accompanied by a frown. "Are you sure that's what you want?"

"Yes," I reply.

He nods slowly. "All right." He looks down at his sweater hanging off my shoulder, and then glances at his watch. "Why don't you go up and change. I'll take you back to the office."

I glance at the clock on the dashboard—it's almost five. "I'm done for the day."

He gives me a suggestive look. "So are you going to invite me up?"

I smirk. "Don't push your luck. I don't even like you yet."

"But you will." His voice is confident. I climb out of the car, already regretting not inviting him up, but I just want to hold a little back, at least for now. "Tony will let you know the travel details," he says, starting the engine. "See you soon."

With that, he's gone, the car purring softly as he drives away, leaving me wondering what on earth I've gotten myself into.

CHAPTER 9

"*I* have no idea what I'm doing," I tell Laurie over the phone the next day. She's working late. I, on the other hand, am packing for my trip. After exchanging notes from our meeting and discussing a little more about the article, Tony Gillies informed me that I would be leaving for San Francisco with Landon in the evening.

"Don't overthink it," Laurie replies. "Personally, I think it's exciting. You'll have your affair and get to write your article at the same time."

"Affair." I grimace. "That's such an old-fashioned word."

"Just like 'lover.'" I hear her snicker. "You're going to San Francisco with your *lover*," she says in her best *Downton Abbey* accent.

"All my dreams are coming true," I say sarcastically.

"Don't be so negative. You know you're creaming your panties at the thought of being with him for a whole week." She ignores my protest. "Just make sure you pack some good lingerie and condoms. You don't want to be caught unprepared."

I look at the box on my bed, which arrived at the same time I got home from the office. It contains a blouse, very much like the one Landon ripped off me yesterday but with a label that makes it much more expensive than my regular wardrobe, as well as two sets of matching lingerie to replace the panties he ripped. "Laurie," I say patiently, "it's still, first and foremost, a work trip."

"Yeah, tell yourself that." Laurie scoffs. "Just like it was a work thing when you ended up having sex in his office."

"Jeez, Laurie! I knew I should never have told you about that."

"Like you could keep it to yourself." I can almost hear the smirk in her voice.

Later, in the luxurious interior of the car Landon's office sends for me, my mind goes to the items of lingerie in my suitcase and I blush in the darkness. Luckily, aside from the driver, the same guy who took me home after my night at the Insomnia Lounge and who hasn't said anything after introducing himself as Joe, I'm alone in the car.

At the airport, Joe drives straight to the hangar where a uniformed steward retrieves my suitcase from the trunk and leads me to a sleek aircraft waiting on the runway. Following the steward, I climb into the plane. A blonde stewardess with a bouncy ponytail welcomes me with a smile and points me in the direction of the main cabin.

I step inside, and pause at the entrance. It is grand, no argument about that. The décor is muted yet luxurious and comfortable, with leather seats and low tables. On one of the seats, a leather sofa with space for two, Landon is sitting with one ankle placed jauntily on the knee of his other leg while he flicks a finger across the screen of a tablet. His striped shirt is open at the collar and the sleeves are rolled up to his elbows, revealing the light dusting of golden hairs on his arms.

I swallow, once again unable to process how good-looking he is. I haven't seen or spoken to him since he left me outside my apartment yesterday, but just looking at him, my body stirs with lust. I want this man, again and again, and I'm suddenly aware that a week will not be enough.

As if he can hear my thoughts, he looks up at me and smiles.

"Hey," he says.

"Hey," I reply, stepping into the cabin.

"Come sit." He pats the seat beside him. "We should be leaving in a few minutes, so buckle up."

I do as he says. Moments later, the stewardess comes to warn us to prepare for takeoff then disappears as quietly as she appeared. The plane starts to move, the engines whirring softly. The takeoff is smooth and in almost no time, we're cruising.

Landon sits back on his chair and closes his eyes. I noticed that he looked a little tired before, and I wonder if he has fallen asleep. His hair is tousled, and his perfect face oddly relaxed, making me want to reach out and stroke it. The thought is so ridiculous, I look away and chuckle silently.

"What's funny?"

His voice startles me and I turn back to him. Unlike a few seconds ago, he looks awake and alert.

"Nothing."

He gives me a skeptical look then reaches for his tablet again. His movements are strong and graceful, and I wonder if it's possible to be around him without finding reasons to lust after him any time he moves or says something.

"I thought Tony would be here," I mention, wondering where his efficient assistant is as I retrieve my MacBook from my bag. I know that the photographers, a husband and wife team with a photography firm named Litte and Parker, have been in San Francisco documenting the stages of the refurbishment for weeks.

"Tony will arrive tomorrow," Landon replies without looking up from whatever he's reading on the tablet.

I start to go over my notes on the article. I had a meeting with Mark Willis earlier in the day to discuss the outline, and now I type in new ideas in addition to the ones I've already put down. I've been doing my research and learning more about the history of the hotel, from the high-profile people who've stayed there over the years, including presidents and movie stars, to the mismanagement by the previous owner, a career playboy named Evans Sinclair. I've read about the coup in which the members of the board, all of whom were members of the extended Sinclair family, forced him to agree to sell the hotel to Landon.

After a few minutes of working, I look up to see Landon looking at me. Our eyes meet and my stomach twists. I look away quickly, concentrating on the screen of my computer.

He interrupts the nervous silence. "If you need anything, a drink, food, there's a button right there." He points to a yellow button on the arm of my seat. "If you'd like to lie down, there's a bedroom through the doors at the back." I look from the doors back to him, my mind already full of images of the bed that's in there and the things we could do on it.

"You're the one who looks in need of a bed," I say lightly, doing my best to disguise my carnal thoughts.

"Yes, but I have no intention of going in there without you." His eyes cut a sensual path from my face down my body. "And if I get you in there, neither of us will be getting any sleep."

Oh boy. My thighs clench and I tear my eyes away from him, fixing them on my screen and forcing my mind to thoughts of the article. I can feel his eyes on me, but he doesn't make any move toward me.

"I have some questions," I say, breaking the silence.

"Shoot."

I ask him about his reasons for acquiring the Gold Dust and his inspiration for the refurbishment. He answers my questions, displaying a love for the hospitality industry he was born into and the hotel brand he successfully expanded in such a short time.

"I've learned to see past appearances, to look at something and see its potential. I could see the possibilities in the Gold Dust even at the height of its misman-agement when the standards kept falling, and I know exactly how to ensure it reaches its full potential."

"Why are you keeping the old name?" I ask. "Why not Swanson Court San Francisco? Wouldn't that be more decisive in announcing that the hotel is entering a new era in its management?"

"It was an agreement I made with the Sinclair family."

I ask some more questions, and after I'm done, he calls the stewardess and orders two glasses of orange juice then goes back to reading whatever he has on his tablet.

I must have fallen asleep after drinking my juice. When I wake up, my head is resting on Landon's shoulder and I'm curled against his side. I straighten, blinking the sleep away from my eyes.

"I fell asleep," I say unnecessarily, embarrassed and sure I look disheveled.

"So you did." Landon's voice is strangely gentle. "I hope you enjoyed using me as a pillow."

"I'm sorry," I whisper.

He shrugs. "I didn't mind. I think we've established that my body is here for you any time you want it."

I ignore his teasing grin as color floods my face. "Are we almost there?" I ask, eager to change the subject before I make a fool of myself and jump on the part of his body I really want.

"We're about to land." He leans over me to fasten my seatbelt before he does his.

It's still dark when we land in San Francisco. A car comes to take us from the airport to the hotel where we're staying. I've never been to the city, so even though I'm tired, I keep my eyes focused out the windows, taking in the sights.

The hotel is an eight-story establishment with turn-of-the-century architecture. Set back from the street, it has a black awning over the entrance with the name, Rosemont Royal, written in flowing script. It's the early hours of the morning when we arrive, but there's a crisp-looking man in a suit waiting to greet us.

"Good morning Mr. Court," he says cheerfully. "Welcome back to San Francisco. How was your flight?"

Landon's voice is brisk. "Good Ralph, thanks."

The man turns to me. "Welcome to the Rosemont Royal, Miss Foster. I'm Ralph Groff, the manager. Should you need anything during your stay, I am entirely at your service."

I nod my thanks, admiring the lobby with its thick carpeting, richly ornamented walls and columns, and plush waiting areas. "Your suite has been prepared," Ralph is saying as he leads us to a private elevator. A few steps behind us, a bellboy wheels the cart containing our luggage away from the lobby.

Ralph follows us up to the top floor, all the way to a spacious suite that reminds me of Landon's apartment at the Swanson Court in New York. The foyer has a gleaming black and white diamond marble tile finish, dark-colored walls, and an elaborately framed mirror over a carved side table. The living room is large and richly furnished with thick carpets, heavy curtains, and elegant furniture. There's a grand piano in one corner, and through an archway, a formal dining room boasting about ten seats. A gorgeous sparkling crystal chandelier hangs from the ceiling.

"I imagine you're tired from your journey," Ralph continues in his courteous voice, "but if there's anything you would like, we'll send a chef up."

"No nothing, thank you," I say, enjoying the solicitous service.

Ralph nods. "If you'll excuse me, I believe your luggage has arrived." He disappears through a door leading out of the living room.

"Service elevator and fire escape are through that door," Landon explains. He's watching me with a small frown. "Do you like it?" he asks.

For a second, I wonder if he's serious. "I think it's gorgeous," I tell him.

He smiles. "There's a library too. I'm sure you'll find a poetry book or two."

"Thanks." I return his smile. "So, I take it you've stayed here before."

"Whenever I'm in the city, yes." He turns away from me and walks to the edge of the living room, opening the double doors that lead out to the terrace and letting in a cool breeze that ruffles his hair. He looks perfect standing there, like a gorgeous actor in an old Hollywood movie.

I join him at the terrace, enjoying the view of the bay and the fascinating lights on the Bay Bridge, which I've read about but have never seen outside of pictures. "It's a lovely view," I comment.

He turns around, facing me. "Yes, it is," he says slowly, making me think he's talking about me. He moves toward me, only stopping when he's almost touching me, and runs a finger lightly over my cheek. His eyes are burning with a familiar intensity, and I know if I close the distance between us, I'll feel his erection hard against my thigh. Sweet tension takes hold of my belly as I wait for him to do something, kiss me maybe, and complete the magic of our surroundings with his expert touch.

"I'm sure they're done unpacking," I hear him say. "Let me show you to your room."

My room? I try to hide my confusion. The last thing I want is to be shown to my room—unless he's going to join me there. I look at him from beneath my lashes, wondering what he's planning.

Ralph is nowhere to be seen as Landon leads me through the living room, along a short hallway, to a door that opens into a beautiful bedroom. There's a perfectly made four-poster bed dominating the room, with curtains that match those hanging from the windows. A lounge chair rests at the foot of the bed with a long cylindrical cushion. Beside the window, there's a desk with an impressionist landscape hanging above it. There's also a dressing table with a large mirror, a hanging bookshelf filled with books, and a door that probably leads to the bathroom and dressing room.

"Wow," I say softly, stepping past Landon into the room. I walk to the bed, running my fingers over the soft sheets before turning around to face him. He's still at the door, leaning on the doorframe and watching me.

"Aren't you going to come in?" I ask, cocking my head to the side and giving him an inviting look.

He straightens and walks into the room, right to where I'm standing, and with his hand around my waist, he places a soft kiss on my lips. I can feel the steely control beneath his kiss, almost as if he's determined not to let things go any further.

I have no idea why.

"You must be tired," he says softly, leaving me puzzled. "And you have a lot of work to do tomorrow. I'll see you in the morning, Rachel. Goodnight."

With that, he walks out of the room, unbuttoning his cuff as he leaves. I stand there watching him, aroused and confused, wondering if there's something I'm not getting.

CHAPTER 10

I wake up slightly disoriented, wondering where I am. The memories of the trip and Landon's uncharacteristic behavior last night flood in all at once, and I get up, still wondering what the hell happened. I thought the whole point of being here together was to have sex—again and again, according to him. Yet last night, even though it had been obvious that he was at least as aroused as I was, he had held back. Why?

I could have seduced him, tried at least to shatter that steely control, but I'd held back, mainly because it seemed unnecessary to make it so obvious how much I wanted him. I'm paying for that now as my whole body is highly strung, wanting the release it had been expecting last night.

I'm wearing one of the t-shirts I usually sleep

in, having had no reason to bust out my sexy lingerie last night. I walk over to the windows, admiring the San Francisco skyline and trying to pick out some of the more popular buildings. My phone rings and I hurry back to the bed to pick it up. It's Laurie.

"I just wanted to make sure you arrived safe and sound, and he hasn't kidnapped you and taken you to his lair." She says the last word with a theatrical evil voice.

"Nothing like that," I tell her. "We're at the Rosemont Royal in San Francisco. You won't believe how lavish it is."

"I can imagine." She sighs. "I miss you though. There's nobody to complain about my addiction to reality TV."

"I'll be back before you know it."

"Make sure you enjoy yourself. Brett and I are taking advantage of your absence."

"TMI, Laurie."

"What? We have no secrets between us. So...what happened with Landon?"

"Nothing, actually. We arrived, then went to bed...separately."

"Really?" She sounds doubtful. "That's boring. I thought he was going to make you come until you begged him to stop."

I sigh. "I tell you too much."

"I don't mind." There's a short pause on her end. "I have to go now, meeting."

"Talk later."

"Yes, and make sure you have something to talk about."

After the call, I check the time on the phone. It's already past eight in the morning, far later than I usually wake up. I hurriedly take a shower in the oriental-themed bathroom and dress in a pair of cream pants, a blue cotton shirt, and a jacket. I brush my hair and let it hang loose, applying nude lip gloss and one coat of mascara before leaving my room.

From the living room, the doors to the balcony are open. I find Landon already dressed in one of his exquisitely tailored shirts, a dark gray one this time, with a black silk tie and dark trousers encasing his long legs. He's sitting in the sun at a low, wrought iron table surrounded by four cushioned chairs. His hair is combed back and gleaming golden as he sips from a glass of orange juice with a newspaper spread out on his lap. For a long moment, all I can do is stare at him, my stomach twisting with yearning.

I tear my eyes away from his perfection, transferring my gaze to the view behind him, which is almost as breathtaking as he is.

He notices me standing at the doors. "Good morning," he says pleasantly, his eyes following me as I join him at the table. "Did you have a good night?"

"Perfect," I reply, giving him a bright smile. I'm certainly not going to tell him I spent the whole night wanting him.

He smiles back. "Juice?"

I nod and he pours me a glass of the cool fresh drink. As I savor it, a uniformed waiter wheels in a breakfast tray and starts to set the table. "I asked for toast and fried eggs with some coffee," Landon informs me. "If you would prefer something else, you can let the cook know."

"This is fine." I watch, entranced despite my annoyance with him, as he butters a piece of toast, his fingers moving deftly. How does someone make something as simple as buttering toast look so sexy?

He hands it to me and starts on another one. "Tony is arriving this morning. He's going to be staying a floor below for a few days before he returns to New York."

"Okay."

"We'll leave for the Gold Dust after breakfast," Landon continues. "You've discussed your itinerary with him?"

"Yes. I meet with the hotel manager today, tomorrow the designers, and the photographers after that."

"Good. I'll be busy all day. I'm meeting with the whole refurbishment team then the project managers to iron out a few issues before the project closeout."

Is that his way of telling me he won't have any time for me? I eat my breakfast, wondering if now that I'm available, no longer presenting a challenge, he's lost interest in me. I sneak a glance at him and he's watching me. He doesn't look like someone who has lost interest. No, I'm not getting that vibe at all.

We finish breakfast, and as the waiter clears the plates, Landon glances at his phone. "Tony's here," he tells me. "Are you ready?"

"Yes." I get up, intending to go to my room to pick up my bag, but when he gets up too, he's standing in my way. He lifts a finger to my mouth and wipes a speck of butter from the corner of my lip, a spot the napkin must have missed. Then he lifts the finger to his lips and licks it, making me go weak at the knees.

"I'll wait in the living room," he says softly, as if he's oblivious to the effect that simple action has on me.

I hurry to pick up my bag, legs shaking, heat pooling between my thighs. I don't understand what's going on anymore, and if it continues, well, I'm going to have to confront him. I almost do that on the elevator ride to the ground floor, but it only takes a few seconds for us to get to the lobby, where Tony is waiting.

"Good morning, Mr. Court, Rachel," he greets cheerfully, shaking my hand.

I return his smile. "How was your flight?"

"Smooth."

We walk outside to the entrance where under the awning, a gleaming black car is waiting. Landon is talking on the phone, but he opens the door and waits for me to get in before walking around to the other side.

The interior of the car is black leather and I sink into the seats, thinking how I could get used to the luxury that's par for the course with Landon. In the car, I listen with half an ear as Landon and Tony talk about issues concerning materials and delivery delays.

Unlike the Rosemont Royal, the Gold Dust is set far back from the street. There's a short drive to the entrance, edged with flowers and artwork on the lawns. The front of the building looks newly painted, a testament to the refurbishment going on. The sign over the entrance is still covered with some sort of protective sheet. Inside the lobby, the floors are also covered but the walls are bright, with freshly painted moldings and panels. The high ceiling is a dome, decorated with gold leaf.

"It's lovely," I breathe softly.

"I'm glad you think so," Landon says from beside me. I wasn't even aware he was so close. I look up to see those blue eyes on my face, and my breath catches. "I'll see you later," he says, patting my arm before leaving me to start with his itinerary for the day.

An arm pat—seriously? I came all the way to San Francisco for a pat on the arm.

I also came to write an article, so I concentrate on that, forcing all thoughts of Landon and his mixed signals from my mind. Tony hands me over to the hotel manager, a Frenchman named Claude Devin. "I'm to show you around and tell you everything you need to know," he tells me in a lilting, sexy accent. "I know everything about this place. I worked here when I was younger, when it was still run by the Sinclairs. Then I went back to France. Mr. Court lured me back with the promise of running the finest hotel in San Francisco, and he was perfectly right."

He keeps talking all morning, peppering informa-tion about the hotel with gossip from the old era as he shows me around the facilities, from the world-class gym to the spa, the bar, the meeting rooms, and the restaurants that will all be run by world renowned chefs. There are two ballrooms, several conference rooms, a presidential suite that puts the luxurious suite where I'm staying with Landon to shame, along with indoor and outdoor pools.

"It will be the jewel of San Francisco when it opens," Claude promises. "Court has kept all that was good about the old hotel and brought in everything no one else could have known it lacked."

By lunchtime, Landon is still in his meeting. Claude shows me to one of the furnished offices where I can set up my laptop and start to piece my notes together. I have to send a progress sheet to Mark tomorrow, so I really can't slack off.

Claude leaves me to work, going back to his own office after assuring me he'll let Landon know where I am as soon as the meeting is over.

The sound of the door opening interrupts my work, and I look up to see Landon entering the room. Hours of meetings haven't done anything to lessen the potency of his attractiveness.

"How're you getting on?" he asks.

"Okay. Claude was very helpful."

"Good." He nods. "We'll go out to lunch. After-ward, if you're done with Claude, you can return to the Rosemont. I'm going to be here for a while."

"That's fine." I get up, intending to pack up my stuff, but I stop, unable to repress the question that's been gnawing at me since last night. "Did you change your mind about this trip?" I hold his gaze. "Did you decide you don't want to fuck me anymore?"

His expression doesn't change, his silence seeming to confirm my fears. He turns back to the door, and I almost think he's going to leave. Then as I watch, he turns a button in the door handle, locking it, and turns back to face me.

For some reason, my heart is pounding, but I stay

silent as he comes to stand behind me. My blood is rushing hotly through my veins, my whole body eager and anticipating. As if from a distance, I hear the noise as he pulls my chair out of his way.

My whole back feels heated, as if I'm being seared by being so close to him. I stiffen as he presses a hand flat against my stomach, pulling me back to mold my body against his.

I gasp at the contact, feeling his arousal, hard and thick against my back. He leans forward, his breath teasing my ear and neck. "Does this feel like I don't want to fuck you?"

"No." My voice is a whisper.

Still holding me against his rock-hard body, he uses his other hand to undo the buttons of my top, one by one, until it's hanging open, along with my jacket. He pulls it out of the waistband of my pants and then reaches up to undo the clasp of my bra.

"I want you so much it fucking hurts," he whispers at my ear as his hand finds my breasts under the loose bra. He pinches a nipple between his thumb and forefinger and I groan, loud.

"I can hardly keep my mind on anything else," he continues. "I've never wanted anyone so much."

I know what he means. I feel as if my body has only just been awakened. "But last night…" I manage to ask through the haze of my arousal. "Why…?"

"Why did I stay away? Why did I try to give you a

chance to change your mind? I have no fucking idea. I must have been crazy." The hand on my stomach slides down to my pants, undoing the clasp with one sure flick of his fingers. Then those same fingers are sliding into my panties, over the wet slickness between my legs.

My hips buck, rubbing against his fingers. Releasing my breast, he uses that hand to pull down my pants then abandons his ministrations between my thighs so he can push my panties down over my hips. His fingers find me again, stroking the swollen mass of aroused nerves that my clit has become, while from behind, he inserts two fingers into my wet pulsing core.

"Oh God!" I cry out as he starts to fuck me with his fingers, fast, giving no room for anything else but the sensation of his touch and the maddening sensation of him teasing my clit. *I'm going mad*, I think as pleasure overtakes me, *or else I'm dying*. I cry out, loudly, past the point of caring who hears, as my hips buck uncontrollably.

"Landon!" I scream his name, helpless against the coming orgasm, my brain dying with each stroke of his fingers. "Oh fuck! Landon!"

"Let it go," he whispers against my ear, rubbing harder against my clit at the same moment he presses his fingers against the bundle of nerves inside me. I let out a harsh scream and collapse forward on the table, spent, my body trembling with the aftermath of my orgasm.

My body is slick with sweat, making strands of my hair stick to my face and neck. I try to catch my breath, which is almost impossible as Landon continues to stroke my clit.

He reaches between us to loosen the waistband of his pants, and soon I can feel his cock, warm and hard against my butt. I rub myself against him, eliciting a low growl from him.

"Are you on the pill?"

I nod, impatient to feel him inside me. "Yes."

"I'm clean, Rachel, and I want to fuck you like this, with my skin against yours. I want to feel your heat. I want to come inside you." The finger on my clit moves lower to press against the wet opening to my body.

"Please," I hear myself beg. "Please, now."

Immediately, I feel the warm crown of his cock pushing against me, and in the next moment he plunges deep inside me, filling me so completely, I let out a sob of pure, undiluted pleasure.

He starts to move, his muscles bunching as he goes deeper with each successive thrust. He pulls me up to press my body against his, his hands at my breast and my stomach. I'm helpless against the pleasure of his thrusts, his grunts of pure animalistic pleasure making me even more aroused.

Heat spreads from between my legs, taking over my entire body and drowning me with pleasure. I surrender to the waves of another orgasm just as Landon's body tightens, his muscles stiffening as he thrusts deep inside me, burying himself to the hilt as he groans, coming inside me.

He collapses onto the chair behind us, taking me with him. He's still inside me, still hard even though he just came. He starts to stroke my shoulders, his hands moving over my skin in a slow caress. By the time he gets to my breasts, I'm already moving my hips, riding his still hard cock. He squeezes my breasts, groaning softly as I move up and down his length.

"You're so hot," he whispers.

"You're so hard," I reply breathlessly.

He sighs and drops his hands to my waist, gripping me on both sides and taking control of my movements. Unbelievable pleasure spreads through me, fed by the soft rocking of his hips, the strength with which he moves me up and down, and the low grunts from his lips.

We come at the same time, his cock rocking into me as my body tightens and explodes. He groans as he comes and my pulsing body squeezes everything out of him.

Afterward, I end up sitting on his lap, his arm

around me. I'm exhausted, about to fall asleep. "You said something about lunch," I remind him.

"Yes." I feel the deep rumble in his chest as he chuckles.

"I'm sleepy, but I'm also unbelievably hungry."

His chuckle turns into a wry laugh. "Me too, for some reason."

With his hands around my waist, he lifts me off his lap. Still sitting, he retrieves a handkerchief from his pocket and proceeds to wipe between my legs. He folds the hanky and then wipes himself before folding it again and putting it in his pocket.

I wrinkle my nose. "You're not going to keep that as some sort of weird memento, are you?"

He grins. "I don't need a memento when I have you," he replies, pulling up my pants and redoing the clasp while I button up my blouse. Then he gets up and adjusts his own clothes, going back to his usual impeccable appearance almost immediately.

You only have me for a week, I want to remind him, already mourning the future end of our temporary arrangement. But, I keep silent, helping him pack up my laptop so we can go to lunch. It's when I pick up my phone off the desk, right before we leave, that I see the missed calls—five of them, all from Jack.

CHAPTER 11

"I can't believe you were taking such a huge trip and you only left a message!" my mom complains, "You know I hardly check my messages. I'm sure you did it on purpose so you wouldn't have to hear me complain about you missing Sunday lunch."

I'm back at the Rosemont Royal after lunch with Landon, and while he's gone back to the Gold Dust for another round of meetings or whatever, I have the rest of the afternoon to work on my article in the comfort of the suite. After a quick shower, I'd just settled at the desk in my room when my mother called. "It's not a huge trip, Mom, and I'm sorry, but it was kind of sudden." She's right about the reason I only left a message, but I don't tell her that.

My mom sighs. "At least it's not a promotional article this time."

"It's not." My mom has never hidden the fact that she doesn't think much of the kind of articles I write. She's made a career out of always been true to her art. While she thought I would have made a great editor at the Gilt Review, which she reads religiously, she doesn't approve of the fact that I've spent two years 'hacking' out articles that are a little more than advertising copy.

"Okay." She pauses. "Laurie says you're there with a man, some hotel owner."

"Laurie talks too much," I reply. "I'm really going to kill her someday for telling you everything I tell her."

My mom ignores me as usual. "She was trying to assure me you weren't moping over Jack whatsisname. So, is there a man?"

"Not in the way Laurie made it sound, Mom. It's really just work."

"If you say so," she replies, sounding unconvinced. "Your father says hi."

"Hi Dad," I say loudly.

"Oh, he can't hear you. He's on his rowing machine, working on those biceps." I hear my father's indistinct words, and then her breathy giggle. "Okay, bye dear," she says. "Talk later."

I put down the phone and start to work,

expanding the outline for the article. I manage to shut everything else out of my mind and get a few hours of work done before my phone rings again.

At the sight of the caller's name on the screen, I almost decide to ignore it, the same way I pushed his earlier calls out of my mind. What could Jack want from me? Why is he calling?

Picking up the phone, I swipe my finger across the screen as I raise it to my ear.

"Hello Jack."

"Rachel." He sounds relieved. "I'm so glad you answered."

"Yeah...I'm sorry about your calls earlier. I was busy and I didn't feel the phone vibrate."

"That's a relief. I assumed you didn't want to talk to me." There's a short pause. "I learned you're in San Francisco on an assignment. How's that going?"

"Great."

"Okay." I hear him sigh. "Rachel, the thing is, I'm a little disappointed we didn't get to talk like we planned."

"You wanted to talk," I point out. "I'm not very sure what we have to talk about."

"I miss you," he says simply. "Isn't that enough to talk about?"

"You keep saying you miss me. What exactly do you want? For me to tag along so you can amuse yourself with me when your fiancée isn't available?"

"About that," he says, "I'm going to be in Argentina for about a month starting next week." He pauses. "Claudia and I decided to take a break, see how things go."

I shake my head in disbelief. "What? That doesn't even make any sense."

He is quiet. "I thought you would be glad."

"I'm indifferent."

I hear him take a breath. "Rachel, I'm not saying this because I no longer have a fiancée, but I know I've taken you for granted in the past. I've had time to think about all that, and I'm sorry."

He's never apologized to me before, and it takes me by surprise. My anger toward him dissipates, and I don't know what to say.

He continues. "I shouldn't have sprung the engagement thing on you like that. You're my closest friend, and we have a history. So...I'm sorry. I just wanted you to know that...whatever it's worth."

Whatever it's worth. I sigh. The thing with Jack is that he's so good at straddling that line between a close friend and a romantic interest, I'm never entirely sure if I'm finally being pursued or if I'm still stuck in the friend zone. "I'm sorry about your engagement," I say softly.

"I'll get over it," he replies carelessly.

"I'm sure."

"I heard you were working with Landon Court," he says after a moment.

"I'm writing about his new hotel."

"Yes. I read somewhere about him buying it from right under Evan's Sinclair's feet. Hotel had been in the same family for generations. But then, Court has always been very ruthless in business. He's also known for being heartless with women when he's done with them. Being around him so much, don't fall in love with him."

I almost laugh. "Someone should have told me that when I met you."

"That's not fair."

I sigh. "It's nice that you called Jack."

He laughs. "That sounds like a dismissal."

"I'm working."

"Okay, but just so you know. I'm not giving up on you. You're still my favorite person in the world."

It's an old joke we share. He calls me his favorite person, and I do the same. This time, I keep silent.

I hear him sigh. "Bye Rachel."

I put the phone back on the desk, deep in thought. It makes no sense for Jack to warn me about falling in love with Landon. With Landon, I know where I stand. A week, and then I'll never have to see him again. There's no chance of getting hurt. In a few days, I'll be back home and he'll just be a memory of great sex.

As if he knows I'm thinking about him, Landon's name lights up on my screen. I reach for the phone, my body surging with excitement.

"What are you doing?" he asks without preamble.

That voice. It flows over me like velvet. "Working. You?"

"Thinking about you."

His words cause a fluttering in my stomach. "Aren't you supposed to be in a meeting?"

"I called a recess."

"Lucky you." I'm smiling as I get up and go over to sit on the side of my bed. "When will you be back?"

"In about two-three hours. Why? You missing me?"

"In a way." I laugh. "I'd rather you were here making the most of the time we have. You did promise to make me come until I beg you to stop."

I hear him groan. "Rachel, you're going to drive me crazy." His voice drops to a low murmur. "I wish I was there right now, my tongue in your pussy. You wouldn't be laughing."

My breath is suddenly shallow. "No, I wouldn't."

"I would suck you until you're breathless and coming against my tongue." I hear him breathe. "Would you like that?"

"Yes," I whisper.

"You sound aroused," he says softly. "Tell me where you are."

"In my room. Sitting on my bed."

"What are you wearing?"

"A camisole dress."

"Is it short?"

"Yes. Thigh length."

"Pull it up to your waist," he orders, and I obey, lifting my hips as I pull the dress up with one hand. "What are you wearing underneath?"

"A white bra and thong."

He groans. "Pull down the dress and the bra. I want your beautiful breasts spilling out. They're beautiful—have I told you that? So full and firm, with nipples I want to keep licking. Touch your nipples, baby."

I do as he says, moaning as pleasure shoots through me.

"Now I need you to pull that white thong to the side and touch yourself. Tell me how wet you are."

I do as he says, wondering at how easily I comply, how natural it feels even though I've never done this before. "I'm soaked," I tell him. My voice is a thin, aroused whisper. I rub my fingers over my clit, feeling my body tighten, already so close to orgasm. "I'm so wet Landon."

"Wet for me, Rachel. My cock is so hard, I want to put it in your mouth. Let you suck it."

"Yes," I moan, my fingers working my clit. I can almost feel him pumping into my mouth. "I want you in my mouth."

"And also in your hot pussy, fucking you until you can't take any more."

"Oh God!" I moan as the image sends me over the edge. My legs stiffen, my body throbbing as pleasure rolls over me. I fall back on the bed, my body trembling uncontrollably.

I sigh as my heart slows, my body still feeling the little aftershocks of my climax.

"I have to get back to my meeting," Landon says, as if he hasn't just given me an intense orgasm through the phone. "Let's go out to dinner tonight."

I breathe slowly, my body still sluggish. "I'd like that."

"Be ready at seven," he says. "I'll come pick you up."

I only have a few hours, so I quickly finish up my additions to the article and email them to Mark for feedback.

My few clothes have all been neatly unpacked in the dressing room closet. I select a deep blue wrap dress I brought with me, silently thanking the stars for my mom, who taught me to always pack evening wear.

By the time I emerge from my room at seven, I'm fully dressed and made up with my hair styled in the low messy chignon that's the only one I can manage without Laurie's help. Landon is already waiting. He has changed out of the clothes he was wearing earlier and is now dressed in a dark blue evening jacket and another one of his crisp, tailored shirts. His hair is slicked back, shining like burnished gold. He looks unbelievably hot, and I just want to keep looking at him.

"You look amazing," he says with a smile as he takes my hand, dropping a kiss on my right cheek.

If I look amazing, then there are no words to describe how he looks. "You don't look too bad yourself," I reply, inhaling the intoxicating scent of his cologne mixed with the yummy smell of his body wash and shampoo.

He grins. "I aim to please."

"And you never miss," I quip.

His eyes hold mine. "Not if I can help it."

God! I want him again, even now, when we're on our way out. I wish he would change his mind about going out for dinner.

Taking a deep breath to calm my heated body, I follow him to the elevator. Outside, it's very cool, and there's a light fog over the city. Luckily, my dress came with a matching blue shawl. As we wait for the car, Landon takes it from me and wraps it around my shoulders, his fingers trailing along my arms and making me tremble.

On the ride to the restaurant, we're both quiet. His mind seems far away as he looks straight ahead, and I find myself thinking again how good-looking he is. He has the kind of looks women dream about. Combined with his potent sexual magnetism, he's the stuff fantasies are made of. Right now though, he looks almost unapproachable. This is not the first time I've seen him retreat behind that wall. Is he like this with the other women he's dated? Very physical in one moment, then distant in the next?

Or is it just me?

It shouldn't affect me. I shouldn't mind if we have no relationship beyond sex—that's exactly what I want.

When the car stops, he reaches over and strokes a hand over mine, making me look up to see him smiling at me. I feel a pull in my stomach, equal parts desire, longing, and another ache I can't even identify.

He leans across the seat and drops a soft kiss on my lips. When he pulls back, I follow him, wanting another. He obliges me, stroking his tongue along my lower lip before sucking it into his mouth. Hot need shoots through me and I moan.

He releases my lips with a sigh. "I can't imagine why I thought I could make it through the evening without wanting to tear off your clothes," he says, his voice low.

I turn a cautious glance at the driver, who's looking straight ahead, a pair of earphones stuck in his ears. Sliding a hand up Landon's thigh, I stop when I touch the erection already straining through his pants. Slowly, I run my hand along the hard ridge. "I'm not very hungry," I say hopefully.

He catches hold of my hand, taking a deep breath. "I wish we could go back, but there's someone expecting us."

With that, he opens the door, almost immediately appearing at my side to help me out of the car. I'm wondering who could be expecting us while simultaneously trying to compose myself and get in control of the arousal raging through me.

The restaurant is on the ground floor of a building on a hill close to the waterfront. Even from the street, views of the Golden Gate Bridge and the sparkling lights reflecting off the water are simply breathtaking. We enter the restaurant, first going into a quiet reception area, from where a fussy maître d' ushers us upstairs to a dining area overlooking the main restaurant, with less obstructed views.

No sooner has the maître d' shown us to a secluded table than a door at the rear opens and a stocky man with bright red hair and a broad smile bursts into the room. He approaches our table and Landon gets up, an easy smile on his face as he clasps hands with the man before they exchange a bro-hug.

The man faces me and grins. "You must be an angel," he says, taking my hand with an earnest look in his deep green eyes.

Landon does a small head shake. "Rachel, this is Cameron McDaniel. Cameron, Rachel Foster."

"Pleased to meet you," I say.

"Delighted." Cameron raises my hand to his lips, ignoring Landon's narrowed eyes.

"Cameron is an old friend," Landon tells me, "and he only recently opened this restaurant, so he's dying to hear you say it's awesome.

"Definitely awesome," I say with a smile at Cameron, whose grin widens.

"Definitely. I like you already." He pulls out a seat and joins us. "What are you doing with this hand-some devil anyway," he says jovially. "We reds should stick together. I know all the dirt on him, known him for years. I could tell you things that'll make him squirm."

I steal a glance at Landon, who's chuckling silently. He looks almost jovial, so different from the controlled man he usually is in public, and the intensely sexual person he is when he's with me. He sees me looking at him and holds my gaze, and in his eyes I can see the sensual promise that always goes right through to the deepest parts of me.

I turn back to Cameron. "I look forward to hearing the worst."

Cameron responds by clapping his hands excitedly before summoning a hovering waiter who takes our wine order. "For my friend, who I haven't seen in ages, and his lovely girlfriend, I have prepared something special," he informs me. "You don't mind seafood, do you?"

Shaking my head, I wonder if I should correct him about the girlfriend part. Landon, who's watching me, makes no move to say anything, so I leave it.

"Perfect." Cameron grins again. "Now, while we wait, let's gossip."

I haven't enjoyed a meal so much in a long time, laughing so hard at Cameron's quips that more than once, I almost choke on my wine. He's irrepressible, around the same age as Landon, but with a wicked wit and sharply funny commentary that flows very naturally. He tells me how he met Landon when he spent a few years working at the New York Swanson Court in his early twenties before leaving to open his own restaurant. He took courses in management and learned how to expand along the way. Now he owns a chain of restaurants in Northern California.

By the time we leave, I'm not only stuffed, I'm actually sorry to be leaving Cameron. He follows us outside to the sidewalk and gives me a warm hug. "Take good care of her," he warns Landon, making a big show of relinquishing me to him.

"I believe I'm already doing that," is Landon's only reply, his carnal gaze on my body telling me all the ways in which he's going to take care of me.

A flash from across the street makes me raise my head in alarm, and a few more flashes follow. Landon mutters something under his breath and pulls me closer to him.

"They always come here hoping to catch the movie stars leaving," Cameron says, turning dismissively from the paparazzo. He eyes Landon. "You can blame yourself for looking too much like a movie star.

"I agree," I say, giggling as Landon's hand around my waist sends warm heat coursing through my body. *I shouldn't have drunk so much wine*, I decide silently, saying goodnight to Cameron.

Landon helps me into the waiting car, joining me in the back just before the car starts to move. Alone again, the impossible sexual energy that always radiates from him finds me, drawing everything inside me to him. I'm tense again, eager for him to touch me, wanting to touch him so desperately it hurts.

I sneak a look at him at the same moment he turns to me. In the next second, he pulls me to his body, crushing my breasts against his chest as he claims my lips.

He tastes perfect, like the wine we shared, and like warm sexual heat. A low moan comes out from deep within me as my hands roam over his body, trying to touch him through his clothes and wishing I could tear them off.

When he releases me, I'm panting softly, my nipples straining against the fabric of my bra. His chest is rising and falling sharply, his increased body heat enveloping me even through the barrier of our clothing.

"I've been thinking about this all evening," he whispers, his palm tracing a path along my thigh. "No, since we spoke on the phone earlier. I need to fuck you."

"Me too," I admit, my thighs parting of their own accord, needing his touch, even though I know we're in a car, that we have to wait, at least until we get to the hotel.

His fingers tighten on my thigh. "You're going to give yourself to me, every part of you." He traces his lips along the side of my throat. "I want you so much, Rachel, and I'm going to make you mine."

The possessiveness in his words stokes the flames of my desire, making it almost impossible to wait. By the time we get to our hotel, I'm practically burning with need, senseless to everything but the driving desire to have him deep inside me.

Inside the elevator, he looks as if he's barely restraining himself. He stares at the numbers on the panel, his hand tight around my waist. Standing close to him, I can feel how tense he is. It feels like if we so much as look at each other, we're going to end up having sex inside the elevator.

As soon as the doors slide open in the suite, he pulls me inside, pinning me to the walls of the foyer and claiming my lips. His tongue dips into my mouth as he rocks his hips against me, allowing me to feel the steel hard length of his arousal.

I'm panting, fumbling with the tie of my dress in my eagerness to take it off. Landon, thinking along the same lines, tears off his jacket and shirt without bothering to release my lips.

My hands find his chest, running feverishly over the rock-hard muscles before moving down the flat board of his stomach to his waistband, where my fingers get busy undoing his belt.

He pulls my dress apart, leaving my body exposed in only my bra and panties. Then he pulls me from the wall so he can slide the dress off my shoulders. Before my fumbling fingers succeed in undoing his pants, he already has my bra off and is pulling my panties down over my hips, letting them slide 'til they fall around my ankles.

I finally manage to get into his pants, stroking his hard length through his briefs. He groans and slides a finger between my legs, feeling the slickness of my need for him. His groan turns into a low growl, and in a swift motion, he lifts me, spreading my legs around his waist as he pins me to the wall, his hips pressed against my needy, aching center.

I sigh impatiently, and unable to wait anymore, I rub myself against him. My body is pulsing with unbearable, uncontrollable need. "Landon," I moan.

"Shh, baby." With my legs wedged around his waist, he pulls down his trousers and briefs, just enough to free his cock. At the sight of the thick member, my body turns to liquid desire. "Fuck me, Landon." I pant, long past the point of shame. "Fuck me now."

He obliges, spearing me with one sweet plunge that goes so deep inside me, I lose all my senses. Everything disappears but the exquisite sensation of his cock inside me. His tongue works feverishly at my nipple as he thrusts so fast and so deep, it feels less like just sex, more like some kind of intense primal mating. His deep grunts mix with my whimpers, the sounds of uncontrolled and unbridled pleasure filling the room.

He moves his mouth from one breast to another without slowing his pace. I groan, my body tightening around him as warm pleasure courses through me.

"Ah fuck!" His voice is tortured as he leans back, still thrusting, giving me a view of the tightened muscles from his chest to his stomach and the column of his cock as it moves in and out of me. The sight pushes me over the edge and I cry out, helpless and boneless, my body spasming in a long, pulsing orgasm.

He plunges deep, filling me completely as my body contracts with pleasure far beyond anything I've ever experienced. I hear his low groan as his hips jerk, his cock twitching inside me as he comes.

Afterward, he pulls me off the wall and drops to his knees, still inside me. His chest is rising and falling heavily. I wrap my hands around his neck and bury my face in his hair, pressing my sweat-sheened body against his with a strange desire to be as close to him as physically possible.

After a few moments, he rises to his feet, carrying me with his semi-hard cock still buried inside me. He carries me to his room and lays me gently on the bed before starting to pull away.

"Don't," I whisper, not wanting to release him. "Don't go."

He settles between my legs, leaning his weight on an elbow. He leans down and covers my mouth with his, kissing me with an intensity that feels as if he's getting to the very depths of my soul. With his free hand, he caresses my sensitive skin. I feel him harden again within me, and the full feeling makes me moan into his mouth.

He pulls his lips away from mine, his blue eyes dark with desire. Holding my gaze like some kind of erotic hypnotist, he starts to move, this time doing it slowly, sliding in and out of me, stroking my already sensitive walls to the edge of pleasure.

I can't look away from his eyes. As the pleasure intensifies and his control begins to slip, it feels as if I'm looking into his soul and he's looking into mine. As if, in that moment, there are no barriers. As if we're not lovers just in our bodies, but somehow to the very depths of our souls.

I come with a long drawn-out whimper, my body tightening as pleasure rocks me. His soft groan follows, and his hands tighten reflexively around my waist as he spills himself inside me.

He pulls out, sending aftershocks rolling through me, and pulls me close to him, holding me against his warmth. I feel tears teasing at my eyelids and I blink them away, concentrating instead on how good it feels to be so close to him.

Enjoy it while it lasts, an inner voice warns, *because it'll soon be over*.

CHAPTER 12

I wake up sometime during the night, still in Landon's bed. The room is dark, with only a dim light from outside the open curtains. Landon is not with me on the bed, nor anywhere in the room.

I find a white hotel robe in the dressing room. Putting it on, I find my way through the suite, finally going through the open doors that lead to the terrace. There I find him standing by the stone railings, looking out at the city in the night.

I stand by the doors, just looking at him. He's wearing pajama bottoms riding low on his lean hips. The air is cold, but he doesn't seem to feel it. As I watch, he runs a hand through his dark gold mane then leans forward on the railing, releasing a sigh as the muscles of his back flex with the movement.

I find myself wondering what he's thinking. There's something melancholy about his solitude and I'm hesitant to disturb him, but almost as if he can feel me standing there, he turns around and straightens.

"You should be asleep," he says.

"So should you. What are you doing out here?"

"Just thinking." There's a hint of tiredness in his eyes.

I join him at the railing. "What about?"

"Work."

I turn to look at him. He's looking straight ahead, his eyes focused on the darkness beyond the lights. Did I really expect he would tell me what was on his mind? His monosyllabic answers remind me that even though last night it felt as though something shifted in our relationship, it was just my imagination.

We're still practically strangers—strangers with good sexual chemistry, but still strangers.

The wind moves, causing me to shiver slightly. Landon notices. "You're cold," he says. "Come on. Let's go back inside."

He puts his arms around me and his skin is warm, even though he's been standing outside shirtless. In his room, he takes off the robe I'm wearing and pulls the covers back on the bed, lying down with his arm around me until the steady rise and fall of his chest lulls me to sleep.

I feel it when he gets up not long after, the loss of his warmth almost jerking me out of sleep. He doesn't return until it's getting light outside. I wake up when he joins me on the bed, and after another tender round of intense sex, we lie in each other's arms, not speaking, and not asleep either. Eventually he gets up to go to the bathroom, and I leave for my room to prepare for the day ahead.

DESPITE HARDLY GETTING ANY SLEEP, LANDON looks wide awake and alert in the morning when we go back to the Gold Dust. He leaves me almost as soon as we get there, joining the project managers for a meeting.

Tony introduces me to the interior designer Lydia Khan, a vibrant middle-aged woman who, according to my research, has done refurbishment work in many big-name hotels all over the world. We spend the morning talking about her work creating distinctive properties and enriching the experience of visitors through compelling design.

Landon calls me around midmorning. I've just left Mrs. Khan, and Claude is showing me around the hotel bar where refurbishment has been completed. It's luxurious and glistening, with black leather seats surrounding low, dark oak tables. The bar itself covers one large expanse of wall, and a raised stage allows for small performances.

I excuse myself from Claude's enthusiastic descriptions and answer the call.

"I have to go to New York," Landon starts. "I'll leave in about an hour, and I'll be back tomorrow."

"Oh." I have no other words to articulate the devastating sense of loss.

I think he senses the disappointment in my voice. "It's very important," he says, "or else I wouldn't leave... I wouldn't go."

I wouldn't leave you. That's what he had been about to say. I swallow. I have to tread carefully, or else I'll be ascribing feelings to him that he hasn't communicated, and then I'll end up wanting more from him than he's prepared to give.

"I'll be here when you get back," I say lightly.

"You'd better be." His voice is low, and my breath catches in my throat.

I spend the rest of the day at the Gold Dust, alternatively talking with Claude, the managers of the spa and the world-class gym, who I hadn't met before, and working on my Mac in the quiet of the office Claude has assigned to me. There, during every little break from my work, my head fills with the memories of Landon thrusting into me from behind while I stood over the desk.

In the evening, I order dinner from room service,

and I eat alone while downing half a bottle of wine. Afterward, I explore the suite, ending up at the library, where I find, among many exciting books, an old classic novel I've read at least a hundred times. I start reading it again, getting to a very dramatic proposal scene before I decide to call Laurie.

"At last!" she exclaims. "I was wondering when you would take a break from Landon long enough to remember me."

"I'm mad at you," I reply. "What did you tell my mom?"

"Nothing," she denies. "I said, very innocently, that your work in San Francisco involved a guy named Landon Court."

"I don't believe you."

"So how's it going?" she says quickly, changing the subject.

I shrug. "Landon's gone back to New York. He'll be back tomorrow though."

"He probably has to give his equipment a rest after you used him with a vengeance to end that incredibly long dry spell."

"It wasn't that long," I protest, "and believe me, Landon's equipment does not require rest to perform at optimum capacity." *He doesn't even need to sleep*, I add silently, still puzzled by his apparent inability to rest like a normal person.

Laurie giggles in delight. "Before I forget"—I hear

the beeping sounds as she does something with her phone—"I sent you a link. No idea why I forgot to send it earlier. It's pretty exciting."

The message appears on my phone and I put the call on speaker while I follow the link. It's one of the entertainment websites, and it has a picture of me, Landon, and Cameron McDaniel. Landon has his hand around my waist, his face impassive as he looks at the camera. Cameron is standing a little to the side, also glaring in the direction of the camera. My face is turned toward Landon so that only my side profile is visible in the shot.

The article is just a short blurb.

New York hotel and real estate billionaire Landon Court spotted in San Fran with longtime friend restaurateur Cameron McDaniel and a mystery woman. Is the most eligible bachelor in New York going off the market?

"Jeez!" I exclaim. "All we did was go out to dinner."

"I know, right?" Laurie sounds impressed. "You're hanging with the big boys now. Enjoy it. I gotta go, Brett will be here any minute."

With that, she's gone. I end up following the link highlighting Landon's name and land on a search result of all the articles the website has published about him. Most of them are about his public appearances with women. I've read the rumors about the women he's been linked with before, so I skip those articles. There are pictures of him at an acclaimed off-Broadway play directed by his brother Aidan. There're other pictures of him with his brother, who is slightly darker but has the same blue eyes and arrow-straight nose. He's the brother who was supposed to have sent 'hooker' me to Landon's apartment. *How awkward*, I think. At least I know we're never going to meet and be put in a position where he would remember that Landon once thought I was a whore. When we get back to New York, Landon and I will go our separate ways.

I shake the feeling of sadness that comes with the thought, instead concentrating on the articles I'm reading. My mother has had articles written about her work and exhibitions, and Trent & Taylor has been featured in some popular publications. Even Aunt Jacie used to be a very popular model before she became the face of Trent & Taylor and married my uncle. However, all that is nothing compared to the volume of news that has been written about Landon's family. There's so much, going back to his great-grandfather, Gabriel Swanson, who built the Swanson hotel in New York in the forties, soon after the war ended. A few years later, he almost lost it, but was saved by Landon's grandfather, Alexander Court, who used his money to turn the hotel into a world-class name in luxury. He also married Lily Swanson, Gabriel's daughter, one of the most desired women in

New York in her day, and changed the name of the hotel to the Swanson Court Hotel.

Then there's Landon's father, Preston Court, who seems to have been a playboy in his time. The archived articles are full of rumors of affairs, some of them dated after he had already married Alicia Creighton, a well-known ballerina and socialite. After she died, he turned into a recluse, hardly seen in public until his death a few years later.

I forget my novel, concentrating instead on Landon's life and wondering how his experiences have affected him. I bury myself in reading about him, going from the social and gossip sites to the business reports and online encyclopedia articles, until it feels as if I could write a paper about him if I wanted.

I know instinctively that there's a lot more to him than even what I've read. The people behind the articles and profiles haven't even scratched the surface of who he is. I doubt anybody has, and as I finally get into bed, very late, I know I'd like to be the one who does.

∼

THE NEXT DAY, I SPEND THE MORNING AT THE Gold Dust. Most of the refurbishment work is completed, and the project team is slowly giving way for the operations people, who are starting to prepare the hotel for opening night. I spend most of the morning with the photographers, a husband and wife team who met in art school and established a firm together. They set up and take pictures while letting me scroll through a folder on their tablet that contains pictures documenting the refurbishment of the hotel from the first day.

Later, I have lunch at a small restaurant close to Union Square, on the advice of the concierge at the Rosemont Royal, who makes the reservation for me. While I eat, I watch the tourists outside at the square. Back at the Rosemont, the manager reminds me that the spa services are available. With nothing else to do, I decide to spend the afternoon being pampered, and I emerge with my muscles loosened, and my hair, nails, and brows done to perfection. After that, I laze around the apartment, a little sullen that Landon hasn't called to tell me he's back or on his way. In fact, he hasn't called at all since he left. I start to feel like I imagine jealous wives feel, and it annoys me.

When my phone rings, I practically pounce on it, thinking it's Landon. I'm surprised by the severity of my disappointment when it's only Jack.

"Hi Jack."

"You could try to sound a little more excited to hear from me," he teases.

"I could try, but why should I?"

"Okay, I deserve that." He pauses. "So, what's going on with you?"

I look around the empty suite. "Nothing in particular."

"I'm in luck then. Guess who's in San Fran?"

I frown. "Not you?"

"Definitely me." I can hear the grin in his voice. "Let's hang out. I'm sure you've worked so much you deserve to take a break."

"What are you doing here?"

"Isn't it possible that I missed you so much, I flew across the country to see you?"

"No."

"Well, I'm hurt that you think so, and I'd like to rectify that. So what do you say to a night out?"

"Not unless you tell me what you're really doing here."

"I'm here to see you," he insists. "I didn't want to leave the country without saying goodbye."

I'm not buying it. "You could have said goodbye on the phone."

"I could have, but I chose not to. Come on Rachel. Come out and see me. It'll be fun."

I almost refuse. I know how impulsive Jack can be, but I've never been on the receiving end of his grand gestures before. A month ago, I would have been over the moon. Now I'm just confused by my lack of interest.

However, it doesn't seem fair for me to spend the rest of the evening just waiting for Landon when Jack has supposedly flown halfway across the country to see me.

"Sure," I tell him. "When and where?"

"Let's see," he says, "I'm staying at this excellent hotel close to Union Square. There's a lounge here I've heard a lot about. We can go there."

He tells me the name of the hotel and I agree to meet him. I dress in a simple pale blue sheath dress and navy heels, leaving my hair to hang around my shoulders. Downstairs in the lobby, I run into Ralph.

"I hope you're enjoying your stay," he says solic- itously.

I smile at the man. "I am, thanks." He's been attentive to all my needs in my short stay. Of course, I know it's being paid for, but I'm grateful nonetheless.

Outside, the chauffeured car I've had at my disposal since Landon left is waiting under the awning. I tell the driver where to take me, wondering what Landon would think if he found out that the resources he left at my disposal were now being used to facilitate my date with another man.

I don't fool myself into thinking he would care.

The drive to the hotel where Jack is staying

doesn't take too long. The entrance is adjacent to the sidewalk and Jack is standing there, his hands shoved into the pockets of his stylish black pants as he radiates calm, confidence, and serious cool. Two women walk by, stealing glances at him, one of them almost missing her step as they pass by.

"Hello beautiful," he greets me with a hug. I can't help but notice how good he smells.

Just good though, not divine, like Landon.

"Hello to you too," I reply.

Pulling back, Jack's eyes skip from me to the chauffeured car now pulling away toward the hotel parking lot. If he has any thoughts on it, he keeps them to himself.

The lounge is on one of the top floors of the building, overlooking the square. From all the windows, there are fantastic views of the city, with the breathtaking sunset that turns the sky into a beautiful burst of purple, orange, and gold. The décor is heavy luxury, with thick rugs, damask curtains pulled back from the windows, soft lights, and deep red velvet chairs that look like luxurious half-moon pods. A chanteuse on the stage is singing covers of mellow love songs while smartly dressed waiters carry trays around the room.

A waiter leads us to a table by a window. "Now tell me what you're really doing here," I say to Jack as soon as we take our seats.

"I already told you," he replies.

We order drinks—scotch for him and a cocktail for me—and the waiter recommends the bacon and deviled eggs small plate.

The chanteuse launches into an Adele song about turning tables. It's sad and emotional, and we both listen silently.

"What are you working on?" I ask finally, uncomfortable with the silence.

He shrugs. "At the moment, nothing interesting. I'm joining a team of high-profile climbers in the Andes, but my heart's not in it. I think I'd like to try something new, maybe submarine tourism—I'd like to explore the ocean depths."

I grimace. "It doesn't sound very safe."

"I'm sure it could be. Safe is boring, by the way."

I smile. "You always say that."

Right as we finish eating, a DJ takes over from the chanteuse. By now, there are more people around, and a few are dancing. Outside, it's already getting dark, but the whole city is ablaze with lights.

"We should dance," Jack suggests.

"Noooo." I finish my cocktail—my second—and grin at him, feeling slightly wobbly. "I don't want to dance with you."

Hurt flares in his gray eyes. "Why not?"

"Because I don't like you very much right now."

He stares at the ice melting in his drink then looks back up at me. "Maybe that will change."

"I doubt it." I pause. "So you and Claudia..."

He shakes his head. "It was rash, and maybe a little silly to get engaged in the first place. It's easy to fall in love with someone after you jump out of a plane with them."

"I guess."

"She was fun, very spontaneous. You know she got famous after a rodeo campaign where she actually rode the bulls?" He pauses. "I think I saw us being a team of adventurers, but we didn't really know each other. She didn't know me, at least not like you do."

He looks so serious, and he's doing the thing where he's looking at me as if I'm the only person in the world. I get up from my seat, not eager to pursue the line of conversation he's starting. "You know what?" I say, "We should dance."

He obliges. The DJ is playing some upbeat songs, and I let Jack twirl me around the floor. By the time we return to our table, I'm smiling and breathless from the exertion.

"Another drink?"

I bat my eyelashes at him, doing my best imitation of old Hollywood glamor. "Now, sir, you wouldn't be trying to get me drunk, would you?"

"Why, Miss Foster, I wouldn't dream of it." We

both laugh. It feels so much like old times, except this time, I'm not as full of longing.

My phone rings suddenly, interrupting our laughter.

"Sorry," I tell Jack as I glance at the screen.

It's Landon.

I signal to Jack to give me a few minutes and get up from the table, walking in the direction of the ladies room.

"Hello," I say.

"Where are you?" Landon asks without preamble.

"Have you returned?"

"I have. I landed about half an hour ago."

"You could have let me know you were on your way."

"Why? I told you I was going to return today."

"Yes, but..." I stop myself. I'd been about to complain about the silence. He didn't call me once while he was gone, and it rankled. It really shouldn't have, because even though my emotions are telling me otherwise, I'm not his girlfriend. He doesn't owe me calls every other hour to check on me, just as I don't owe him any explanation for going out.

"I went out," I say, not offering any further explanation.

"I gathered." His voice is terse. "Are you alone?"

I pause. "No, I'm not, but I'm about to leave."

There's a charged silence on his end. "Where are you?" he says finally.

I tell him the name of the lounge.

"I'm on my way," I hear him say.

"You don't have to—"

"I'm on my way," he repeats, his voice crisp as he ends the call. I stare helplessly at the phone then turn back to the table where Jack is waiting for me.

CHAPTER 13

"*E*VERYTHING all right?" Jack asks when I join him again.

I nod. "Yeah, I think."

"You sure?"

"Yes." I look toward the entrance, wondering how long it will be before Landon arrives.

"You sure you don't want another drink?"

I shake my head. If Landon is coming here, I'm going to need all my senses intact.

"I'm leaving tomorrow," Jack is saying. He starts to tell me about his travel plans, but I'm not really listening. I have one eye on the door, waiting for Landon to appear. The tension in my stomach is as much eagerness to see him as it is anxiety about his reasons for coming, and what his reaction will be when he sees me with Jack.

Will he be jealous?

The idea is oddly appealing, but I dismiss it almost instantly. Why would he care who I hang out with?

Jack is waiting for me to say something, and I realize I have no idea what he's been telling me. He leans across the table and put his hand over mine. "You're not listening," he says, smiling. "Where's your mind?"

Before I can answer, my eyes skip past him to the entrance again, and Landon is just walking into the room. As always, seeing him, seeing all that strength and power encased in a body that's almost too raw in its beauty—it takes my breath away. He's wearing one of his magnificent suits with no tie, and the top buttons of his shirt are undone.

As I admire him, his eyes skim over the other people in the lounge and land on me. He takes in Jack, whose hand is still over mine on the table, and as I watch, his eyes grow a few degrees colder.

Still, he walks toward our table, his eyes never leaving mine. I don't even feel Jack pull his hand away or see him as he follows my gaze to see Landon. All my attention, my whole being is focused on the insanely sexy man walking toward me.

When he reaches me, he surprises me by taking my face in his hands and giving me a deep toe-curling kiss that leaves me flushed and breathless.

He releases me, and I sway on my seat. Then he straightens and turns to Jack—who's looking at me as if I've committed some huge betrayal—and stretches out a hand. "Landon Court," he says.

Jack rises to his feet and takes the proffered hand. "Jack Weyland."

"Pleased to meet you," Landon says, though there's no trace of the stated pleasure in his voice or face. "You write for Gilt as well, don't you? Are you here for work?"

Jack looks at me, then back at Landon. "No, I'm here to see Rachel."

The challenge in his voice is not lost on me, and Landon notices it too, I'm sure. He just chooses to ignore it. He turns to me. "You ready?"

"You're leaving?" If I didn't know better, I would say Jack sounds hurt.

"Yes," I reply, getting up without looking at him. I'm still reeling from Landon's kiss. "I had a great time."

"Yeah," Jack says woodenly. "Me too."

Jack doesn't follow us outside, for which I'm grateful. I can't even imagine how awkward it would have been for the three of us, especially with Landon's arm positioned possessively around my waist.

I don't complain, not only because Landon fried my brain when he kissed me, but because I felt a little pleasure from seeing the expression on Jack's face as I left with Landon. It's an inadequate revenge for the two years I spent pining for him, but nevertheless, it makes me feel good.

I follow Landon to the elevator. His hand is still around my waist, building a slow heat on the surface of my skin. As soon as the doors slide closed, I turn to face him.

"What was that about?"

His face is bland. "What exactly?"

"Coming here. Kissing me in front of Jack. Acting as if I did something wrong by going out—"

"I wasn't aware my actions were so out of place." His eyes are fixed on my face. "I came here because I wanted to see you and I was tired of waiting. I kissed you because I wanted to." He stops. "What exactly is the problem? That I interrupted your reunion with your boyfriend?"

Before I can answer, the elevator stops and the doors slide open. I follow him across the lobby to the street and a few seconds later, a car parks in front of us.

"I came in one of the Rosemont cars," I tell Landon.

"Your driver has already returned," he replies, pulling open the door of the car.

I get in with a sigh, waiting for him to join me. "First of all," I say calmly, "Jack's not my boyfriend.

Secondly, I don't think it was necessary for you to flaunt our...arrangement in his face like that."

"Why do you care so much?" Landon asks. "What is he to you?"

"It's not about him," I retort.

"Isn't it?" he challenges. "I seem to recall that exclusivity was one of your conditions for agreeing to this arrangement. Did that particular condition apply only to me? Am I supposed to sit back and accept the fact that you went out with him, the same man with whom you had a fight in my hotel the day we met? He's the reason you were crying in the elevator, and he came all the way here to see you. Talk about a grand gesture."

My planned response freezes on my tongue. How had he known about my fight with Jack in the Swanson Court, and about me crying in the elevator?

He takes in my puzzled expression. "Security cameras, Rachel. How do you think I found you? I had dinner with my brother that night. He was trying to convince me that hookers were a better deal than relationships, and he offered to send me one. I refused. When you appeared in the elevator, I thought he'd ignored me, as usual. You didn't leave your number, and I couldn't get you out of my mind. So, I called him, and it turned out he had no idea what I was talking about. I had the security team at the hotel review the tapes to find out who you were, and I saw them too. I saw your argument with Jack Weyland, and I saw how distressed you were afterward."

I'd wondered how he found me. Now I knew, and I couldn't stop wondering how many other things he knew about me. With the resources he had at his disposal, he could probably find out anything he wanted—not that I had much to hide, but still.

"Did he come here to apologize?" he continues. "Am I standing in the way of some romantic reunion?"

"Would you care?" I mutter.

"No." He utters the words so carelessly it pisses me off. "Let's just be clear, for as long as this arrangement lasts, I have every right to be extremely selfish when it comes to you. I don't give a fuck about what he wants, because right now, you belong to me."

Why do those possessive words start a sweet ache in my belly, one that grows and spreads until every inch of my skin is waiting impatiently for his touch?

I shake my head. "I don't belong to anyone," I say stubbornly. "I sure as hell don't belong to you."

He leans forward and places a finger under my chin, bringing my face close to his. "Unless you're telling me you want to stop this, to end this...arrangement right now, then you belong to me." His blue eyes are almost hypnotizing. "Is that what you want?"

I want to tell him to go to hell. I can do that. I

can go back to the suite and concentrate on my article while he remains in the next room. I can stay here for two more days without touching him. I can tame the craving my body has for him. I can.

I can't.

I shake my head, too ashamed of my need for him to say the words out loud.

"Say it," he demands.

"No," I whisper, "that's not what I want."

I see the smile of triumph on his face right before he lowers his lips to mine. The kiss is soft, possessive, and sensual. He's so skilled. He makes me forget everything but the feel of his lips over mine, the warmth as he sucks my bottom lip into his mouth before releasing it to slide his tongue into mine, licking and tasting. He's gentle, tender, and so sweet, I immediately lose myself, moving across the seat to lean into his body.

He pulls me onto his lap, deepening the kiss as his hands move down from my arms to my waist, setting fire to every inch of my skin he touches.

I barely register it when the car stops, but I groan in protest when Landon tears his lips from mine.

"We're here," he says softly, smoothing my hair.

I nod, my body aroused and wanting, resenting the time it will take to make the trip up to the suite.

He starts to open the door, then stops and looks back at me. "I'm sorry I didn't call," he says, surprising me. "I wasn't sure..." He stops. "I was very busy, but I should have called."

"Okay." I watch him leave the car, barely having time to wonder what he'd been about to say before he's opening the door at my side. As soon as I step out, his hand closes around my waist, and he doesn't let go even as we cross the spacious lobby.

Once in the elevator, he starts to kiss me again, pressing my hips against the wall with his, giving me no doubt as to his desire for me.

"I couldn't stop thinking about you." His voice is a rasp against my ear. "Every single minute I had you in my head."

I respond by pressing my hips forward and rubbing against the bulge in his trousers. He groans. "If you don't stop that, we're going to end up fucking in here."

I want to tell him I don't care, but the elevator stops just in time and he lifts me in his arms, carrying me all the way inside the suite to his room. He lays me on the bed then starts to remove his clothes. Rising up to my knees, I pull my dress over my head, eager to be naked by the time he's done undressing. I remove my bra and pull off my panties just as he pulls down his briefs, letting his glorious erection spring free. At the sight of the thick, hard length and the veins bulging under the silky skin, heat spreads from below my stomach to pool between my thighs.

He joins me on the bed, gently pushing me to lie on my back. He lowers his head to lick along the seam of my lips, making me shiver in pleasure. Then he starts to trace a path from my lips, over my throat, down to my breasts. I squirm as he takes one nipple in his mouth while he rubs the other one between his finger and thumb. He moves his lips to the other nipple, licking and sucking it before moving downward over my stomach, kissing the mound at the juncture of my thighs before he nudges my legs apart and lowers his lips to my sex.

I groan at the first contact of his tongue, my hips bucking as he licks my clit. He grips my thighs and spreads them a little more, sucking me greedily before moving down to rim the pulsing slit of my sex. I moan loudly, my fingers threading through his hair as he drives me to the point of madness.

I moan his name, unable to bear the heat and pleasure coursing through me.

"Hmm." The sound vibrates through my body as he moves his mouth back to my clit, teasing me to the point of climax before moving back to my wet aching slit. My hips start to move of their own volition, matching the licking movements of his tongue. I feel his fingers teasing at the entrance to my body, hovering there for a moment before sliding inside.

I squirm, my insides tightening and demanding more. He moves his fingers without stopping the teasing of his tongue, rubbing them against the tight bundle of nerves inside me. I cry out and jerk off the bed, my whole body exploding in a shattering climax.

He removes his fingers and I draw my legs up, wanting to turn on my side and press my legs together to still the trembling all over my body, but he doesn't let me. He kneels between my legs and positions himself, rubbing the wide head of his cock over my sensitive clit and down over my slick folds. I spread my legs wider, inviting him in.

Slowly, he slides into me, drawing out the pleasure as he fills me. I moan softly, rubbing my hands over the muscles of his chest as he surges forward with a groan. His muscles tighten, and he expels a slow breath before he pulls out almost entirely then pushes in again. I wrap my legs around his waist, tightening my inner muscles as I urge him deeper inside.

"Fuck," he groans, his hands moving feverishly along my thighs, his hips grinding as he thrusts into me again and again. My soft cries blend with the sound of his groans as pleasure builds uncontrollably inside me, but still I want more. My hands find the tight muscles of his buttocks, and I press my fingers against them, urging him deeper. He starts to move faster, his body covered with sweat, his eyes shut, his face tightened in an expression of primal male lust.

My body seizes, unable to bear the pleasure

anymore. I come with a loud, helpless cry, and Landon moans my name as he thrusts hard into me. Then he stiffens too, his hips jerking as he comes.

A moment later, he leans down to lay kisses on the sensitive tips of both my breasts, then pulls out and lies back on the bed beside me. He draws me close to him and I relax into his body, luxuriating in the feel of his skin against mine, of his heart beating against my chest.

I fall asleep soon after. A few hours later, I wake up and find myself alone on the bed. This time, I find Landon in the library, where a temporary office has already been set up for him, same as before he left. He's sitting in the dark, his face lit only by the glow from his computer screen as he types something really quickly. The door is open, and I watch him from the doorway, wondering if he ever sleeps.

He doesn't see me standing there, and after a while, I go back to bed. This time, without him beside me, it's harder to fall asleep. I finally drift off, but for the rest of the night, even in my sleep, I'm aware of his absence beside me on the bed.

CHAPTER 14

I wake up missing Landon. The feeling is acute, real, and sad, almost as if I've gone forward in time to when our arrangement is completed and he's no longer a part of my life. It makes no sense, because for one, our arrangement isn't over, and two, even when it ends, there should be no reason for me to be sad. It's not as if we're in a real relationship.

Still, I can't shake the feelings of depression and emptiness. Confused by the intensity of what I'm feeling and my inability to rationalize it, I get up from the bed, wondering if Landon is still working in the library. Wrapping myself in one of the sheets, I walk over to the bathroom.

The dressing room and bathroom are combined in one large suite, and as I step in through the door,

Landon emerges from the shower, totally naked. His hair is wet, plastered to his face and neck. His body is glistening with moisture as little drops of water run down his skin. A cloud of steam comes out with him, carrying the tangy scent of his body wash.

He stops when he notices me standing by the door, and his eyes linger on me for a moment. "Good morning," he says, going to a carved wooden shelf next to the shower and picking up one of the hotel towels. He goes to sit on a low bench that runs along the wall by the marble bath and starts to dry his hair. I watch the bunching of his muscles as his arms move, my body responding almost immediately. This part I get, the wanting him. It's only normal; no woman could see him and not want him. It's the other part I don't get, the way my feelings have started to become a mess that even I don't understand.

"Are you going to stand there staring at me all day?"

He's teasing, and it makes me smile. "Would you mind?"

He grins. "Not at all." For someone who has had so little sleep, he doesn't look tired at all. How does he do it?

"You hardly slept last night."

He shrugs. "I was working." Something in his face tells me he doesn't want to talk about it, and I drop the topic. He drops the towel beside him on the bench and combs his hair with his fingers. I could watch him all day, I realize. Everything about his body is amazing.

I'm staring, and from the smirk on his face, he knows why.

"I know I said I didn't mind you staring at me," he says, "but it seems I mind if that's all you do."

"Really?" I chew on my lower lip. "What else would you like me to do?"

"What would you like to do?" he asks. "I'm entirely at your service."

My eyes travel over his body, from his tousled hair to his naked cock, lying thick and hard on his lap and growing harder by the second. I lick my lips and free the sheet I'm holding around my body, letting it drop to the floor before walking over to him. Dropping to my knees in front of him, I run my hands along his thighs then look up at him before I take him in my hand, stroking up and down his length.

His breath deepens and his hips move forward. I bend my head and lick around the head of his cock while still stroking him up and down. He groans and throws his head back.

"Fuck!" The word comes out as a low, harsh whisper. His fingers thread in my hair, flexing over my scalp, and I respond by taking him into my mouth and flicking my tongue around the head of his cock before taking him all the way in, until I can feel him at the back of my throat.

His hands tighten in my hair and I hollow my cheeks, sucking deeply as I pull my lips back up then do a deep suck on the head of his cock.

"Rachel!" he groans, removing one hand from my hair to brace it on the bench while the other remains to help him move my head to match the movements of his hips as he strokes his cock in and out of my mouth.

It's so blatantly erotic, what we're doing. I feel as if I could come just from sucking on him. My eyes rise to meet his and he groans again, throwing his head back as his hips continue to move.

I cup his balls with one hand, the other busy exploring the tense muscles in his thighs. I love the sounds he's making, the way his muscles flex as his hips thrust. I love the heady feeling of feminine power I get from seeing how aroused he is. I want him to lose control, and I want to be the reason why.

I tighten my lips around him, my tongue licking at the underside of his cock. His fingers flex in my hair and a tortured sigh escapes him, followed by hoarse words. "I'm coming," he says breathlessly. "Fuck! I'm coming."

I respond with a moan, taking him deeper inside my mouth. His hips thrust forward, his muscles stiffening and his whole body shuddering as he comes into my mouth in a warm rush.

I swallow, milking him for every last drop. When I'm done, he leans down and kisses me deeply, his chest still heaving.

He releases me and I start to get up, but he grabs me and pulls me onto his lap. "You're not going anywhere," he growls, "not until I make you scream."

His lips cover mine again and his hands cup my breasts, but I take hold of his wrists and pull away from his kiss. "You don't have to," I tell him. "I sucked you off because I wanted to, not because I want you to return the favor. Anyway," I continue, "you should be resting. I'm sure you need to recover your strength, and I want to take a shower."

I start to get off his lap, but he doesn't release me. "I wasn't trying to return the favor," he says. "I happen to like making you come. I'm very fond of the way your face looks when you lose control, and the sounds you make are addictive." He gets up, still carrying me, and moves like that to the shower stall.

"What are you doing?" I ask when he sets me down.

He gives me a look. "You wanted to shower."

"Yes…"

"Shh." He turns on the water, testing it to get the right temperature, and then he reaches for the bottle of body wash. Even in the steamy enclosure, I notice that he's hard again. *How on earth does he do it?*

He pours some of the soapy liquid on his palm. "Turn around," he orders.

I do as he says, already aroused. He spreads the soap on my back then my arms, his hands snaking in front of my body to soap my breasts, and then my stomach. By the time he starts working on my buttocks, my legs are weak, and my sex is pulsing with desire.

He rubs the soapy liquid across my ass and my hips, spreading my cheeks with each repeated motion. Hooking an arm around my waist, he pulls my butt back toward him. I steady myself by placing my hands on the glass wall of the stall and gasp when he parts my butt cheeks with his free hand, one finger coming to rest on the puckered opening between them.

As he moves his finger, massaging the tight ring, the feeling is unlike anything I've ever felt before, and I don't want him to stop. At the same time, I can feel his erection pressing against the back of my thighs, intensifying my need to have him inside me.

The hand on my stomach slides down between my legs. It slips between my folds and finds my clit, and a loud moan escapes me when he starts to stroke it.

"What was it you said about recovering my strength?" he asks.

My only response is another moan, which intensifies when the finger at my rear dips inside the entrance. My hips roll of their own accord, my body taken over by need verging on desperation.

"I don't need to recover my strength when it comes to you," Landon whispers. "I could fuck you all day long."

I want him to fuck me now. I reach behind me, wanting to touch him at least, to feel his thick hardness in my hands, but he doesn't let me. He pushes my hand away and leaves me hanging for a couple seconds before I feel the head of his cock pushing into me from behind. Even as he slides fully inside me, his finger is still playing with my puckered rear opening, sending unbearable sensation through me as he rocks his hips, using his cock to drive me to an explosive dimension of pleasure.

With only a few strokes, my entire body is shaking, the pleasure nearly overwhelming me. My skin is covered with sweat and water and steam, and my whole body is pulsing, suffused with pleasure so intense, I can't stand it. My hands flex against the glass wall of the stall, a scream tearing from my throat as I come so hard my legs give out.

Landon holds me up, his own climax coming at the end of mine. He slams into me and comes in a hot surge, his growl full of ecstasy that mirrors what I feel.

Later, after he has washed me all over and shampooed my hair, he wraps me in a towel and carries me over to his bed.

I snuggle against him, happy and contented. "What's the plan for today?"

"I already said I was going to spend all day fucking you."

"Ha!" I laugh softly. "I'd probably be dead by lunchtime—though it wouldn't be so bad, dying of pleasure."

His chest rumbles as he joins in my laughter. "I'd probably be the one dying from trying to keep up with you." He nuzzles my ear. "After breakfast, I have a few calls to make, then we're going out."

I raise a questioning brow. "Out to where?"

"It's a surprise."

"I hate surprises," I declare with a pout.

"I'm sure you'll like this one," he says, getting off the bed, his tight muscles flexing as he walks toward the dressing room.

I leave his bed, retrieving my clothes from the floor before going to my room, where I get dressed and make myself presentable. By the time I come back to the living room, Landon is already dressed. He asks what I'd like for breakfast, and then places the order. When he's done, we go outside to the terrace, where he reads his newspaper while I check my phone for emails and messages.

I had a great time yesterday, a text from Jack reads. *Looking forward to hanging out when I get back.*

There's no mention of Landon at all, but somehow, he's there between Jack and me, even in the message. In a moment of clarity, I realize that whatever my feelings for Jack were before, after Landon, they're almost certainly gone.

Acting on a suspicion I've had since yesterday, I do a search on Claudia Sever. The first few results are news articles from entertainment sites, and they confirm my suspicions. According to the sites, Claudia Sever has rekindled her on-again, off-again relationship with billionaire Reese Fletcher after ending a short engagement with American writer and TV personality Jack Weyland.

I'm glad I don't even care enough to be disappointed in Jack. Why would he tell me he was dumped? It didn't gel with his image—he was usually the one doing the dumping.

There's a message from my mother, asking how I am, and as I type my reply, an email from Laurie pops up with the subject line *FAMOUS*.

The email contains a screenshot. There's Landon, opening the car door for me outside Jack's hotel last night, and below it, part of an article.

New York hotelier and real estate mogul Landon Court

spotted in a passionate clinch with a mystery lady in San Francisco.

All over New York, hearts are breaking as Landon Court is spotted with this woman for the second time. We're still trying to find out who she is, and how she managed to get the elusive bachelor on lockdown.

The screenshot is cropped after that last sentence. I glance up at Landon, who's frowning at something he's reading. I don't have him on lockdown, although at the moment, I kind of wish I did.

He catches me staring at him. "You want to tell me something?"

I shake my head. "No."

He smiles. "Then stop looking at me like that, or else I won't be able to get anything done this morning."

I pull in a sharp breath, helpless against the way even those simple words affect me. I turn back to my phone, finishing the reply to my mom and starting a messenger chat with Laurie.

Breakfast arrives, and right after we eat, Landon disappears to the library. I finish my chat with Laurie, giving her the latest updates while purposely neglecting to tell her anything about Jack's visit. Then I get my Mac and start on a couple revisions to the article, getting lost in my work and not looking up until Landon emerges from the library some hours later.

I feel him looking at me, and when my eyes meet his, I briefly forget what I'm doing. It's not just that he's attractive; it's that there's a power that radiates from him that gets me every time. It's obvious just from looking at him that he's a powerful man, a rich one, someone who controls a lot more than almost all of his peers. It's obvious in his carriage, in everything about him.

And he wants me.

It's in the way he's looking at me right now. My stomach tightens as his gaze warms my skin. *It's never going to be like this with anyone else*, I realize. It's just not possible.

I swallow. "Are you going to say something? Or are you going to keep looking at me like that?"

He folds his arms across his chest and leans back on the wall. "Looking at you like how?"

Like you're a hypnotist and I'm your willing victim? Like you're a vortex sucking me in? I shrug. "I don't know, like you can see inside me?"

"Believe me, I wish I could."

I frown at the cryptic words, my eyes following him as he leaves his position by the wall to approach me. He comes to stand behind the sofa and leans over me. I can feel him behind me even before he touches me, his hand gently stroking my hair.

I set my Mac down beside me on the sofa, my eyes fluttering closed as I relax into his touch.

"I love your hair," I hear him say, the words soft and slightly rough. "Sometimes it's red, sometimes gold, and sometimes it's both." He lifts a few strands in his fingers and lets them fall back down.

I shift in my seat, turning around to face him. Resting my chin on the back of the sofa, I look up at him. "Is that the only thing you love?"

His eyes darken. "You have no idea," he says, straightening suddenly and pushing his hands into his pockets. "You should pack an overnight bag," he tells me. "We're leaving in about an hour."

"You still won't tell me where we're going?"

He shakes his head. "You'll see soon enough."

I do as he says and pack a change of clothes and fresh underwear before changing into a pair of cream pants and a white linen blouse. I leave my hair down, joining him for the trip downstairs after applying mascara and lip gloss. He's dressed casually too in pants and a short-sleeved cotton shirt that leaves his forearms exposed.

His hand curls possessively around my waist from the moment we leave the suite to when we get into the car. During the short ride, he's busy talking on the phone. I try to find something else to interest me other than the easy sexiness he exudes, something other than the overwhelming desire to do something about how much I want him, even now, in the car.

After a few minutes, we arrive at what looks like a

private estate or a club, and the car drops us off at the dock where a long, gleaming white boat is waiting in the water.

Landon is standing beside me, watching as the chauffeur carries our overnight bags onto the boat. "Do you like sailing?"

"I don't know," I reply. "I've never done it."

He takes my hand, the small contact sending a small shock of excitement through me. "Well, come on then."

The boat has a captain and a steward, and they welcome us pleasantly before showing us around. In the stateroom, there's a box on the bed containing a bikini that's exactly my size.

"You didn't have to rent a whole boat just because you want to see me in my bikini," I tease.

"I've seen you in a lot less," he reminds me, eyeing my curves in the small white bikini. He's changed—faster than me—into a pair of shorts appropriate for a day of relaxing the deck of a luxury boat. His bare chest is a study in perfection, hard slabs of muscle that continue all the way over his flat stomach to end below his navel in a hard V that disappears into his shorts.

"Yes you have," I agree.

His eyes fix on mine, then he sighs. "Come on. They're laying out our lunch. If we don't leave this cabin now, I probably won't let you out all day."

On the deck, we have lunch as the boat sails across the bay, and Landon points out the sights from the water. I'm more impressed by Alcatraz Island than anything else, especially when Landon starts to tell me about a famous escape from the former high-security prison. His face is animated as he tells me about a movie about the escape that was made in the seventies.

"In the seventies?" I tease. "You weren't even born."

He shrugs. "I have a thing for old movies. *The Maltese Falcon*, *Citizen Kane*." He looks at me and smiles. "*The Good, the Bad and the Ugly*."

"Ugh." I do an exaggerated shudder. "I have a thing for Disney movies, Michael Bay type action-fests, and anything with Ralph Fiennes."

He gives me a look. "Well, at least there's hope that you'll find me attractive when I'm that age."

"I'll always find you attractive," I say softly, looking at him. It's almost as if we're both pretending this thing we have isn't going to end in only two days.

I disguise the sad direction of my thought with a cheerful smile and a funny comment. He responds in kind, and we spend the rest of the afternoon just talking. As evening arrives, the boat docks close to a rocky island where a wooden berth connects the dock to a flight of stairs that leads up to a small but exquisite house with wide sunny patios, a sparkling blue swimming pool, and inside, the most amazing mixture of both homey and classy décor.

"Wow!" is all I can say. "How do you even find places like this?"

"You build them." He ignores my look of surprise. "Sometimes, I need to get away, you know, watch old movies and forget about my phone."

"That totally explains it." I laugh, going from room to room to look at the mesmerizing views.

He follows me, seeming to take pleasure in my almost childish enjoyment of the house. In the kitchen, he checks the fridge, his eyes scanning over all the contents.

"I'm famished," I tell him, realizing even as I say it just how hungry I really am.

"Hmm." He closes the fridge. "I asked the retainer to get some food items. Why don't you go change, explore, whatever, and I'll make dinner."

My mouth hangs open. "You cook?"

"I practically grew up in a hotel," he says. "Sometimes I hung out in the kitchen with the chefs."

"I'm not going anywhere," I tell him, pulling out one of the stools at the kitchen island. "I have to watch this."

I watch him cook, helping only a little, since my culinary skills are severely limited. After we've polished off the tender steak with a delicious sauce and a crisp tomato salad, I relax with my head on his lap while we watch one of his old movies in a den with a very large widescreen TV.

The movie, a tragic story about an aging actress and a struggling writer, is surprisingly good, even though it's in black and white. When it's over, we go to the master bedroom, another beautiful room with a tremendous view, and before we go to sleep, we make love with an intensity that brings tears to my eyes. He falls asleep before I do, his breaths slowing as his chest rises and falls. I listen to him breathe, my head on his chest as exhaustion from his lovemaking competes with my desire to enjoy the sound of his heartbeat for a little while longer. When I finally fall asleep with my arm around his waist, I know without a doubt that I never want to let him go.

CHAPTER 15

I wake up with the knowledge that something is wrong. Rising from the bed, I start to look around the darkened room before realizing it's Landon who woke me up.

He's still asleep, but his muscles are tense and straining, his hands into curled into fists by his side. His eyes are tightly closed, and he's moaning words in his sleep, the sounds barely comprehensible.

"No," he says, his head moving from side to side. "No, please, let me go," then a long strained, "Mom."

I look up at his face, and it's drawn into a tight mixture of desperation and despair. I have no idea what to do. My only experience of nightmares is the boogeyman my little brother Dylan struggled with for about two months when he was six.

Landon makes another tortured sound and,

unsure of what to do, I put my arms around him, stroking his chest as I pray for his nightmare to end. It finally does, his body relaxing as sleep takes over. I stay awake long after, still stroking him lightly, until finally, I fall asleep again.

～

"WHEN ARE YOU COMING BACK?" LAURIE MOCK-wails on the phone. "I just managed to escape from the moms. They were driving me crazy asking-but-not-asking when me and Brett are planning to get married."

"Hehe." I laugh gleefully, pleased that I had a valid reason to avoid the Foster family Sunday lunch. Though I'd have liked to see my dad, Dylan, Uncle Taylor, who always proclaims that I'm his favorite niece no matter how many times I remind him that I'm his only niece, and Aunt Jacie, even though she always conspires with my mom as if they're the twins in the family. "Did they make their signature Foster family everything salad?" I ask Laurie.

"Arghh, don't remind me. Brett loved it though." I hear the sound of a kiss. "He says hurry back home, and that you're not fooling anyone into thinking you're getting any work done over there."

"Tell him I said boo."

She laughs. "I miss you, but don't hurry back just because of me."

After we hang up, Landon looks up from whatever he's reading on his tablet. He looks handsome and well rested, his wavy hair gleaming, making me want to run a hand through the silky strands. "Your cousin?"

"Yup," I reply. We're back in the city, on our way back to the hotel after spending the morning exploring the rocky beach, lying in the sun, and making love in the warmth of the patio. I haven't mentioned his nightmare, and I'm not sure I should. I don't know what I can do to help, or if I'm even equipped to.

"She must miss you," he says, still talking about Laurie.

"Nah, she just misses having someone to torture with her teasing." I chuckle at Landon's frown. "I'm joking, I miss her too."

He considers me for a moment. "Maybe I can cheer you up," he suggests. "How would you like to go to a party tonight?"

"A party?"

"Well, not really a party per se. It's the opening night gala for the San Francisco Ballet."

A gala? "Isn't that a big deal?"

He shrugs. "I wasn't planning to go, but I thought you might want to. My mother used to be part of the company before she was hired away to New York. I've always been a sponsor."

My first thought is that I have nothing to wear to a high society gala. "Well, thanks for telling me now," I say, lips pursed, "instead of when I could have actually packed a dress to wear to a ball."

He smiles at my petulance. "Don't worry about what to wear—that's what fairy godmothers are for."

"If you were the fairy godmother, Cinderella would never have made it to the ball," I tease. "She wouldn't even want to, not with the multiple orgasms she'd be getting in the pumpkin carriage."

"I wouldn't ruin a children's fairy tale just for sex," he replies, chuckling, "but thanks for letting me know you think I'm more desirable than Prince Charming."

I laugh softly. "I love how humble you are."

His blue eyes hold mine. "Is that all you love?"

The question is a replay of the one I asked him in an earlier conversation, so I repeat the same words he replied the first time. "You have no idea."

True to Landon's promise, there are delivery boxes on my bed when we arrive back at the suite. The larger box contains a dress covered in layers of tissue, another contains underwear, and yet another contains matching shoes which are exactly my size. I pull the dress out of the box, feeling the exquisite material brush against my skin. It's a deep purple gown made out of the softest, most luxurious silk. Holding it against my body, I walk over to the adjoining dressing room to look in the mirror. It's gorgeous.

After hanging up the dress, I return to my room to find Landon waiting for me at the door. "I'm going to be in the library. I have a long call to make."

On a Sunday? is my first thought, but I suppose with everything he has to take care of, he probably works every single day. "Thanks for the dress."

"I should be thanking you. You'll save me from drowning in socialites, I promise."

"I can look fierce and glare at any woman who comes within two feet of you."

"That would be ideal," he says, his blue eyes serious. "There're going to be a few people here later to help you get ready.

I grin. "Yay! Pampering!"

He looks amused. "I'll just hide out in the library 'til they're gone."

"You're scared of makeup brushes and hair styling tools?"

"Not scared." He pauses. "Just wary of the whole process, although I have no doubt I'll appreciate the results."

"You will," I say confidently.

"As I said, I have no doubt." He makes no move to go, leaning on the door frame as he looks at me.

There's a strange half-smile on his face. "A week has never seemed so short," he says finally before leaving me reeling with all the possible implications and interpretations of that simple statement.

∾

LANDON'S FEW PEOPLE TURN OUT TO BE AN army of five from the hotel spa. They arrive after I finally finish working on Mark's comments and sending the second draft of the article to him so he can read it first thing tomorrow morning.

After I take a quick shower, they give me the hair, nail, and makeup treatment. By the time they're done, I look and feel like a glamorous Hollywood star on the red carpet.

When I'm ready, I leave my room and find Landon waiting in the living room. At the sight of him, my breath catches in my throat.

It's really unfair for one man to have so much, to look so perfect, to achieve all that he has and still be blessed with such incredible sex appeal. His black tuxedo is perfectly molded to his figure like it was custom made for him—which it probably was. His hair is brushed backward into sleek waves that curl at the ends, but the dark gold strands are already finding their way out of the orderly arrangement. As I enter the room, he turns to look at me, his eyes gleaming with sensual intensity as they travel over my body.

He strides toward me, his movements both sure and graceful. "You look ravishing." His eyes make no attempt to hide the fact that he'd like to be doing the ravishing.

"I had help."

He makes a dismissive sound. "No, this is all you."

My stomach tingling with the compliment, I follow him out of the suite.

There's a limo downstairs and once we're inside, he pulls a black velvet box from his inner jacket pocket and opens it to reveal a glittering diamond choker and earrings. The colors are perfect for my gown, and they are beautiful.

"God, it's perfect," I whisper.

"I'm glad you think so." He takes the choker out of the box. "May I?"

"I don't..." I look from the obviously expensive piece of jewelry to him. "I don't think I can take this."

He looks surprised. "Why not? It's just jewelry."

"Very expensive jewelry."

He looks at me. "You wouldn't feel better about it if it were cheap."

"That's not the point." I pause. "How many women have you given jewelry?"

There's a short pause before he replies. "A few."

"Well, this makes me feel like one of 'your' women, and I don't want to feel like I'm being given expensive gifts for spending time with you."

He grins, his teeth gleaming white in the dimness of the car. "Even if I had any 'women,' I'd never consider you as 'one of them.' He clasps the choker around my neck, his hands lingering at my nape before he pulls them back and gives me the earrings. "Consider it a loan then, just for tonight. They look wonderful on you."

The limo drops us off, and we walk up a flight of steps to the entrance of the public building where the pre-performance reception and dinner is being held. There are flashing lights everywhere as cameras go off. We walk into the lobby, where cocktails are being served, and I spot a few famous faces. There are politicians and Hollywood stars liberally sprinkled among the designer-suited moguls, trophy wives dripping with diamonds, and powerful women with the aura of confidence that only comes from facing the world on their own terms. Landon navigates a politely reserved path through them all, stopping for a word here, a handshake there, and a compliment for some of the women.

I'm enjoying myself, sipping my champagne while watching Landon engage in light conversation with a couple he just introduced to me, when a man who, though handsome, looks as if he's already drunk too much, steps directly into our path.

"I suppose now you have more reason to be in San Francisco," he says to Landon, his expression practically dripping with hatred. He turns to look at me, his eyes traveling insolently up and down my body. "Something else you've bought, I presume."

"You need to learn to control your tongue if you don't want to get your nose broken," Landon replies, his expression retaining the mask of politeness even though I can hear a dangerous bite in his voice. "You already lost too much to risk losing that pretty face of yours too, haven't you, Sinclair?"

I recognize the name as the man blanches, involuntarily rubbing the nose in question before turning and walking away. He's Evans Sinclair, the former owner of the Gold Dust Hotel.

Landon watches his retreating form with hard, uncompromising eyes, and I'm reminded of Jack's warning about his ruthlessness in business. "Well, that's one person who doesn't like you," I say lightly.

"He happens to be one person whose good opinion I can do without."

"Hey Red," a familiar voice says from behind me. I turn around and see Cameron McDaniel's broad smile and friendly eyes. "Don't tell me you're still hanging out with this one." He nods in Landon's direction.

I smile back. "I hate to disappoint you, but I am indeed."

He shakes his head in an exaggerated gesture of mournfulness. "More's the pity," he intones.

"Shut up and stop badmouthing me," Landon says good-naturedly. They grin at each other and do the quick bro-hug thing before Landon turns to the person beside Cameron, a slightly built dark-haired woman whose tummy has a slight roundness that hints at early pregnancy.

"Hey Jules," he says, kissing her on both cheeks. "How are you?"

"Knocked up." She sighs and turns to me. "I'm Jules McDaniel, Cameron's wife."

"Rachel Foster. I'm here with Landon."

"Okay." She takes my hand and turns to her husband and Landon. "Where's our table, or are you two planning to keep a pregnant woman standing all night?"

It's almost comic the way her words galvanize them into action. They start off to find the table, engaging the help of an usher, who checks his chart and leads us to a table close to the raised podium, where a slideshow of dancers is showing on a huge screen.

The table is empty except for us. While Cameron is busy pulling out a seat for Jules, two additions show up to join us.

"I'm glad you could make it," the distinguished older man with short silver hair and sparkling eyes says to Landon before his eyes skip to me. "Please introduce me to your lovely companion."

Landon introduces us. The man is Nelson Bledsoe, a self-made cosmetics billionaire who made his fortune developing and selling a line of men's skin and hair care products. He's also a sponsor of the ballet company. While Landon speaks, the man's companion, a beautiful dark-haired girl with olive skin, sloe eyes, and a striking red mermaid gown, never takes her eyes off him.

While I'm still wondering if she's his trophy girlfriend, Nelson turns to Landon. "I'm sure you don't remember my daughter Davina. You only met her once."

"At my father's funeral ten years ago," Landon says, looking at her. "You've changed."

She smiles. "So have you."

Something about the exchange puts me on edge. Ten years ago, Landon was nineteen, and since the girl looks at least a few years younger than me, that puts her at about twelve or less, so definitely nothing could have happened between them at the time. Even so, there's just something about the way she's looking at him that makes me think maybe she wants a lot more from this reunion than just hello.

"Davina served on the board for the gala this

year," her father says proudly. "She's now a swan in her own right."

"In San Francisco at least," Davina says in a tone that makes me think she's more interested in conquering the rest of the world.

"Let's sit." Nelson pulls out a chair for his daughter while Landon does the same for me, and I can't help but notice that Davina is on his other side. He says something to her and she smiles, and I feel a thin sliver of jealousy slice its way through my stomach.

This is ridiculous, I tell myself, ignoring the rich sound of Landon's laughter as he discusses something with Nelson. I have absolutely no reason, no right to be jealous. I turn to Jules on my other side. She's asking about my gown while looking longingly at the glasses of champagne being consumed around the table. I answer her questions, and while Cameron joins the conversation Landon is having with Nelson, Jules tells me about her work in restaurant management, through which she met her husband.

I hear Landon laugh again, and I turn to look at him, admiring the raw beauty in his profile. At that moment, he looks toward me and catches me staring. His piercing blue eyes hold mine, and he reaches for my hand under the table, squeezing it gently. In that moment, it's just the two of us; nobody else exists, nobody else matters.

I turn away from his gaze, feeling confused and emotional.

"So Rachel," Nelson says from across the table with a smile in my direction. "How would you compare the new San Francisco version to Swanson Court in New York?"

"I haven't visited the New York hotel extensively, but from what I've seen, I'd say San Francisco tends more toward modern luxury, while New York is time-less elegance."

"Well put." Nelson nods.

"Modern luxury is the exact concept we had in mind for the refurbishment," Landon adds. "It's very gratifying that Rachel thinks we succeeded."

I meet his eyes, and he's looking at me, a small smile playing on his lips. "Your team did an excellent job bringing out the concept in their design."

"Landon lives at the Swanson Court," Davina says pointedly, her eyes on me. "If you haven't spent a lot of time there, then you two are not very close."

Oh, we're close, I want to tell her, just to wipe the smirk from her face, but I resist the urge. "We're as close as we need to be—I'm only writing a feature on his hotel."

"Hmm." She smiles. "Of course."

"Landon here has a knack for building hotels people can't resist," Nelson tells me. "His father would be so proud of him. Preston had all these dreams for expanding the Swanson Court hotels, and Landon is bringing them to life."

My interest is piqued. "You knew Landon's father?"

"Yes, I did," he says. "Preston and Alicia were close friends of mine, and they were spectacular, I tell you. Alicia was the pride of the New York City Ballet, and Preston, well he was Preston. I remember when Alicia danced Odette in Swan Lake. It was phenomenal. I believe Gilt Style did a feature on her, called her the 'Swan of New York'."

Landon is still holding my hand, and I feel his fingers stiffen. Then he releases my hand and places his on the table, turning his gaze toward the exhibition of pictures on the large screen. His face is suddenly blank, his expression inscrutable, and I remember the nightmare he had last night. All Nelson's talk about his parents can only be awakening the painful memories from the day he lost his mother.

Feeling sad for him, I manage to change the subject, steering Nelson to conversations about his company. Food is served by solicitous waiters while the sponsors and chairs give their speeches. Later, we all move to the opera house across the street where the opening night performances will take place.

From the moment the curtain rises the first time to the end of the last performance, the audience is transfixed. I enjoy the performances, thinking how Laurie would have loved to see them. I'm also worried about Landon, seeing how he might be reminded of his mother.

After the last performances, we go back across the street for the after party. Landon leads me to the dance floor, his hand at my waist molding my body to his as he moves in time to the slow ballad a popular singer is belting out from the stage.

I rest my head on his chest, breathing in the seductive scent of his cologne, the expertise with which he moves his body making me think of how well he uses it to give pleasure.

"Enjoying yourself?" He whispers the question into my ear.

I look up at him. "I am."

He nods and continues to lead me in the dance.

"Are you enjoying yourself?" I ask, still looking at his face.

His smile is sensual. "I have a lot to look forward to."

The words make me shiver in anticipation. I know exactly what he's talking about, and I feel the same way.

I take a breath, knowing I should change the subject before the lust that's suddenly growing in my body takes over me completely.

"When Nelson was talking about your parents

earlier..." I start, almost faltering when a frown creases his brow, but I soldier on. "I just...I read about you on the internet, so obviously, I found some news stories. I noticed that you were upset. I don't know how it feels to lose someone, but I'm sorry."

He sighs. "I wasn't upset. I would just rather not think about it."

I nod. "I can imagine."

He shakes his head. "You can't. Not really." He's looking straight ahead. "They were all in love with her, you know, every single man in their circle—including Nelson Bledsoe—but she was crazy about my father. The rumors made her crazy. No matter how often he told her that they were lies, if he wasn't right in front of her, she drove herself to jealousy imagining that he was with someone else."

I'd read the tabloid rumors about Preston Court's affairs. It would have been so easy for someone to believe them, especially someone who loved him.

"The day we had the accident, some busy body called her about yet another rumor. My father had recently decided to expand the hotels. He was trying to acquire property in L.A. She didn't wait to hear his side. She took off her ring and left a note then bundled us in the car with all our favorite books and toys, so I knew wherever we were going, we wouldn't be back for a long time." He takes a deep breath. "We never found out where she meant to take us. Car crashed. She died. End of story."

I stare at him, unable to process how painful it must have been. "Landon..."

"Aidan didn't utter a word for the next five years," he continues without emotion. "My father was never the same. People like to say he became a recluse, but the truth is, he abandoned me and Aidan in the hotel under the care of the staff and locked himself up in the house in Sand's Point, trying to drink himself to death. One winter, he left the house in the middle of the night and went out into the water. By the time they found him in the morning, it was too late. He died of hypothermia, at forty-nine, a few feet away from a warm house."

"I'm so sorry," I tell him, feeling the inadequacy of the words even as I say them. For one person to have so much pain, so many wounds...I can't even begin to comprehend. An overwhelming instinct to comfort him takes over me, and I tighten my arms around him, holding him close as we dance. He doesn't pull away, so I lay my head on his shoulder, feeling the reassuring thump of his heartbeat, so close to me.

"I don't know why I told you all that," I hear him say. "You shouldn't think too much about it. It's all ancient history."

I look up at him. "But you dream about it."

He stiffens. "What?"

I take a breath, wondering how he'll take the knowledge that I witnessed his pain. "Last night, you were dreaming, and you said a few things. I didn't want to wake you, because I was afraid you wouldn't go back to sleep." I pause. "It's why you hardly sleep isn't it? Because you still dream about it."

He doesn't answer, but he moves back a little, putting some distance between us.

"Have you talked to anyone about it?" I ask, unwilling to leave the issue.

He considers me for a few moments. "Let it go," he says finally.

I frown. "I'm just trying to help."

"I don't need your help," he says quietly, "and just to be clear, it's really none of your business."

My body stiffens at the words that firmly and resolutely put me in my place. It's not my business because, regardless of all the time we've spent together, I'm still just a girl he's sleeping with.

I swallow, unwilling to acknowledge the tightness in my stomach, the shard of pain suddenly lodged in my chest. I force a smile to my lips. "You're right, it isn't."

After that, we dance in silence until Nelson cuts in, leaving Landon free to give Jules McDaniel a few twirls on the floor.

I dance with Cameron, and then another man, and yet another, determined to enjoy myself. The singer leaves the stage and a DJ takes over. The tempo of the music picks up and I dance with a white-haired man who twirls me round and round with much too much energy for someone his age.

I can feel Landon's eyes on me most of the time, but I ignore him. Even when I see the swans converge on him, the beautiful socialites who had chaired the gala, I force myself to look away. I can't pretend, even to myself, that his words didn't hurt me. Why do I care so much? So what if he didn't want to open up to me? It shouldn't matter, and it wouldn't if I had just kept my feelings out of our arrangement.

When I get tired, I leave the ballroom to find the ladies room. Facing the large mirror over the sinks, I do the best I can to touch up my makeup before returning to the hall. Almost immediately, I see Landon at one end of the room with Davina Bledsoe, who is obviously flirting with him.

I don't care. After tonight, he's free to pursue her to the ends of the earth if that's what he wants. In fact, I decide, he can start right now if he likes. There's nothing preventing me from leaving this place. I turn toward the entrance and walk only two steps before someone blocks my way.

It's the sneering man from earlier. "We didn't get introduced before," he says, leaning toward me. "I'm Evans Sinclair."

I recoil from the heavy smell of alcohol on his breath. "I know."

"Well then, you have me at a disadvantage. What's your name?"

I hesitate. "Rachel Foster."

"So, Rachel Foster. Why don't we have a little dance, you and I?"

"I'm sorry." I manage a polite smile. "I'm tired."

"Come on," he cajoles. "If you can put it out for Landon then you can do the same for me."

I look him up and down, annoyance at his rudeness making me want to say something nasty to him, but I control myself. "Go find someone else to insult," I say dismissively. "You're only making me bored."

For a moment, he looks surprised. Then he looks across the room to where Landon is still talking with Davina.

He smirks. "He's abandoned you already, hasn't he? And you're fucking him. Bastard. A few months ago, that was my sister. He's been fucking her for years, told her he loved her. Then the moment he got her to convince the board of my hotel to make me sell it to him, he dropped her like the hot smelly potato she is. The bitch."

He has a hateful expression on his face as he speaks, his anger coming off him in waves. I'm suddenly afraid he might hurt me, just to spite Landon. I want to tell him it wouldn't be worth it, because Landon obviously does not give a damn about me.

"I don't know why you're telling me this," I say in a measured tone. "It's none of my business."

"You're a coward as well as a whore, aren't you? You can't even face the truth about the man you're fucking."

"I don't know who you think you are, but don't ever insult me again." I push past him, dodging the hand he holds out to restrain me. *What a douchebag!*

I stalk to the entrance. The photographers are gone, and without the crush of people and cars from earlier, it feels cold and windy. I'm about to retrieve my phone from my purse and try to find a way to get a cab when Landon appears beside me.

"Where're you going?"

"What do you care?" I snap without looking at him.

There's a short pause. "What's that supposed to mean?"

"You should go back in there. I'm sure Davina is waiting, and you seemed to enjoy flirting with her. I don't mind. I just don't want to sit there and endure being harassed by someone who hates your guts."

IIis jaw tightens. "What did Sinclair say to you?"

"Who cares? I've already forgotten." I look up at

his eyes. "Like everything else about you, it's really none of my business."

His face turns to granite. "Fine," he says. "You want to leave, let's go." He brings out his phone to call the chauffeur, and the limo arrives almost immediately. I get in, staying on my side of the car and looking determinedly out of the window. *Tomorrow, I'll be back home,* I keep telling myself, and then I can put him—all this—behind me. I'll never have to see him again.

The thought of never seeing him again hurts so much, my eyes start to ache with unshed tears.

At the Rosemont, I leave him in the car and hurry through the lobby, getting to the elevator before he catches up with me. When he joins me, I move as far away from him as I can, keeping my eyes on the display panel. I can feel his eyes on me, but I ignore him.

As soon as the elevator doors open to the suite, I start to walk toward my room.

"Rachel." His voice makes me stop in my tracks.

Slowly, I turn to face him. "What?"

He sighs. "Look, whatever Sinclair said to you... I'm sorry. I'm the one he hates, not you, and he really doesn't matter."

"Yeah...and neither do I, or this...whatever it is we're doing. It doesn't matter, because by tomorrow, we'll be back home and it'll be over." I sigh. "Which is for the best anyway."

He is silent for a long moment. "If you're so eager for it to end," he says finally, his voice cold, "we don't have to wait 'til tomorrow."

"Is that what you want?" I demand. "Is that why you told me so bluntly how your nightmares are none of my business and then spent the rest of the night flirting with every single socialite in San Francisco?"

"First of all, yes, I believe my nightmares are my problem. I've dealt with them for twenty years, and to answer your question, I have spoken with people—therapists, doctors, you name it—and they haven't helped at all. I didn't ask for your pity, Rachel, and I don't need it."

I asked because I care. I really care, and to hear him dismiss it as pity is hurtful.

He's not done. "And I wasn't 'flirting' with anyone, so there's no reason for you to be jealous."

"There's no reason for me to be jealous," I retort, angry at myself because he was right—I was jealous. "Why would I be? You're just some guy I'm having sex with, for now."

His jaw tightens and I falter. The words are so far off from what I really feel that I almost take them back, but my resentment wins and I don't.

"Thanks for clearing that up," he says quietly.

I fold my arms, stubbornly meeting the anger in his eyes. "It should never have been in doubt."

"Of course not." His movements are jerky as he starts to loosen his tie. "After all, only a few days ago, you were entertaining your ex-boyfriend. Were you ironing out your issues? Deciding you'd made a mistake agreeing to come here with me? Arranging how to get back together once this pesky little situation with me was out of the way?"

"Maybe we were," I spit at him.

His face hardens. "Then you must be a glutton for punishment," he says scornfully. "Why don't you go to him now? Pack your bags, the plane will take you to join him wherever he is. You might have to compete with another woman for his attention, but it wouldn't be the first time, would it?"

The things he's saying, the disdain in his voice... I swallow my hurt. "Fuck you, Landon." Turning on my heel, I start to leave, but he stops me with a hand at my waist, pulling me against his body.

"I have and I will," he says through gritted teeth. "You're not going anywhere, Rachel. You're going to stay here and I'm going to make you come, over and over, with my hands and my mouth, and then I'll fuck you properly just to remind you that when you're with me, there's no room for him."

With his proximity and his words, my body has already turned to liquid desire, but I'd rather die than give in to him. "Why are you so concerned about him?" I ask heatedly. "Why do you care so much?"

"Why?" He threads his fingers in my hair and lifts my face to his. With his other hand, he gathers my dress up, his fingers finding their way between my legs. "Because right now, you're mine."

He starts to stroke me through my panties, the sensual gleam in his eyes telling me he's aware of how wet I already am, how much I want him, even now. His fingers move and my hips grind involuntarily. "I'm not yours," I spit at him.

"Aren't you?" He pulls the crotch of my panties aside, his fingers moving over my wet sex. "You're so turned on," he continues before plunging his fingers inside me, making me gasp in shock and pleasure. With his other hand, he unzips my dress, freeing the bodice enough to pull it down along with my strapless bra. My breasts are heaving, the pink tips fully extended. A sound escapes him, the mixture of aggravation and arousal equal to what I'm feeling. "Does he make you feel like this?" Landon continues, his fingers driving me crazy. "Does he make you so hungry to fuck even when you know you should be angry?"

I can't think past his fingers inside me, his hot mouth as he bends to take a nipple between his lips, but I'm not ready to let go of my anger. "Maybe he does," I taunt. "Maybe I'm thinking about him right now."

His hand stiffens, and I feel his fingers press deeply inside me, until I can feel his knuckles pressing against the wet surface of my sex. Involuntarily, my hips roll, rubbing my body against his hand.

"You don't mean that," he cautions.

"Don't I?" I force a breathless laugh. "Maybe you think you're the only one who's allowed to be an ass."

He releases me, his fingers pulling out of me as he lets my dress fall back to the ground. I sway slightly, unable to balance on my feet, and my hand reaches out to steady myself on the back of the sofa. My body is pulsing, inches away from coming, my exposed breasts aching with each heavy breath I take.

His face is tight with control. I can see the hard ridge of his erection in his pants, but he makes no move toward me. He's really going to leave me like this.

Furiously, I reach behind me and pull down the zipper of my dress all the way, tearing it off and bundling it a huge ball before I throw it at Landon's face. "Fuck you." I hurl the words at him.

He advances toward me, his movement lightning quick. One moment he's standing in front of me, the next I'm bent over the back of the sofa. "I already said I was going to." His whisper is rough against my ear.

I hear his buckle and the ripping of fabric as he tears off my panties. The next moment he's probing my wet sex with his cock, giving me no warning before he plunges deep inside.

There's no gentleness in what he's doing, and it's exactly what I need. He fucks me hard, pulling my arms up and pinning my wrists together. With each thrust, my nipples rub roughly on the leather of the sofa. I feel helpless, boneless, as if nothing matters but his cock inside me, stretching me, stroking me, setting me on hot, sweet fire.

He bends over me, reaching for my hair and turning my head to the side.

"Look at me," he commands.

I do as he says, crying out with each hard thrust. His face is drawn into an expression of stark arousal. "I want you to be sure who's fucking you right now," he says, his voice rough as he pumps hard into me.

My eyes glaze and I let out a long moan. "Don't stop," I beg.

He releases my hair and squeezes one of my breasts. "You like it, don't you?"

My hips are shaking. "I love it," I moan, close to coming.

"Fuck! Rachel," he groans loudly, growing harder inside me. "Fuck, fuck, fuck!"

The helpless arousal in his voice sends me over the edge. I cry out, my legs giving way as I come. He continues to pound into me, his hand tightening on my breast and a deep growl tearing from his lips as he explodes inside me.

He buries his face in my hair. "Rachel." He says my name as if it's a prayer. "God, Rachel, you have no idea how you make me feel...no idea how crazy you make me."

My brain is foggy, unable to focus, but his words penetrate my clouded mind. *How I make him feel?*

He pulls me up, gathering me into his arms. "I'm sorry," he whispers. "I lost my head for a moment, but thinking about you with him, remembering you two having that cozy moment at the lounge the day I returned from New York...it makes me feel..." He searches for the right word.

I remember what I felt earlier, when he was talking with Davina Bledsoe, and I turn my face to look up at him. "Jealous? Possessive?"

He chuckles. "Crazy...enraged?"

I sigh, confusion and sadness taking over me. He hurt me by dismissing me when I asked about his dreams, and he hurt me again by throwing Jack in my face. I hurt him, too, by taunting him with Jack—but we shouldn't have been able to hurt each other. The whole idea of our arrangement had been the sex.

I take a shuddering breath. "Landon," I start softly, "you weren't...we weren't supposed to feel anything at all."

"No," he agrees quietly. "We weren't."

He's still holding me, and in the warmth of his arms, I start to wonder what kind of chance we have after tonight. I was the one who insisted our arrangement would only last for a week, but he'd agreed, which had to mean it was what he wanted too...or did it?

I pull back from his arms. I'm naked, with only my bra hanging somewhere around my middle. He unhooks it, dropping it to the ground. It's so clear in my mind that I don't want this to be the end. I want to tell him I want us to keep seeing each other, but I'm afraid. The last time I opened up to a guy emotionally, he threw my feelings back in my face.

Looking up at Landon, I know that if he ever rejects me, I won't be able to bear it.

I link my arms around his neck. If this is going to be our final night together, I want to make the most of it. Pulling his face toward mine, I start to kiss him. His hands tighten on my back, his fingers flexing as he pulls me flush against him.

He lifts me off my feet, still kissing me as he carries me into my room, where he makes short work of his remaining clothes.

"I'm addicted to your body," he says almost reverently, tracing his fingers over my arms. "I can't get enough of you."

I sigh and pull his face down so I can kiss him

again. My whole body is trembling, not just from arousal, but because I feel so emotional, on the verge of tears. I feel as if I'm breaking, and I just want him to touch me, to make me forget that the thought of losing him is driving me crazy.

He lays me on the bed, his mouth tracing a path from my lips to my breasts. He takes a nipple in his mouth, sucking deeply while simultaneously slipping a finger between my legs, spreading my wet lips, and sliding a finger over my clit. Of their own accord, my legs spread wider, opening up to him, and I hear him moan against my breast.

He looks up. "I love how ready you always are, how wet." His voice is a seductive whisper as he continues to play with my clit. His eyes are looking deep into mine, inviting me to drown in their depths as his fingers work between my legs, driving me to another round of sweet, helpless pleasure.

"Yes," I moan, moving my hips. He lowers his head back to my breasts, moving his mouth from one swollen nipple to the other, grazing the aching skin with his teeth.

He plunges his fingers inside me then pulls them out slowly. my body clenches around them, aching for more. I feel his erection against my leg and almost come just from the thought of him inside me again.

Removing his fingers from between my legs, he moves lower on the bed, stroking the insides of my thighs lightly before wrapping his hands around them and holding them apart while he bends his head to stroke me with his tongue.

I almost explode from pleasure. His tongue moves in sure flicks, licking my clit then sucking deeply. Heat spreads like flames through my body, incoherent pleas escaping my lips as I beg him never to stop. When his fingers join his tongue, I feel as if I'm hovering on the point of madness. My fingers grip the sheets. My hips buck uncontrollably against his mouth, a tight scream escaping me as I lose myself in a bone-shaking climax.

He lifts his head, watching my face as I recover. I rise from the bed, getting on my knees as I push him to lie on his back. His cock is erect, facing upward like a thick, hard mast. Bracing my hands on his chest, I straddle him, slowly lowering my body until he's completely sheathed inside me.

His hips grind up into me, a small groan escaping his lips. "You feel so good," he says.

His hand grips my hip as I move up then slide back down. His lips open. "Fuck," he breathes.

My body clenches around him as I ride him again. Sweat beads on my skin, and his low grunts blend with my soft moans. He grips my waist, holding me still as he braces his back on the bed, pounding his hips up at me. He's fucking me so hard, so fast, making me a helpless mass of warm, hot pleasure. My body starts to pulse uncontrollably, and then I'm exploding, spiraling into a sea of nothing but pure ecstasy.

His hands tighten around my waist, his hips pumping as he thrusts deep into me with an explosive groan. The movement lifts my knees off the bed, and I feel the warmth as he spurts his pleasure inside me. I fall onto his chest and his arms cover me, holding me to him. I'm almost drifting to sleep when he moves, laying me on my side and pulling the covers over me. Then he picks up his clothes from the floor, putting on his pants before he leaves the room, and me.

CHAPTER 16

WE leave for New York the next day after spending the morning at the Gold Dust, which has made so much progress in one week that to my eyes, it's ready for the grand opening. I can only assume Landon's presence had something to do with the speedy progress, as the opening night is still weeks away.

Landon hardly says a word to me, even on the flight back. Apart from a few polite words, we might as well be strangers again.

What did I expect after last night? We made love then he left, and it was obviously his way of saying goodbye, of telling me that whatever we had, it ended last night.

The truth is, I don't feel like talking either. The less we say to each other, the less I'll be tempted to dwell on the things we both said in the heat of our fight, and afterward. I don't want to hope that maybe, just maybe we have something that can be parlayed into a real relationship. It's safer to stick with the original arrangement—a short time together then a clean break. It's what I asked for. It's what I wanted. Only, now I don't feel as if I'm getting what I want. I feel like I'm losing something I can never replace.

His driver is at the airport to pick us up, the same one who took me to the airport when I was on my way to San Francisco. *God!* How different I'd felt that day, excited about what lay ahead and confident that afterward, I'd easily be able to walk away.

How wrong I'd been.

On the drive to my apartment, the silence continues. The knowledge that getting out of the car will signify the end of what we had fills me with something close to panic. It's unreasonable, and I push it to the back of my mind, concentrating on other thoughts, like how glad I'll be to see Laurie—anything other than him.

At my building, as soon as the car stops, I reach for the door handle. Joe is already retrieving my things from the trunk to take them to my door. I don't want to wait around in hope that Landon will say something to change the direction we're going. The sooner I'm away from him, the sooner I can start to face the fact that whatever it is we had is truly over.

"Rachel."

I pause, my hand still on the door handle as I turn toward him. It's hard to look at his perfect face, the sensational body clad in another beautiful suit, and not feel excruciating pain at the fact that I'll never get to touch him again. My mind floods with all the things I want, making me emotional. I want to him to tell me he wants to see me again. I want to tell him I wasn't thinking right when I demanded that our arrangement would last only as long as the trip. I want him to tell me we have something that's much more than just sex. I want confirmation that I'm not the only one feeling something I didn't plan to feel.

"Yes, Landon?" How I manage to keep everything I'm feeling out of my voice, I have no idea, but I manage to sound like I'm not dying inside at the thought of leaving the car, of leaving him. I even manage a small smile.

His eyes linger on my face. "About this past week..."

I pull in a sharp breath. Here comes the goodbye. This is where he'll tell me it was great and then dismiss me with a few nice words. There's no need— he already said goodbye when he left my room last night.

"It was perfect," I say quickly, interrupting what

ever it was he wanted to say. I don't want to hear the words that'll tell me he's done with me. "Last week was exactly what I needed."

He nods, then turns away from me. "I'm glad you had a good time."

I open the door then pause, and some instinct makes me turn back to him, lean over, and place a light kiss on his cheek. His hand is resting on his knee, and I notice the fingers flex, but he doesn't say anything.

"Goodbye Landon."

"Goodbye Rachel." When he turns back to look at me, the shutters are down, his eyes impersonal and so remote, I could be a stranger.

I leave him and walk into the building, going up to my apartment, where Joe has set my luggage on the floor by the door.

I give him a small smile. "Thank you, Joe. I can manage from here."

He nods and leaves me standing there. I let myself into the apartment, and Laurie flies into the living room as soon as I enter, running across the room to envelope me in a warm hug.

"I missed you!" she cries enthusiastically before pulling back to look at my face. "Are you crying?" she asks with a frown.

"No, of course not." I force a laugh. "I'm not that happy to see you."

She sighs. "It's him, isn't it? What happened?"

My voice is shaking with unshed tears, and suddenly I can't hold them back anymore. "I don't know. It went exactly as I planned. I have no idea why I'm so fucking sad."

"Oh sweetie." Laurie envelopes me in another hug. "Stop crying. Tell you what? Why don't I get your bags inside then I'll make you something hot to drink and you can tell me all about it."

∿

YOU HAVE FEELINGS FOR HIM.

Those were Laurie's words yesterday, after I told her everything.

I do have feelings for Landon. I'm hung up on him, strung out because of him. It wasn't part of the plan, but somewhere along the way, the strong physical attraction I felt toward him turned to something else, something that makes me think of little things about him and smile, even as the thought that I'll probably never see him again leaves me close to tears.

I meet with Mark Willis in the morning, along with a few other people from the features team and the photography and copy people. We do a final walk-through of the article, and then afterward I start the research for my next assignment, trying my best not to think about Landon.

Not that it helps. Every few moments, he creeps into my thoughts, leaving me wondering what he's doing now, and if just maybe, he's thinking about me too.

Probably not. More likely he's busy acquiring another hotel and forgetting he ever met me.

A few hours into the day, I use the office messenger service to send a package to Landon's office at the Swanson Court Tower. It's the jewelry he gave me in San Francisco. I forgot to give them back to him before we left, and the staff had packed them with my luggage. I send them back with regret, not because of their monetary value, but because he gave them to me.

I spend the rest of the morning working. At lunchtime, Chelsea and Sonali invite me to join them so I can give them the dish about Landon Court. The office grapevine has been busy, especially since the pictures from the charity gala appeared online. They both plead and cajole, but I politely refuse, giving an excuse about having to finish up some work.

When my desk phone rings a few minutes after they leave, I answer it, and it's the ground floor reception calling to tell me I have a package being sent up to my office. Almost as soon as I put down the phone, the delivery guy arrives.

The package he gives me contains the box I just sent to Landon's office. It also includes a note on

Swanson Court stationery, written in Landon's firm slanted handwriting.

Keep them.

Just that. I stare at the words, disappointment flooding me. What was I expecting? Some heartfelt communication to show me I still meant something to him?

Well, I'm not going to keep a gift from a guy who can't be bothered to expend more than two words on me.

My phone rings just as I'm about to call the office messenger service again. I don't care that I might have to come up with an explanation as to why I'm using office facilities for personal stuff. I just want to let Landon know I don't need his diamonds, and I won't take orders from him.

Keep them indeed.

Too caught up in my thoughts, I slide my phone to answer without looking at the screen.

"Hello," I say impatiently.

"Don't even think of returning them. I'll just send them back, and I can do this all year."

Landon.

My heart almost stops. Somehow, I had convinced myself I would never hear his voice again, that the delicious blend of perfect timbre and raspy smooth-ness was lost to me forever. I luxuriate in the sound, wanting to store it somewhere so I can listen to it whenever I want.

"Are you there?"

I recover myself enough to realize I have to say something. "Landon, I can't keep them. We agreed that they were a loan."

"And now I want you to have them."

Why? I almost ask him. *Do you need to give me something you can consider as payment for the time we spent together? So you don't feel like you owe me anything? Well, you owe me nothing. I'm a big girl, and I knew what I was getting into.*

Except I didn't.

I close my eyes, my throat tight. "It's not enough that you want me to keep them. Maybe you always get what you want, but this time—"

"Rachel, stop. I don't carry expensive jewelry around in case I'll need to give gifts to random women. I bought them for *you*, because I thought they would look great on *you*."

I'm silent.

"And contrary to what I said to you a long time ago"—he exhales audibly—"I don't always get what I want."

I swallow, suddenly confused. What does he mean? My eyes go to the package on my desk. "I'm not going to keep them Landon."

"Okay." There's a short pause on his side. "Why

don't we talk about it then, face to face?"

The instinct to say no is defeated by my desire to see him, which is so strong that every other thought is instantly pushed out of my head. I have to pause and try to get control of my brain. "I don't think…"

"Let's have lunch," he suggests. "I'll come to you. Is that okay?"

I want to see him—so badly. "It's fine. I'm free at one."

"Perfect."

In the few minutes before one, I hover nervously by my phone, smoothing my hair and checking my clothes. By the time he calls to let me know he's close to my building, I'm a mess of nervousness, eagerness, and desire.

Downstairs, he's waiting on the curb, gold waves windblown, his sensational body clad in another perfect suit. He's leaning on the gleaming black car like a ridiculously gorgeous model in a photoshoot.

"Oh fuck," I mumble at the sight of him, a bolt of awareness moving through me. Why does he have to look so good? How am I supposed to stop thinking about him when he insists on reminding me just how delicious he is?

He unfolds himself from the car and faces me, spearing me with his intense blue gaze. Somehow, I manage to walk up to him without swooning. "Hey."

"Hey Rachel." His eyes are roaming my face,

stormy and intense. The look goes straight to my core, where it starts a slow heat. He opens the door for me then walks around the car to join me, settling into the seat beside me while Joe pulls away from the curb.

I resist the urge to make small talk. I'm feeling too much to pretend I care about things like the weather or traffic. He doesn't seem to want to talk either. His eyes are in front, his fingers tapping on the armrest between us. When I steal a glance at him, his face looks as if he's deep in thought.

"How's your day been?" he asks when the silence has stretched to breaking point.

"Okay, just...work."

He nods. Then he turns to look at me, and his eyes are blazing with hunger that matches what I'm feeling. Trapped in that gaze, I can't move. I fully expect him to do something, touch me, kiss me, and I know I won't resist—but then Joe stops at the entrance of a glass-fronted building and we have to leave the car.

Lunch is at a swanky restaurant close to the top floor of the building. There's an excellent view of the city from where we're sitting in a secluded part of the restaurant, shielded from other lunchers by a creative arrangement of furniture and indoor plants.

A waiter takes our order and while we wait, I try to keep my eyes on the table, the view, anything but

Landon. I feel drawn to him, like a moth to a flame, like he's a magnet and I'm a helpless piece of metal.

When I finally get the courage to look at him, his eyes are on me.

I breathe. "You said you wanted to talk."

He nods. "I did."

He doesn't offer more, so I start. "There was no need for us to come here because of your jewelry."

"Your jewelry," he replies. "I gave them to you, but that's not why we're here. I wanted to see you."

I swallow, silent, as hope fans in my chest.

"I wanted to see you," he says again, his eyes burning into mine.

Something is squeezing at my heart. "Why?" I ask, my voice soft.

"Why?" He runs a hand through his hair and lets out a short laugh, but there's no amusement in the sound. "Because you've gotten under my skin in a way I didn't think was possible."

I stay silent, not trusting myself to speak.

"I want to keep seeing you," he continues. "I haven't been able to stop thinking about you."

My heart is beating a staccato rhythm against my chest. This is what I want. I want to keep seeing him, and I haven't been able to stop thinking about him either, but now I know that for me, it's not just sex. Laurie is right—I have feelings for him. If what he wants is just an extension of our arrangement, will I be able to handle that?

Our food arrives, and we're both silent as the waiter serves us. When we're alone again, Landon leans forward. "When I asked you to take the trip with me to San Francisco, you insisted you only wanted our arrangement to last for a week." His eyes hold mine. "I want to know why."

Because even then, I knew there was a chance I would fall in love with him, and I thought if we only spent a short time together, I'd be safe.

But I still fell in love with him. The realization tears through me like a slice of physical pain. *I'm in love with him.* I want him, every part of him, everything about him, more than I've ever wanted anyone or anything.

He's still waiting for me to say something.

"I was in a bad place," I tell him, remembering Jack and the feelings of heartbreak I thought were real at the time. "I thought a short physical relationship would help to get me back on track."

"You thought." His eyes are questioning.

I shake my head. How do I tell him that instead of forgetting Jack as I'd planned, I'd realized my feelings for Jack had been nothing, totally inconsequential compared to the way I feel now, as if not only my heart but my whole being is at stake.

"What are you asking, Landon?"

"I want to know if..." He stops and mutters something under his breath. "What I'm saying is, I want you. I have from the moment I saw you, and I still do. I can't let you go."

I stare at him, my emotions running high. I have to make a decision. I should tell him I want more than sex, that I want him to...

To what? Return my feelings? Love me back?

It's just been a week.

I can't let you go.

And I don't want him to. That's all that matters, at least for now.

"You don't have to let me go," I respond, my voice barely audible. "I don't want you to."

I hear him breathe, the sound threaded with something like relief. Then he leans back on his seat. "The food is getting cold," he says. "We should eat."

Food is the last thing on my mind. There's a ball of excitement and relief building in my stomach, and I can tell he feels the same way. I smile at him, he smiles back, and I feel as if the weight of the past few days has been lifted from me. There are still so many things to consider—like what exactly our relationship is now—but I push the questions out of my mind.

We talk about different things while we eat—the article, his work, how happy I was to see Laurie again.

"What are you doing tonight?" he asks when we're almost done with the food.

I shrug. "Nothing. Why?"

"Aidan, my brother, has been working on a play. It's still in the preview stage, but tonight is a press night, and I'm going to lend my support." His lips quirk. "Will you come?"

It's probably the play Sonali was talking about when we went out to lunch what seems like a lifetime ago. "I'd love to."

"Good." His eyes linger on my lips, and then he lets out a ragged breath. "Now I'm going to take you back to your office, because if I don't, I'm going to have to find a place to fuck you."

I'm shocked at the raw statement, but also, more than anything, I want him to do exactly that. I take a deep breath. "I can get away with another hour or so."

He stares at my face for a split second then gets up, taking my elbow as I rise from my seat. He leads me out of the restaurant, his urgency obvious even from the heat of his fingers on my skin, and I feel exactly the same way.

"Where are we going?" I ask as we wait for the elevator.

"The nearest place with a bed."

The elevator doors open and he pulls me inside, not waiting for the doors to close before he covers my mouth with his. His lips are warm and hungry, and his tongue delves into my mouth, making me moan and arch against him.

"My place is closer than your hotel and your office," I whisper to him when he releases my lips. I'm panting, my words breathy. His hands are on my waist, holding my body flush against his, and I can feel his arousal, hard and insistent against my thighs.

"Your place it is." He reaches for my lips again and just as he claims them, the bell dings and the elevator stops.

He pulls away with a muttered oath just as the doors slide open. Immediately, he takes my hand and resumes his brisk stride toward the entrance. He's already calling Joe, who pulls up to the curb just as we exit the building. Landon orders him to drive to my apartment in a curt voice then leans back on the seat, his body tense as his fingers tap an impatient rhythm on his thigh.

The journey to my apartment is mercilessly long. Joe does his best to weave through the traffic, but by the time we get to my building, I'm desperate with need. We hurry up the stairs, and once inside, Landon doesn't wait to get to my room before he pulls me to him and starts to kiss me again.

His hands are everywhere as I lead him to my room, our tongues entwined. He pulls my top over my head and unclasps my bra, tossing them both to the floor. Inside my room, I start to work on his trousers while he loosens his tie and tosses his jacket on my chair. I undo his belt and pull down his briefs to free his erection. He is so hard, fully erect, and warm against my fingers. Hungrily, I get on my knees to take him in my mouth, sucking on the head as I stroke the length from top to root.

His hips jerk as I flick my tongue over him. "Fuck, Rachel. I need to be inside you right now."

I look up at him, meeting his eyes while still sucking on him. He groans and throws his head back, my name escaping his lips like a prayer.

He stills the hand I'm stroking him with and pulls out of my mouth, kicking off his trousers and briefs before pulling me up and laying me gently on the bed. He lifts my skirt and pulls off my panties, his movements almost frantic in their urgency. Covering my body with his, he moves my legs apart as he positions himself between them.

He lowers his head again, sucking on my lower lip as he slides inside me in one hot surge of his hips. I moan loudly, and he releases my lips. His eyes are darker than I've ever seen them, full of his desire for me. He moves his hips backward then slams into me again. I cry out, wrapping my legs around his waist and urging him deeper.

He takes my lips again, his tongue plunging into my mouth. My nipples are grazing against his chest, aching and tender, and between my legs, each delicious thrust is bringing me closer and closer to my climax.

My body clenches around him, eager to feel every inch of him. He answers with a groan, rotating his hips as he starts to pump faster, the wide head of his cock hitting the tight mass of nerves within me as he strokes the explosion of pleasure building inside. Warm, pulsing sweetness builds between my legs and starts to spread through my limbs. My body stiffens, tightening around him, and a deep groan escapes his lips, the sound sending me over the edge. I shatter completely, my whole body shaking uncontrollably.

Still inside me, he gathers me in his arms and pulls me up, getting to his knees at the same time. My legs are still around his waist, so he's carrying me. I brace my arms around his neck and he takes hold of my waist, thrusting his hips even as he moves me up and down his rock-hard cock.

I feel as if I'm dying of pleasure. Another climax builds, taking over my body. His lips claim mine just as I lose my mind, coming apart in a burst of pure exquisite sensation and luxuriating in the unrestrained sound of his own pleasure as he pumps into me one last time, spilling his warmth inside me.

CHAPTER 17

"SO are you guys like dating now?" Laurie asks.

"Hmmm." I don't hear her at first. I'm sitting on one of the smaller chairs in the living room putting on my shoes, my mind on Landon and everything that happened earlier in the day.

After giving me two incredible orgasms, he cleaned me up and dressed me, smoothing my clothes and getting me presentable enough to return to the office. It had been tender and sweet, so sweet that I can't think about it without smiling. Of course, he left the jewelry box on my dresser, and I'd only noticed when I finally returned from work.

"Rach...did you even hear me?"

I look up at where Laurie is lying on the couch,

her head on Brett's lap while he feeds her grapes with the decadence of a Roman emperor. "Not really."

"I said, are you guys dating now?"

"I don't know... We like each other, and we want to see where it goes."

"So...dating," Laurie concludes.

"Don't assume," Brett offers, popping a grape into his mouth. "Set the terms. What exactly is he offering? Long-term commitment? Exclusivity? Will there be a ring at the end of the tunnel?"

"What?" Both Laurie and I burst into laughter. "Has anybody ever told you that you have such a way with words?" I ask.

"Once or twice." He grins.

"He's right though," Laurie says. "Find out what the deal is so you're not left hanging in the end."

In the end.

"We're just taking it one day at a time," I say nonchalantly, frowning as Brett feeds Laurie another grape and she licks his fingers. "That's kind of gross. Can't you just maybe wait for me to leave?"

"Nope." Laurie grins. "We want to make you so uncomfortable you have to leave."

I snort and get up to go to my room, where I study my reflection in the full-length mirror and judge the effect of my cream bandage dress and my nude heels. Landon will be here any moment to pick me up for his brother's play, and I want to be ready when he comes.

I'm still looking at myself in the mirror when I hear the buzzer. I was expecting Landon to call when he was downstairs, so the sound of his voice in the living room as he says hello to Laurie and Brett takes me by surprise.

I take a deep breath and go to join them, stopping by my door to drink in the sight of him looking delicious in a dark blazer over a crisp blue shirt.

He raises his head immediately, and his eyes meet mine. "Hey baby."

The endearment makes me warm. "Hey," I reply.

He grins and walks over to me, dropping a very light kiss on my lips. "You ready?"

"Almost." I scoot back into my room to pick up my purse, doing one last check in the mirror before joining them again. Laurie blows me a kiss. "Have fun," she tells me before turning to Landon. "Take good care of her."

He smiles at her before transferring his gaze back to me. His eyes are hot and full of all the sensual promise I've come to expect. "I fully intend to," he says, and then takes my hand and leads me out the door.

~

WE HAVE DINNER BEFORE GOING TO THE THEATER, which is one of the bigger ones on Broadway. I've been to a few plays before, with my parents and also with Laurie, but the press viewing is a different experience. The theater is not packed, and in the front rows, serious-faced critics and bloggers are looking intently at the activities on the stage and typing quick notes into phones and tablets.

We're seated on the gallery, which is almost empty. From that spot there's a good view of the stage, the critics, and Landon's brother Aidan in a darkened corner opposite us, looking down at the stage, his intense expression so like Landon's that it's almost eerie.

I don't know if he's worried, but even I can see he has no reason to be. The play is superb, with beautiful costumes, props, and excellent actors, especially the lead, a dark-haired girl who doesn't look a day over seventeen but commands the stage like a pro.

"Who's she?" I whisper to Landon.

"Elizabeth McKay. It's her first role. Her father produced the play, and Aidan can't stand her, for some reason."

"What reason? She's so talented."

"Which is why Aidan had to grin and swallow whatever he's feeling." Landon smiles when he says his brother's name, and I can see the pride clearly in his eyes.

My eyes find Aidan on the other side of the gallery, and I follow the direction of his gaze. He's looking intently at Elizabeth McKay, his eyes so focused that I start to wonder if there's more to his dislike.

"Maybe he likes her," I whisper, leaning toward Landon. "Sometimes attraction can manifest as dislike."

"Hmm." Landon nuzzles my neck. "Is that why you disliked me so much at first?"

I smile. "Maybe I still do."

"Do you?" I feel his hand on my thigh, inching up toward the hem of my dress. "Or maybe now you like me just a little."

I pull in a breath as his hand disappears under the hem of my dress, moving slowly upward to stop at the juncture of my thighs. "Just a little," I agree.

His voice is a warm whisper so close to my ear. "I guess I have to work on that. Open your legs Rachel."

I obey without thinking, not even pausing to spare a glance at the other people in the darkened theater. Immediately his fingers cup my sex, moving over the silk of my panties in a slow sensuous rhythm, applying only a light pressure as he works my folds, using them to massage my clit.

I sigh and my legs fall farther apart, giving him more space. He slides his fingers into the crotch of my panties, stroking me from my wet inner lips to my swollen clit. I moan softly, my hips lifting from the seat. If he continues, I'm going to come, right here, in a public theater.

"You're so wet," he whispers, "so ready. I want to fuck you right here, Rachel, and it's killing me that I can't."

"It's killing me too," I reply, desperation making me rub myself against his fingers, wanting to feel all of him. He slips two fingers inside me, stroking them in and out while he leans back on his seat and concentrates his gaze on the stage.

He looks as if he has all his attention on the play, but his fingers...his fingers are driving me crazy. He finds a sensitive spot inside me and rubs against it, and I grip the arm of my chair, biting back a loud moan as I hover on the edge of coming.

He turns from the stage to look at me, and from the stage lights, I can see the stark arousal on his face, the lust in his dazzling blue eyes. I can't stop myself from spiraling over the edge. I cover my mouth with my hand, biting my lips as ecstasy ripples through me. He doesn't stop until my body stops shaking; only then does he pull his fingers out and pull my dress down over my thighs.

He leans close to me. "Do you like me better now?"

I'm still trying to catch my breath. "You're

growing on me," I manage. "Perhaps you can keep trying."

He chuckles. "I'm certainly up to that."

After the play, we descend from the gallery and go downstairs to the circulation area, where most of the press and critics are standing, some of them discussing the show. Landon stops to talk to a few of them, his demeanor charming and friendly. He keeps me beside him, his arm around my waist in a gesture that feels both protective and possessive, and he introduces me to a few people.

After a while, we're joined by Aidan Court, who looks just like a younger version of Landon except that his hair is dark and his eyes are a lighter shade of blue.

His gaze immediately lands on me and he smiles, his eyes sparkling with a mixture of friendliness and mischief. "You must be Rachel," he says. "I'm Aidan."

He looks almost too young to be directing a play on Broadway, but I don't say so. "It's great to meet you," I reply, "and your play was very enjoyable."

"I hope the critics think so," he says with an easy laugh. "But let's forget about work. What's a nice girl like you doing with my brother?"

"None of your business," Landon tells him, sounding both good-natured and affectionate.

Aidan wiggles his eyebrows at me, making me laugh.

Landon shakes his head. "How're you coping with your ingénue?"

Aidan shudders. "Don't ask."

"I thought she was wonderful," I proffer.

"Spellbinding actually," Aidan corrects me, his eyes clouding for a moment. "But as I said, let's forget about the play. Landon promised to take me out for a drink. I hope you're coming?"

Landon's hand tightens around my waist. "Of course she is," he says, looking into my face for assent.

I nod. "I would love to."

We end up at a bar close to the theater, where we find a private table and order drinks while Aidan regales me with stories about Landon. He's five years younger, and from the way he talks about his brother, it's plain to see that he idolizes him.

Some of the stories are hilarious, and Aidan is a gifted storyteller. I find myself laughing delightedly while Landon mock-threatens his unrepentant brother.

At some point in the evening, Landon has to take a call, leaving me alone at the table with Aidan.

"Now's your chance to dig for dirt," he says with a wink. "Ask me anything—I've been spilling on my brother since I could talk."

I laugh. "Nah, I'm good."

He nods, his voice turning serious. "Landon's my

big brother, and he's saved my life...not just the one time everybody knows about. It's great to see him looking as happy as he does with you."

"You think he looks happy?"

"Are you kidding? I've seen him smile more tonight than I have since our mother died. In fact, I should be thanking you. Last week he was chewing my head off when I abandoned the play and went up north to hide out. He knew where to find me, and he talked me out of the funk I was in. He brought me back here, to the delight of the producer and investors. He was mad, now he's not, and I'm sure I have you to thank for that."

"Last week?"

"Yeah," Aidan says with a shrug. "Occasionally, I go off the deep end, but I'm working on it."

I'm not really listening anymore. When Landon left me in San Francisco, it was to take care of his brother, not work, as I'd imagined. There are so many sides to him, and each side I discover makes me love him more.

"Last call to dig for dirt," Aidan announces, downing his drink. "I'll tell you anything."

"Come to think of it," I start. "I just wondered... the day we met, Landon thought I was a hooker you sent to his suite."

"Ouch." Aidan manages to look shamefaced. "The thing is...it was his birthday, and I was so caught up in the play, I forgot to give him a present. We were having dinner and somehow, we started to have a conversation about the benefits of paid sex versus relationships. I've paid for sex. He hasn't. I offered to prove the benefits by sending him a hooker, but he refused. When you arrived, he must have assumed I'd ignored his wishes, as I have been known to do."

"Oh."

Aidan shrugs. "I hope I cleared that up."

"Cleared what up?"

I look up to see Landon. "Nothing." I smile at him. "We were just talking about the play."

He looks as if he doesn't believe me, but he takes his seat and Aidan resumes his good-natured story-telling.

"Are you ready to go home?" Landon asks me after a while.

"Yes." I turn to Aidan. "It was really great to meet you."

He grins. "Likewise."

After we say goodnight, Landon follows me to the street, where Joe is waiting at the curb. Standing beside the car, he takes my face in his hands and gives me a deep kiss. "I have to stay, Aidan and I have some things to discuss, but Joe will take you home."

I try to keep the disappointment out of my face. I assumed the night would end with us finding

inevitable pleasure in each other's arms. "Okay."
I sigh.

"See you soon," he says, opening the door for me.

"Yeah," I reply. "See you soon."

❧

LAURIE IS STILL AWAKE WHEN I GET HOME. SHE'S
sitting yoga style on the couch while watching a late-
night reality show.

"Where's Brett," I ask.

She shakes her head slowly. "He left. We had a
fight."

Frowning, I move closer to peer at her face, and
just as I thought, her eyes are red-rimmed. "What
happened?"

She sighs. "Some girl. Her name's Emily...she
started working at the gym a couple of weeks ago,
and yesterday she came on to him. The skank."

I collapse on one of the chairs and kick off my
shoes. "How did you find out?"

"Brett told me."

"And you fought with him? That's nuts."

"It's not nuts when I knew she was interested in
him. I told him she might misunderstand his flirta-
tiousness."

I sigh. Laurie has always felt that Brett pays too

much unnecessary attention to members of the opposite sex. "You mean friendliness."

She rolls her eyes. "Come on. You and I both know how easy it is for some women to mistake his friendliness for flirtation. I don't know why he can't be a little more reserved."

"I'm sorry Laurie," I say with a shrug. "But if some bimbo tried to get in his pants, so what? He didn't let her."

"I know." She gives me a small smile. "I didn't plan to get angry. I just...couldn't help myself after a while. I said some things Rach." She puts her head in her hands. "God, I hate it when we fight."

"I know." I move to join her on the couch and put an arm around her shoulders. "It never lasts though."

"Thank the stars for that." She frowns. "So how did your date go?"

"Okay."

"Come on." Laurie cranes her neck to look at me. "You've got to give me more than that."

"I met his brother," I say with a smile.

"The hot one I saw online? Cool." She wiggles her eyebrows. "So, you've met the family. This is definitely dating."

"It's not like he introduced me as the love of his life."

Laurie studies my face. "Is that what you want?"

I sigh. "I don't want to think about what I want. If I do, I won't be able to enjoy what we have."

"How long will you be able to enjoy it? You're in love with him. Soon you won't be able to take it if you don't know for sure that he feels the same way."

I'm silent. Of course, Laurie knows how I feel. She knows me too well not to have picked up on it.

"Do you know how he feels?" she asks gently.

"He says he wants me, and can't stop thinking about me." I sigh. "When we're together it feels like nothing else matters. I've never felt something so intense."

She nods. "He might feel the same way, you know. I saw the way he looked at you earlier. It seemed like way more than lust and chemistry to me."

Yes, but is it love? Anything else is temporary. Anything else means that one day, he'll be through with me, and then I'll have to deal with his rejection.

I change the subject, steering Laurie into telling me more about her fight with Brett. Afterward, I say goodnight and go to my room, where, as soon as I'm alone, my mind goes back to Landon.

He wants me—I don't doubt that—but how does he feel about me? How long will I be able to love him without knowing if there's any chance he'll ever feel the same?

I wash the makeup off my face and change into a tank top and shorts, but when I get into bed, I'm still unable to fall asleep. In the distance, a car alarm goes off, and I start to wonder what Landon is doing. He would have finished talking with Aidan long ago. Is he back at his apartment now? Is he alone? An unbidden, unwanted thought of him with another woman flashes across my mind. It's far-fetched, improbable, but it still makes me feel desperate.

My phone starts to ring, rescuing me from my thoughts. I grab it from my nightstand and see Landon's name on the screen. The surge of relief weakens me.

"Hey," I say softly.

"Did I wake you?"

"No," I reply. "I wasn't asleep."

"Oh?" He sounds surprised. "What are you doing?"

Thinking about you. "Nothing. I'm just lying in bed."

"Alone?"

I smile. "Very funny."

I hear him breathe. "Were you thinking of me?"

Always. "What if I was?"

"I'd tell you I was thinking about you too. I haven't been able to stop thinking about you all night."

My breath catches. "You should stop," I tell him. "You're in danger of starting to sound romantic."

"Do you have anything against romance?"

"Not really," I whisper. "Do you?"

"I cannot be opposed to anything that would bring you pleasure."

I close my eyes. "My world is officially rocked."

He laughs. "Did you have a good time tonight?"

"Mmhmm," I tell him. "I loved the play, and Aidan is really great."

"I think he may have fallen in love with you. He's usually more reserved with women."

I chuckle. "That's ridiculous."

He laughs too. "It is. I'd have to challenge him to a duel or something."

"You wouldn't," I say, giggling.

"I'd have to." He pauses. "I want to see you."

My heart quickens. "Now?"

"I know it's late, and you should be asleep, but I'm standing outside your building looking up at your window, wondering what the fuck is wrong with me."

"You're here?" I throw off the covers and run to the window. There's his silver Jaguar, parked close to the building entrance on the tree-lined street. The windows are up, so I can't see inside the car except for a small glow that might be the screen of his phone, but as I watch, the door opens and he climbs out.

My breath catches in my throat. Seeing him always has that effect on me. He's wearing the shirt from earlier with the same black pants, but he's discarded the blazer. He looks up at my window, almost as if he can see me from where he's standing. "Can I come up?" he asks.

"Yes."

He cuts the connection, and I watch him lower his phone to his pocket and walk toward the entrance of the building. Hurrying to the living room to buzz him in, I start to wish there was enough time to change into something sexier.

When I open the door, he's already bounding up the last step. He takes the few steps toward me and without a word, gathers me in his arms and presses his lips to mine.

He smells so good, and he feels so warm, so hard and male. His lips tease mine, parting them as he moves inside the apartment with me in his arms and closes the door behind him.

I melt into him, wanting nothing more than to be consumed by him. His tongue caresses mine, his hands at my back holding me close to him, so I can feel his erection pressing against my thigh.

He releases my lips and leans back against the door, his hands still holding me to his body as he smiles down at me.

"Thanks for letting me up," he says. "I'd have felt very much like a fool if I'd had to drive back home."

"I doubt you've ever felt like a fool," I reply, breathing heavily.

"No," he agrees. "But around you, it's hard to know how I feel."

I search his face, desperately wanting proof that his words point to feelings for me on his part that could perhaps equal mine. "I'm glad I have such an effect on you."

"I kept thinking about San Francisco, about falling asleep with you in my arms." He pulls in a deep breath, making his chest expand. "What were you thinking earlier? When you were thinking about me."

"I was wondering what you were doing."

"Only that?" He lowers his head and nuzzles my neck. "You weren't thinking about my lips on your skin, like this?"

A small moan escapes me as his lips draw a line along my chin up to my lips. "Were you thinking about me kissing you, my fingers touching you?" I feel his hand slide up my thigh, stopping at the juncture of my legs. I can already feel the warmth pooling between my thighs as my body prepares to surrender to him.

"Is that what you were thinking?"

He grins. "Always. All the time. Everywhere."

He pulls the crotch of my shorts aside and as he touches me, all my thoughts disappear. My hips grind of their own volition, rubbing my core against his stroking fingers.

He growls in my ear before lowering his head to bite my nipple through the fabric of my tank top. Sighing in pleasure, I put my arms around his neck. He takes that as an invitation to lift me in his arms and carry me into my room, where he lays me gently down on the bed.

I watch as he takes off his shirt, then his trousers and briefs. He comes back to the bed, covering my body with his as he kisses from my lips down to my neckline before reaching down to pull the tank top over my head.

He cups both my breasts in his hands, squeezing gently before he takes a hard nipple in his mouth and sucks it deeply. He rolls his tongue around the swollen nub then releases it, moving his attention and his tongue to the flesh of my breast. When I'm moaning and squirming beneath him, he moves on to the other breast, giving it the same treatment.

Without stopping, he moves his hand back to the juncture of my thighs and pulls my shorts aside. His fingers reach inside, stroking me and spreading the slickness between my thighs before sliding inside me.

I spread my legs for him, pleasure spiraling inside me as I start to move my hips in time with the movement of his fingers. He shifts his attention from my breast, moving lower, over my stomach, to the waistband of my shorts. Then he pulls his fingers out of me and I lift my hips, helping him to get the shorts off me.

As soon as I'm totally naked, his lips find me, kissing and sucking every tender spot. I can hardly bear it. A long frantic moan tears from my throat as his tongue delves deep inside me.

I clutch at his hair, my hips bucking, and he presses my body down on the bed with one arm, holding me still as he continues the sweet assault with his tongue.

Pleasure builds inside me, ready to explode. When I'm sure I can't take it anymore, he surrounds my clit with his lips, sucking deeply, at the same time plunging his fingers inside me again. I scream, my body seizing in an uncontrollable rush of sensation. He continues the movement of his fingers until my body stops shaking. Then he pulls them out and replaces them with his cock.

I almost lose my mind at the pleasure. I'm spinning out of control, losing myself in him. His arms are at my side, caging me in. His chest is grazing my breasts as he thrusts into me. Warm, liquid pleasure fills my veins, and I feel another climax coming. My body shatters, ripping a scream from my throat, but still he doesn't stop. He keeps on moving, stroking my insides and prolonging my orgasm. Even when I'm weak and spent, he's still moving inside me. By the time the pleasure takes over me again, I'm screaming incoherently, completely and utterly lost in the insane ecstasy he's giving me. He grinds into me, riding my climax, and a deep groan escapes him as he comes inside me in a warm rush of pleasure.

Afterward, he doesn't let go. He holds me close while our bodies cool, and I fall asleep in his arms.

CHAPTER 18

I wake up to Landon lifting the covers and getting out of bed. It's still dark outside, so I know it must be very early. I reach for him, still sleepy but feeling the loss of his arms around my body.

He stops, his body relaxing as he lies back and pulls me into his arms. "You should go back to sleep," he whispers in my ear.

I don't miss the fact that he slept through the night for the first time since he's been with me. I don't want to mention it, because I don't know yet how he'll react. So, I cuddle contentedly into him. "I will, and so should you."

"I wish I could, but I have to get to work." I feel his lips against my hair. "I love the way you cuddle, like you're going to burrow into my skin."

"It's not my fault you're so warm and comfortable."

"Warm and comfortable? I must be losing my touch."

I smile against his neck. "Also sexy and irresistible."

"That's more like it." His lips trail down to my shoulder and his hand traces a path to the small of my back. "Turn around," he whispers.

Excitement courses through my sleepy brain, and I do as he says. Immediately he molds my body to his. I can feel the thrust of his arousal against my naked butt and I move my hips, rubbing against him.

"How are you always so hard?" I moan.

"It's all you," he replies. He has his arms around me, and one hand slides over my stomach, moving slowly down to my sex, where he starts to caress me gently. I sigh softly, hot arousal flooding through me. I feel his cock probe me from behind, slowly but surely sliding into my warmth.

He fills me so deeply, the sensation is incredible. His fingers continue their work, playing with my clit while his cock stretches me to my limits.

I wait for him to start moving. My body is already clenching around him, eager and wanting, but his hand between my legs, leisurely stroking me, ensures that I can't move. I feel hot, my skin is flushed, and my breath is a desperate pant. I moan and tighten my hips, wordlessly begging him to fuck me.

He groans, but only continues to stroke my clit, his cock hot and sweet inside me. With his free hand, he cups one of my breasts, squeezing gently. I want to beg him to please just fuck me, but already my body is weakening into loose-limbed pleasure, my insides pulsing around his hard length.

"You're going to come," he whispers, his breath hot against the back of my neck. I believe him— already my legs are quaking, my whole body suffusing with delight. He kisses my neck, my hair, my ear, whispering soft endearments the whole time.

I let go, my body giving in to his. Already, my senses are slipping, my whole body tingling. He rocks his hips, just once, and I explode, my entire body jerking furiously as a massive orgasm ripples through me.

I hear him groan, his cock twitching inside me as he comes. My body doesn't stop shaking until his hips finally still. I feel weak, replete with pleasure.

He pulls out of me, and I tremble with the after-shocks. I turn around to face him. "Good morning."

He grins, sliding down to kiss my lips. "Wonderful morning," he corrects. "Go back to sleep."

"Not if you won't be here when I wake up."

He chuckles. "I can't promise that I will, but we

can have dinner tonight, at my place. I'll even cook if you want."

I grin. "I want."

I watch him get up and walk naked into the adjoining bathroom. By the time he comes out a few minutes later, I'm already drifting off, but I feel the soft kiss he places on my cheek before he leaves.

⌇

BY THE TIME I FINALLY WAKE UP, TAKE A QUICK shower, and go to the kitchen for my wake-up cup of coffee, Laurie is already fully dressed, sipping from a large coffee mug.

"Good morning," I mumble, going to pour myself a cup.

"You can walk!" She smirks teasingly. "I'm surprised."

I meet her eyes and blush. "Shut up."

"I won't." She gives me a dirty wink. "I couldn't sleep. I heard everything."

"No, you didn't. The walls aren't that thin. Anyway, now you know what I have to put up with whenever Brett spends the night."

She nods and a small frown covers her face. I notice the frown and cluck sympathetically. "Don't worry about him. Everything's going to be fine. You're a tyrant, but he loves you too much."

She sighs. "I hope so." She picks up her purse. "I'm leaving now. See you later."

≈

AT THE OFFICE, I WORK ON SOME OF MY ARTICLES, attend a few meetings, and even listen to Chelsea complain that she suspects her next-door neighbor at her expensive Park Avenue apartment is a bodyguard hired by her father.

"He's insanely hot though," she tells me. "Maybe I'll just seduce him to piss off my dad."

"Your dad will just hire someone else."

"He probably will." She groans. "He's so hung up on the idea that someone is going to kidnap me or something. Seriously! That went out of fashion with Patty Hearst!"

Back in my office, my phone rings, and I'm pleased, almost giddy to find that it's Landon.

"What're you doing?" he asks.

"Earning my income. You?"

"Resenting the fact that I can't come over there and whisk you away."

"We'll see each other tonight," I remind him.

He sighs. "No, we won't. I have to go to Europe. In fact, I'm at the airport now. There's a little crisis concerning a property I'm planning to purchase."

"You're going away?" I frown, dismayed at the fact

that I won't see him tonight, and maybe for a while after. "For how long?"

"A few days. Maybe a week."

I sigh. "I wish you didn't have to go."

There's a pause at his end. "Will you miss me?"

I miss him already. "I'll miss a lot of things about you."

He chuckles. "Like what?"

"You know what."

"Maybe I want to hear you say it."

I look at the closed door of my office. "Your tongue, for one."

"What else?"

"Your fingers." I take a breath, suddenly feeling hot. "The way you know exactly what to do with your cock."

He makes a frustrated sound. "You have such a dirty mouth."

"No, I don't."

"Yes you do baby, and when I return, I'm going to do dirty things to it."

I swallow. "I will miss you," I say softly.

There's a long pause at his end. "Same here," he says. "I have to go now, Rachel. Let's talk later."

He ends the call, leaving me wondering how I'm going to survive a week without him. It scares me how dependent on him I've become. This happened before, with Jack. It was less intense, less in every way, but still, when it ended, I was devastated.

With Landon, I can't even think of an end without wanting to cry.

At lunchtime, Laurie calls me on the office line, and we talk on the phone over my Chinese takeout.

"Brett asked me out to dinner," she tells me.

"Isn't that a good thing?"

"I don't know," she says, sounding worried. "I just have this feeling. I was so unreasonable last night. What if I pushed him too far? What if he wants to break up with me?"

The idea is ridiculous. "That's the most unlikely thing that could ever happen," I reassure her. "I mean, you guys are so in love it's disgusting."

She chuckles. "So what's up with your boy toy?"

"Don't call him that." I sigh. "He's gone to Europe."

"Ha." She teases. "So last night he was leaving his mark—imprinting on you."

I shake my head. "Go away. He didn't even know last night that he would have to travel."

"So that was a regular performance? Wow!" She laughs. "Seriously, I'm glad you're having fun. He's a nice guy, and I think he really likes you, unlike some other guy I will not even name."

She's talking about Jack. I suddenly realize how long it's been since I even really thought about him.

At least Laurie was right about Landon helping me get over Jack. "I didn't tell you while I was in San Francisco, but Jack came to see me there."

"No he didn't."

I tell her everything that happened, listening to her expressions of outrage.

"How could you not tell me?" she exclaims. "And that Jack... I'm sure he saw one of the pictures of you and Landon and it temporarily did something to his ego. Some guys just can't stand it when a girl moves on."

"Now you've done something to my ego." I laugh. "Couldn't it just be that he really felt something and wanted to get me back?"

"Yeah, so where has he been after the initial rush of passion that made him fly out to see you?"

"He said he was going to Argentina."

"There are cell phones in Argentina, and internet, and Skype." She snorts. "He's probably taken up with some model or telenovela actress, as usual. Then when he comes back he'll suddenly remember you."

"The truth is I haven't really thought about him that much."

"Halleluiah!" Laurie crows.

"You don't have to be so glad."

"Oh, but I am. I'll see you tonight," she says when she's done gloating. "With good news, hopefully."

"Maybe he'll propose," I suggest.

"You think?"

"It's possible."

After our conversation, I start thinking about Jack. For so long, I thought he was the one, and now, even though I know without a doubt that what I felt for him doesn't even come close to what I feel for Landon, I still feel a little ache.

I go back to work with a small sigh, and I manage to keep my thoughts of the men in my life at bay by burying myself in the things I have to do.

I WORK UNTIL LATE, GETTING HOME AT ALMOST eight PM. My phone starts to ring right after I walk into the apartment. It's Laurie.

Her voice is cracking. "Rach, please be home."

My heart constricts with dread. "Laurie, what is it?"

"Just be home," she sobs. "I'm on my way."

The line goes dead.

I close the door behind me and sit on the couch, kicking off my shoes as I wait for her to get home. What could have happened with Brett? I don't even want to entertain the fears sneaking into my mind.

A few minutes later, I hear her at the door and get up. She enters the apartment and rushes into my arms, sobbing as if she's going to die.

I get her to sit, rubbing her back to calm her down. "What happened?"

"He thinks we need to take a break." She sniffs. When she looks at me, her makeup is all over her face, but she still manages to look beautiful. "He says if I don't trust him after all these years then I don't know him, that maybe I'm subconsciously trying to find a reason to break us up." She starts to sob again. "I can't bear it. I love him so much."

I put my arms around her, stroking her hair. "Did you tell him that?"

She shakes her head. "No. I was so hurt and angry, I told him to do whatever he wants. Then I walked out."

"Lauric…"

"He tried to follow me, but I told him to get lost. He probably thinks I hate him, and I do, a little, but I don't think I can live without him." She starts to cry again.

"Shh." I do my best to comfort her. "It'll be all right."

"What if it won't? What if this is just an excuse so he can be with someone else, like that girl from the gym. Oh God!" I hand her a tissue from my purse and she blows her nose. "Rachel, I can't even imagine being with anyone else. What am I going to do? I love him too much."

At that moment, I'm so angry with Brett. I know

how emotional Laurie is underneath the seemingly unflappable skin, and he knows too, which is all the more reason why he shouldn't have hurt her like this.

Laurie cries for a while. Even after I finally convince her to change her clothes, take a warm shower, and get into bed, she keeps on crying, finally falling asleep cuddled against me. When I'm sure she's asleep, I go to take a shower and change into my pajamas before returning to her room. Even in sleep, she looks sad, as if even in her dreams she can't escape the threat of her relationship ending.

I'm about to call Brett when he calls me. I step into the living room to answer.

"Is she okay?" he asks.

"What do you think? I snap.

"Rachel..." He sighs. "I just...I wish she would give me a little more credit, trust me a little bit more. If we don't have trust then what do we have? I want her to be happy, but she can't be happy if she thinks the minute any girl bats an eyelash at me, I'm going to do something wrong."

"You want her to be happy and you thought the best way to achieve that was to break her heart. She's crying, Brett."

"I'm so sorry." He sounds as unhappy as Laurie does.

I sigh. It's not the first time I've had to be a moderator in a fight between them, but it's the first time Brett has asked for a break. "She's the one who needs to hear that, Brett, not me. Why couldn't you guys just discuss how you felt? Taking a break is seriously going too far."

He exhales audibly. "You think we haven't discussed it? I don't know what to do anymore. I can't promise that I'm not going to hurt her if she's going to keep finding reasons to be hurt without me doing anything."

I close my eyes. It's been so long since their last fight that I assumed they'd finally passed that stage in their relationship. "I don't know what you want me to say. You have to decide what's most important to you."

I go back into Laurie's room and watch her cry in her sleep. It's real and it's scary. It's also frustrating that they would waste their time fighting when they both know how they feel about each other. If I knew for sure that Landon felt something for me, would I waste any emotion on fighting with him? I can't imagine that I would.

As if he knows I'm thinking about him, he calls me. I leave Laurie's room again, going to sit on the couch in the living room.

"I thought you might be asleep," he says when I answer. "What's up?"

"Nothing. What're you doing?"

"Having a late lunch."

"How was your flight?"

"Uneventful." He lets out a tired sound. "I spent the whole afternoon trying to convince someone who suddenly changed her mind about selling me a property."

"Did you succeed?"

"Barely."

I find that hard to believe. I can't imagine any woman being able to resist even the slightest argument from him. I wonder what tools exactly he had to employ in his convincing, and a stab of jealousy fills my heart.

"The next issue of Gilt Traveler will be out soon," I tell him, "with the article about your hotel."

"I'm looking forward to reading it."

I hear someone say something to him in the background then his voice responding in rapid flowing French. Suddenly, I'm filled with an intense longing for him, so intense that it feels like I'm going to cry.

"Baby, are you there?"

The endearment makes it even worse. *I miss you*, I want to tell him. *I've fallen in love with you.*

"I'm here," I say instead.

"Are you okay?"

"Yes." I sigh. "Brett and Laurie... He told her they needed a break. She's been crying all night."

He is silent for a moment. "Did he say why?"

"Long story. He says she has trust issues...thinks if

she's not happy, then what's the point?" I shake my head. "But she's miserable without him, and he knew she would be. Why would you hurt someone purposely when you're supposed to love them?"

"I wouldn't know, but if she doesn't trust him, maybe it's for the best."

I remember what he told me about his parents, his mother's jealousy and distrust. "You're not here Landon. She's miserable."

"She'll get over it."

I shake my head. "You don't understand. They've been together for four years. You can't just get over someone you've loved for so long. It's not that easy."

"Well..." His voice is quiet. "You are speaking from exprcience."

I bite my lip. Jack again. How long do I have to wait before he stops coming between us? I have to think of a way to communicate that Jack means nothing to me now, that he's meant nothing for a long time.

"Give Laurie my best," Landon says abruptly.

"I will." My voice is low. "Do you know when you'll be back?"

"Weekend, at the latest." He pauses. "Why don't you go to bed now, we'll talk some other time."

Later, after I've switched off the TV, I go to join Laurie in her room, sighing as she cuddles against me before I fall asleep.

THE NEXT DAY, I TRY TO CONVINCE LAURIE TO call in sick, but she is adamant that she won't. She leaves for work before I even shower with her eyes dry, though slightly swollen.

The days that follow are more of the same. She cries herself to sleep at night while I try to comfort her. Landon calls me every night, and it becomes kind of a ritual. On Friday night, we get a delivery of chocolates and a bottle of red wine, along with a DVD of a stand-up comedy show. It's from Landon, and while we eat the chocolates and get buzzed on the wine, I'm glad to see Laurie laughing at the jokes about mundane things like work, traffic, movies, and children.

On Saturday, my mother insists that we come to the house. Laurie's parents will be there, as well as my brother, who is spending the weekend at home. I suspect that Aunt Jacie has told my mom about Laurie and Brett, and she thinks spending time with family will make Laurie less miserable.

Even though I'm worried she might not want to go, seeing as only last weekend she was there with Brett, Laurie doesn't argue when I tell her, instead, she actually seems excited at the prospect.

After the one-hour taxi ride to Huntington, we walk down the short drive to the front door of my parents' two-story brick house. They moved away from the city as soon as Dylan started college, joining Uncle Taylor and Aunt Jacie, who'd left earlier.

"There are two beautiful young ladies at the door," my dad teases when he opens the door for Laurie and me. "I think I recognize this one," he says, kissing me on both cheeks after giving me a hug. "Though I'm not sure what her name is." He hugs Laurie too. "This one looks like Lauren, but she's prettier than I remember."

"Ha ha, Uncle Trent," Laurie says, but she's smiling.

He steps aside so we can enter. My dad is still fit, tall with graying hair and gray eyes that always look amused.

"Everyone's in the kitchen," he tells us. "Apart from Dylan. He's blowing things to pieces in his room."

I'm not surprised. My brother plays computer games with zeal and passion. How he finds the time for his studies, I've never been able to deduce.

Uncle Taylor is cooking, which is a relief, as he's a much better cook than any of the other adults. He looks almost exactly like my dad, and telling them apart, for me, is more a matter of instinct than actual facial characteristics. He's calmly preparing grilled sandwiches while my mother and Aunt Jacie slice vegetables for a salad.

"Look who's here," he exclaims when he sees us at the door. He leaves the kitchen island as we walk toward him. "Hello Tweedledee." He kisses my cheek. "Tweedledum." He hugs Laurie, who leans into his embrace, looking as if she might burst into tears.

Our moms are next. After a series of warm, perfumed hugs and earnest how-are-yous, Laurie escapes upstairs to my brother's room, leaving alone with the parents.

"How is she?" Aunt Jacie asks, her beautiful face a picture of concern.

"She's still crying a lot."

"You think it's only temporary?" my mom asks.

"I don't know. It's lasted longer than any other fight."

Uncle Taylor sighs. "I always liked Brett, but now I want to beat the shit out of him."

Aunt Jacie pats his shoulder. "How're you doing?" she asks me.

I shrug. "Okay. I'm going to check on Dylan too."

My mother follows me out of the kitchen, wiping her hands on a dishcloth. Her hair is piled high on her head with tendrils drifting down her face, and even in a plain cotton blouse and loose pants, she still doesn't look her age. "When are you planning to tell me about your new boyfriend?"

I stop at the foot of the stairs. "Did someone tell you I have a boyfriend?"

She manages to look shamefaced. "Laurie may have mentioned that you're still seeing that hotelier you went to San Francisco with."

I sigh, wishing Laurie wasn't in so much pain so I could beat her or something. "Mom, I'm not going to talk about it with you, not right now." *Not ever.*

"But you're seeing him?"

I purse my lips.

"Okay." She holds up her palms. "I'm going, though you shouldn't underestimate the value of a mother's advice," she adds, turning back toward the kitchen. "Especially when it comes to men."

Upstairs, Dylan and Laurie are playing some game that involves a lot of shooting. I slump on Dylan's bed. "Hey doc."

"Hey sis." He barely looks up from his game. He's the image of my dad, tall and lanky, but with the green eyes we both got from my mom. "What's up?"

"Nothing."

"You have to shoot down the helicopter," Laurie says urgently.

"What?" I reply, puzzled.

"On it," Dylan says simultaneously, and I hear electronic gunfire. I roll my eyes, relieved when my phone vibrates in my pocket.

I look at the screen, and anticipation fills my chest at the sight of Landon's name. I slide to answer and hold the phone to my ear. "Hello hotness."

"Hmm, hotness, I like that."

His voice washes over me like warm velvet. I've missed him so much...too much. "Are you back?"

"Just arrived. Where are you?"

"At my parents'."

"Where is that?"

"I thought you knew everything about me," I tease.

"It's probably in a file somewhere," he admits, "but you can tell me."

"Why?"

"Because I want to see you."

I let out a slow breath. There's an urgency in his simple statement that mirrors my own desire. "I'll be back by evening."

"I can't wait that long," he says. "I want to come over."

"To my parents' house?"

"Yes. Is that a problem?"

Of course! My mom would put two and two together and come up with wedding bells.

I shake my head. "I don't think you want to meet my parents."

"Why not?"

Because that's not the kind of relationship we have! Because I won't be able to deal with their questions when you leave me.

"Because they're parents. My mom will probably start planning our wedding."

He laughs. "Really? That sounds interesting." I hear a series of beeps from his side. He's probably searching some electronic device for my parents' address among all the information his security team gathered on me. "Just tell them we're friends," he continues. "Tell them I'm in the area, and I'm picking you up or something. I really want to see you."

I sigh. "Fine."

"I'm already on my way."

I look at my phone, realizing the call is already disconnected. Laurie turns back to look at me. "Who was that?"

"It's Landon." I frown. "He wants to come here."

Her brows go up. Then she smiles, no doubt thinking about my mom's reaction. "Good luck," she mouths at me before turning back to the game.

"Who's Landon?" Dylan says without turning around.

"Rachel's booty call," Laurie replies.

"Nooo." He shudders exaggeratedly. "I didn't need to know that."

I pull myself off the bed and go back to the kitchen to find my mom. Lunch is starting to look good. "Well done, Uncle Taylor," I tell him before sidling up to my mom.

"Mom," I start, dreading her reaction. "That guy Laurie told you about...he's coming over."

Aunt Jacie turns to me. "Your new boyfriend?"

"He's not my boyfriend," I protest loudly, eliciting puzzled looks from both my dad and uncle.

"Laurie said he was."

My mom gives me that *Didn't I tell you?* look, and I decide right then that I'm going to kill Laurie, or at least hide her favorite pair of shoes. "Well, he's not my boyfriend, and he's on his way, so please don't refer to him as my boyfriend."

"The lady doth protest too much," my dad teases.

"Is he driving all the way from the city?" Uncle Taylor asks. "If so, you may be wrong about the boyfriend part."

"I think I'll just go back home," I exclaim. "I don't trust you guys not to embarrass me when he gets here."

Aunt Jacie grins. "If you care about that, then you like him more than you're letting on."

"Exactly," my mom says, smoothing my hair. She pulls off the clip holding it in place before I can wiggle away. "That's more like it," she says, fluffing it out.

"This is where I disappear," I announce theatrically, making for the door. "Tell Laurie and Dylan I love them, and if they never see me again, they have you all to blame." I leave the kitchen to the sound of their teasing laughter, reminding me of when I was a child. Smiling despite myself, I go to the living room and pick up a magazine to thumb through while I wait for Landon to arrive.

He does, about half an hour later. I'm thinking about him when the doorbell rings, and I hurry into the hall to let him in.

He looks beautiful as always, sexy in a black leather jacket over a long-sleeved gray t-shirt. His hair is carefree and windblown, his blue eyes gleaming and focused on me. My heart tightens at the impact of looking at him alone. I've missed him, no argument.

"Your security guys obviously know what they're doing," I say lightly. "Did they unearth a copy of my birth certificate too?"

He grins, making me catch my breath. "I only hire people who know what they're doing," he says, pulling me into his arms and dropping a light kiss on my lips. He releases me just as my father walks into the hall.

"Good afternoon, Mr. Foster," Landon says confidently. "I'm Landon Court."

"Good afternoon." My father comes toward us, giving Landon a measuring look. "Don't just stand there. Come in."

Landon steps past me and shakes the hand my dad holds out to him. I follow them into the living room, where my mom and Aunt Jacie are waiting to pounce on him. I'm too embarrassed to listen to the questions they're throwing at him, and after I hear, "So where did you two meet?" I escape to the kitchen to join Uncle Taylor.

The table is already set, so I help bring out the food, occasionally catching Landon's eye from the living room as he charms my mom and aunt, making them giggle like teenagers. Even my dad seems impressed.

"I can't imagine why you were so adamant about him not being your boyfriend," Uncle Taylor comments when he sees Landon. "With a guy who looks like that, most girls would rather say the opposite."

"I'm not most girls," I reply. "And what's the point of saying it if it's not true?"

When it's time, Laurie and Dylan join us. Landon says hi to Laurie without mentioning Brett, which she seems grateful for. During lunch, the conversation flows. Landon seems genuinely interested in everyone. Even Dylan—who never has anything to say to people he doesn't know—soon starts talking with him about school and medicine.

I'm the only one who's quiet, watching as Landon charms my family. I listen to him discuss Trent & Taylor with my dad and uncle, referencing instances from a high-street fashion brand he invested in. In the next breath he's discussing painting with my mom and speaking Italian with Aunt Jacie, who picked up the language when she was a teenage model in Italy. A desperate voice inside my head is screaming that I shouldn't let this happen. I shouldn't have let him come. It's enough that I'm in love with him—I don't want my family to fall for him too. They'll only end up disappointed when Landon and I finally go our separate ways.

That's really the problem, the knowledge that what we have is only temporary.

After we eat, we go to the backyard, and Dylan, Laurie, and Landon play hoops. Of course, Landon is good at that too.

"He's very handsome," Aunt Jacie comments. We're sitting under a shade with my mom, who's doodling in a sketchpad.

"He is," I agree.

"And he seems very nice too."

"Yes."

She gives me a look. "You know, the last time you told us some guy was your boyfriend, he turned out not to be worthy of that title. This one seems like he might be. Just my opinion though."

I put my head on the table. "Aunt Jacie," I moan. "Some people have only two parents."

She grins. "Then you should count yourself lucky."

CHAPTER 19

*I*T'S late in the afternoon by the time we're ready to leave. Laurie decides to stay, though she's not sure yet if she'll go home with her parents, who live only a few minutes away, or stay up all night playing video games with Dylan.

After we say our goodbyes, I follow Landon to his car, the silver Jaguar I've only seen him drive a couple of times. We're both quiet as he pulls out of the gravel drive and onto the road, the only sound, that of the car engine purring beneath us like a jungle cat.

"Do you come home often?" he asks.

"About once a month. My mom's very pushy."

"Is she?" He seems surprised. "I thought she was sweet, and your aunt too."

"Ha," I say, but I'm smiling.

He returns my smile. "Are you eager to get back to the city?"

I give him a teasing look from under my lashes. "Why? Do you have plans for me?"

He nods. "Actually, I do."

I'm staring at his profile, so when he turns, he catches my eye. He gives me a sexy grin before turning back to the road. "My parents had a home in Sand's Point. We split our childhood between there and the hotel. I made a call while we were at your parents, so if you want to go see it, it will be ready for us."

"Yeah, of course." I'd love to see the home where he grew up.

In thirty minutes, we're already there, cruising up the long drive to the front entrance of the two-story, Greek revival mansion.

As soon as we step out of the car, the front door opens and an elderly, gray-haired man walks out onto the front porch. Landon takes my hand and leads me up to the porch steps, grinning affectionately as he shakes the older man's hand. "Good evening Wilson, sorry to disturb you on such short notice."

"It's your home, Landon," the man says with a smile that's almost fatherly. "And we're always happy to see you."

"This is Rachel." Landon turns to me. "Rachel, this is Wilson Hayes. He used to run the Swanson

Court Hotel in New York, and he's been the caretaker here since my father passed away."

Wilson smiles at me. "Welcome Miss Foster. It's great to see a new face at Windbreakers." He holds open the door to let us into a large hallway, while I'm still trying to digest the fact that the house has a name. Inside, I pause to admire the perfectly maintained vision of the shiny marble floors, elegant curved grand staircase, and molded ceiling from which a classic crystal chandelier is hanging.

"I took the liberty of ordering dinner from town," Wilson tells Landon.

Landon nods. "Thanks. We'll eat upstairs at eight. How's Betsy?"

"My wife is coping with me as best she can," Wilson replies, amusement dancing in his eyes.

Landon chuckles and starts in the direction of the stairs. He leads me upstairs, through another hallway into a suite at the end of the hall. From the window of the exquisitely furnished sitting room, I can see the beautifully manicured lawns, and beyond that, the beach and the waters of the Long Island Sound.

I lean my head against the glass. "The view is lovely."

"I agree."

Something in his voice makes me turn around. His eyes are on my body, and he raises them to mine, his expression unrepentantly and blatantly sexual.

"Come," he says, holding out a hand to me. "I want to show you the bedroom."

Warm lust pools in my belly. "You're supposed to show me around the house," I say as I walk toward him on legs that suddenly feel rubbery. "It's the polite thing to do."

"I'm not very polite," he says, leading me toward the bedroom. "What I am is very aroused." He closes the door as soon as we're in the room then gently pushes me back to lean on the door. He drops gracefully onto his knees, pulling my dress up simultaneously. His hands cup my butt, then his fingers link under the waistband of my panties and pull them down, just enough that he can cover the lips of my sex with his tongue.

My legs go weak. If not for his hands holding me up, I would fall. His tongue slips between my folds, hungry and teasing, searching and finding the most sensitive places to drive me completely crazy.

I'm moaning softly, my hands pressed back against the door. Even as he licks and sucks me, he slides my panties farther down, freeing my legs so he can lift one of them onto his shoulder, opening me up to the pleasurable assault of his tongue.

My body is shaking, losing control. My weak moans fill the room, and yet he doesn't stop. He licks my outer lips then sucks on my clit, deftly plunging his tongue inside me again and again until I cry out, coming apart as my body surrenders to the pleasure.

I'm still shaking when he lets my leg drop to the ground and rises to his feet. "Tell me that wasn't better than showing you around the house."

"What house?" I pull his face down toward mine, sliding my lips over his. I can taste myself on his lips, and it makes me so hot. I slide down to my knees and start to unbutton his fly, hurriedly undoing his zipper and pulling down his pants and briefs.

His cock springs free, already erect. I take the rock-hard length in my hands, and his low growl of arousal sets me on fire. I look up at him. His head is thrown back, his eyes closed. Wetting my lips, I take the head of his cock in my mouth, slowly licking around it before sucking in the rest of him, until I can feel him tickling the back of my throat.

He groans loudly, his hands fisting in my hair. I tighten my mouth around him, sucking deeply as I rock my head. He lets out a tortured moan, and one hand leaves my hair to support his weight on the door behind me. His hips are rocking into my mouth. The powerful motion is almost too much for me, but I take it, his carnal enjoyment arousing me too.

"Oh God!" he groans, jerking his hips. "Oh, fuck, Rachel—I'm going to come."

I respond by cupping his balls, letting my fingers skim the soft skin, and he lets out a labored sound, his body stiffening as he spurts his warm seed into my mouth.

I swallow quickly, licking every remaining drop from the tip of his cock. He groans and pulls me up, pulling my dress over my head and dispensing with my bra with lightning speed. He removes the rest of his clothes with the same urgency before carrying me over to the huge king poster bed. He sets me down at one of the posts and pulls my hips back toward him, sliding into me from behind.

I hold on to the post, my whole body sweet and liquid as he thrusts into me with an intensity verging on feral. His hands cover my breasts, his fingers teasing my swollen nipples even as his thick cock strokes every sweet spot inside me. Pleasure permeates me, my climax seizing my whole body. He continues to fuck me even as my shudders subside, his grunts joining with my soft cries. I feel another climax building, and I clutch at the post, my whole body tightening as an orgasm ripples through me. At the same moment, Landon thrusts fiercely inside me, burying himself completely as he groans his release.

Afterward, we lie in a tangle on the bed, sexually sated. He's stroking my hair, and my face is against his chest, where I can hear his heart beating. It feels so natural to be so close to him, it always has, even from the first time.

I look up at his face, wondering if he feels it too.

His hand stills on my hair. "What are you thinking?"

I shrug. "How good this feels, just lying here with you."

He pulls me closer. "I know what you mean. There's nowhere in the world I'd rather be."

I close my eyes, letting the words wash over me. I burrow as close to him as possible, and I hear him laugh, his chest vibrating.

"Are you hungry?" he asks.

I nod. "Starving."

"It's eight," he observes. "Dinner's probably waiting for us." Nudging me to sit up, he gets up from the bed and goes to an adjoining dressing room. He returns with two robes, shrugs one on his perfect frame, and hands the other to me before opening the door to the sitting room.

He's right—there's a dinner tray with covered dishes and an ice bucket with a bottle of wine chilling in the ice.

I watch as Landon uncovers the dishes. "Wilson seems to know what you want when you have guests over," I comment. "Does he have a lot of practice?"

Landon turns a grin in my direction. "You can ask if I've brought a lot of women here. Your jealousy flatters me, actually."

I return his smile. "So? Have you?"

"No, never."

"Not one?"

He shakes his head. "I'm not the playboy the gossip magazines make me out to be. I've had a few relationships, all with women who knew what the terms were."

"Like me?"

He hands me a glass of wine. "There has never been anyone like you."

I search his eyes, wondering if I can dare to hope, but he turns away and busies himself with setting plates on the table.

"What exactly were the terms?" I ask.

"Exclusivity, but no commitment in the long-term."

Just like I'd asked for. "And you never felt tempted to make an exception with any of the women you've been with?"

He shakes his head. "No, never. I've felt pressured, but usually as soon as a woman starts to demand more than I can give, I walk away."

"Oh!" I take the seat and the plate he offers me, trying not to let my feelings show on my face. If he always walks away when a woman shows signs of wanting more from him, then it's only a matter of time—likely very little time—before we're done.

"Lucky for me I never asked you for a long-term commitment," I say with a lightness I don't feel.

His eyes burn into mine. "This is just sex, and I

don't want to pretend it's anything more," he says. "Those were your exact words."

Back when I had no idea I was going to fall in love with him. "Yes," I say in a small voice. "I remember."

He refills my wine. "Do you like the food?"

I nod, and we start to talk about other things. After we eat, he finally shows me around the house. It feels almost decadent, walking around the beautiful rooms in just our robes, but there's no one else in the house. Wilson has retired to the apartment he shares with his wife on the property, and the maid has gone back to her home in town.

We end up on one of the upper balconies, watching the stars while seated on a long divan with a blanket covering us both. The silence is peaceful, with only the sound of the insects in the garden and the distant surf. Farther off, the lights of the city look like fireflies in a fog. I mention it to Landon and he laughs. "Very descriptive," he teases. "I think there might be a poet inside you somewhere."

We talk late into the night, and finally, with his arms around me and the steady rhythm of his heart against my ear, I fall asleep.

I WAKE UP ALONE, LYING IN THE BIG BED WITH

the covers around me. Landon is sitting at the edge of the bed, his head in his hands. I don't need to ask to know he's been dreaming again.

I reach for him, placing a hand on his shoulder. "Are you okay?"

He gets up, moving away from my touch. "Yes, I'm fine. Go back to sleep."

I frown. "No, not when you're going to stay awake the rest of the night." I get up too, pulling the covers with me. "Why don't you tell me about it?"

"Why?" he asks testily. "Because you're curious?"

"Because I care!"

His throat works as he swallows. "Forget about it, Rachel. You've already helped more than you know. These past two weeks with you have been the most peaceful I've had in a very long time."

I cup his cheek with one hand, aching to comfort him. "Come back to bed," I whisper.

Later, when he's lying in my arms, his head on my chest, I listen to his breathing as he sleeps, praying that whatever demons he faces in his dreams won't come back before morning.

WHEN I WAKE UP IN THE MORNING, I'M ALONE again. I find a note in Landon's handwriting on a sheet of Swanson Court stationary, telling me that my clothes are in the attached dressing room.

I take a quick shower and brush my teeth with a new toothbrush that's been thoughtfully placed in a toothbrush holder on the sink. In the dressing room, my dress from yesterday is hanging, freshly laundered, and my undies are folded on a shelf next to it. After putting on my clothes, I find my way downstairs where the smell of breakfast leads me to the kitchen.

I'm disappointed when I don't find Landon there. Instead, a plump woman with a rosy face is making toast and frying strips of bacon.

"Good morning," she greets me with a cheerful smile. "You must be Rachel. I'm Betsy—Mrs. Hayes. Did you have a nice rest?"

"Yes, thank you."

"Why don't you sit," she suggests, going back to her cooking. "Landon is outside looking around the gardens. I'm sure he'll be back in a moment."

At that moment, Landon steps into the kitchen through the back door. He looks freshly showered, dressed in a t-shirt and shorts that show off his broad shoulders, sculpted chest, and long muscular legs.

"You're finally awake," he comments, coming to the table to drop a kiss on my lips. "I thought I was going to have to transport you back to Manhattan unconscious."

My eyes drink in his features. How is it possible to love him now even more than I did yesterday? "I was tired," I reply to his question.

"Understandably." He grins and I try to hide my blush from Betsy, who is smiling.

"Take a seat," she tells Landon. "It's been a while since I had young people around to feed. Eat up."

"Yes ma'am," Landon says, grinning fondly as he does as she says.

Wilson joins us, and we all have breakfast together. The older couple are obviously fond of Landon and proud of both his and Aidan's accomplishments. They're the closest thing Landon has to real parents, I realize, feeling grateful toward them.

The house has a long stretch of beach attached to it, along with a tennis court, a swimming pool, and unending gardens. After breakfast, Landon takes me for a walk along the beach. We find a secluded area, where he takes my clothes off and makes slow, sweet love to me amidst the sound of the surf breaking on the sand. My toes are tingling as we walk back to the house, and when we wash the sand off our bodies, we make love again. This time, I ride him, dictating our movements as I take him deep inside me. By the time we finally start the drive back to the city, I'm drowsy, and pleasantly sore.

I spend the first few minutes on the phone with Laurie while Landon drives. She's back home after spending the night at her parents' place. Afterward, I scroll through Landon's playlists, wrinkling my nose at the hard rock songs before finally settling on some classical music.

I sigh with contentment as the car fills with the sound of "The Blue Danube". Out of the corner of my eye, I see Landon watching me. "What?"

"Nothing." He turns back to the road, smiling.

I swat him on the arm playfully. "Tell me what you were thinking."

"That I love to look at you." His eyes are on the road. "I enjoy the way you enjoy little things."

I'm about to respond when my phone rings. I look at the screen and I'm surprised to see Jack's name. Landon's eyes are on the road, and I frown at the phone. If I don't take the call, Jack will keep calling, and it'll just look weird if I don't answer.

I answer the call. "Hello."

"Hi Rachel. What's up?"

"Nothing much? What's up with you?"

"I'm great now, but I caught a bug before, which you would know if you hadn't abandoned me. Not even a call for an old friend."

I sigh. "How're you now?"

"Perfect, though I had to come back early."

"So you're in New York?"

"Yes." There's a short pause. "I want to see you. How about we hang out tonight?"

"Not tonight."

"Why not? Have pity on someone who's dying to see you." When I don't answer, he sighs. "Tomorrow then, after work. We can go get a drink just like old times."

I steal a glance at Landon. "Yeah," I tell Jack. "Why don't you call me tomorrow?"

"Great. See you then."

After the call, both Landon and I stay silent for the rest of the drive. His face is impassive as he navigates the traffic going into the city. I toy with the phone on my lap, my mind on Jack. It's hard even to remember the feelings I used to have for him. It's almost as if, in my head, I've let go of everything I ever felt before I fell in love with Landon.

I stare at his fingers on the wheel, feeling helpless. I want to tell him I'm in love with him, but I know that will only make him push me away.

He glances at me and sees me looking at him. After a second, he turns back to the road. "That was Jack Weyland on the phone."

It's not a question. "Yes it was."

"And you're going to see him tomorrow."

"Yes."

He doesn't say anything else. At my building, he parks on the street and turns to me. "We're here," he says.

I nod. "I had a great time."

"I'm glad I could be of service," he says drily.

The change in attitude has to be because of my conversation with Jack. I recall Landon's reaction to him back in San Francisco. He admitted then that he was jealous. Does he still feel the same way? Deep down inside me, I accept that maybe I agreed to go out with Jack because I wanted to see a reaction, a sign that Landon would care if he thought he might lose me.

"I'm just going to have a drink with him," I say softly.

His fingers flex on the wheel. "It's fine. You said yourself that you can't just get over someone you've loved for years."

"I was talking about Laurie."

"So it doesn't apply to you and Jack? You're completely over him?"

"Yes."

He exhales and taps his fingers on the wheel. "So why do you need to go out with him?"

I fold my arms. "Because he's also been a friend. Not every relationship is built completely on sex."

He shrugs. "You were the one who demanded that this thing we have had to be based on sex alone."

"Maybe now I want more."

"Do you?"

I want to say yes, but there's that fear niggling at the back of my mind.

As soon as a woman starts to demand more than I can give, I walk away.

I don't know how I'll be able to bear it if he walks away from me.

But, one day, he will. It's inevitable, and the longer I hold on, the harder it will be to finally let go.

He's still waiting for me to say something. I draw in a deep breath. "You can't give me what I want," I say softly.

His jaw tightens, and for a long moment, he doesn't say anything. "I find it very enlightening that we're having this conversation right after you spoke to *him*." He spits out the word. "If you'd rather be with your ex, you don't have to conjure vague reasons why we shouldn't be together. Just let me know, and I won't stop you."

"This has absolutely nothing to do with Jack."

He is silent, and then suddenly, without any warning, he reaches for me, pulling me toward him and covering my lips in a kiss that's hard, hungry, and demanding. Despite the riot of emotions I'm feeling, my body responds immediately, my tongue meeting his, taking and giving.

It feels as if I'm melting into him, as if I'll never know again where he ends and I begin. By the time he releases me, we're both panting. He pulls back and closes his eyes, his chest rising and falling as he tries to get his breathing under control. My thoughts are all jumbled in my head, and I feel as if I'm going to cry.

"I'm sorry," he says roughly.

At that moment, I know I've made a huge mistake. I want to tell him that I'm willing to take whatever he has to give. I want to beg him not to leave, but the words fail me.

He starts the engine, his eyes straight ahead. "I had a great weekend too," he says, his voice dismissive. "Goodbye Rachel."

"Yeah," I say miserably before stumbling out of the car. He waits until I'm at the door before he drives away. By the time I climb the stairs to my apartment, my cheeks are wet with tears, and I don't know if I'm ever going to be happy again.

Addicted to You, the next book in this series, is out now. Find out more at www.serenagrey.com/addicted-to-you

If you want to get an email when the next book comes out, subscribe to my mailing list at www.serenagrey.com/alerts.

I love reviews, so if you liked this book, please leave a review on Goodreads or any of the purchase sites. I would love to know what you think. Do not hesitate to recommend this book to fellow readers. That's the best gift you can give to an author.

Thank you for reading.

Serena is obsessed with books. She reads everything–history, the classics, novels, poetry and comic books, and writes because the stories in her head won't leave her in peace otherwise. She loves all kinds of fiction, but has a soft spot for love, romance, and that flush of pleasure that can only be found at the end of a beautiful love story.

When she's not reading and writing, she enjoys cocktails, coffee, TV shows, and has never gotten over her crush on Leonardo DiCaprio. If she had to choose between a good book and ice cream, she'd take both and make a run for it.

To be the first to find out about new releases from Serena,
sign up for her Mailing List at
www.serenagrey.com/alerts

CONNECT WITH SERENA

Facebook: www.facebook.com/authorserenagrey

Twitter: @s_greyauthor

Goodreads: www.goodreads.com/serenagrey

Website: www.serenagrey.com